TOO HOT TO HANDLE

PORTIA MACINTOSH

B
Boldwood

First published in Great Britain in 2025 by Boldwood Books Ltd.

Copyright © Portia MacIntosh, 2025

Cover Design by Alexandra Allden

Cover Images: Shutterstock

The moral right of Portia MacIntosh to be identified as the author of this work has been asserted in accordance with the Copyright, Designs and Patents Act 1988.

All rights reserved. No part of this book may be reproduced in any form or by any electronic or mechanical means, including information storage and retrieval systems, without written permission from the author, except for the use of brief quotations in a book review. This book is a work of fiction and, except in the case of historical fact, any resemblance to actual persons, living or dead, is purely coincidental.

Every effort has been made to obtain the necessary permissions with reference to copyright material, both illustrative and quoted. We apologise for any omissions in this respect and will be pleased to make the appropriate acknowledgements in any future edition.

A CIP catalogue record for this book is available from the British Library.

Paperback ISBN 978-1-80426-750-9

Large Print ISBN 978-1-80426-749-3

Hardback ISBN 978-1-80426-751-6

Ebook ISBN 978-1-80426-748-6

Kindle ISBN 978-1-80426-747-9

Audio CD ISBN 978-1-80426-756-1

MP3 CD ISBN 978-1-80426-755-4

Digital audio download ISBN 978-1-80426-752-3

This book is printed on certified sustainable paper. Boldwood Books is dedicated to putting sustainability at the heart of our business. For more information please visit https://www.boldwoodbooks.com/about-us/sustainability/

Boldwood Books Ltd, 23 Bowerdean Street, London, SW6 3TN

www.boldwoodbooks.com

For Darcy
Love you, sis.

1

Some people know that they want to get married – and some people are even lucky enough to know the person they want to spend the rest of their lives with. Some are dead certain that marriage isn't for them, and then you have the people in the middle, the ones who are unsure.

And therein lies the problem with proposals because, for women in particular, proposals are usually a surprise.

I often wonder how many men pop the question out of the blue. You would think most men would sound a woman out, make sure it was what she wanted, or at the very least lock in a few conversations over the years, so that everyone knows what everyone wants for the rest of their lives. I get it, most men want it to be this big surprise, but it (sometimes literally) keeps me up at night wondering how many men get shot down in public places, for all to see, when a woman says no – or even worse, how many women say yes, because they're in front of an audience, only to regret it later.

I suppose, in all of the chaos, the proposal itself is probably the best way (or the first step, at least) to figure out if the person asking you is the person you should spend the rest of your life with.

Hear me out.

Some people go all-out with their proposals. It's a whole, choreographed thing. Flash mobs, firework displays, brass bands literally chilling on the top of a mountain in the Swiss Alps, waiting for the right moment to pop out from their hiding place. But then you have the more subtle ones. A ring being placed on the dinner table, a private walk somewhere scenic, with no one else around. For some people, it's not about the show, it's just about the question, and every woman will have her preference, so, how can your partner prove that they are marriage material? By giving you the proposal you want. Not trying to be impressive or flashy or trying to get away with something low effort. Your man should know what you want – whether it's being plastered on the big screen at a Leeds Lions match, while their mascot rappels into the stadium to Abba's 'I Do, I Do, I Do, I Do, I Do' or it's just a quiet moment over breakfast in bed where you realise there is something twinkling in the light, and it's a ring attached to a ribbon that is around your dog's neck.

My point is that there is no one-size-fits-all when it comes to proposals. That said, this one looks pretty perfect to me.

'So, what do you think?' Ellis asks me.

He looks good in his suit. I'm used to seeing him in his scruffy work clothes – even his regular clothes usually have flecks of paint or bits of plaster stuck to them – but he's scrubbed up really well today.

He does look nervous though. I can see a slight shake in his hand, as he holds the ring out in front of him.

He has nothing to worry about. This scene is like something out of a fairy tale. The back garden has been filled with fairy lights, with rose petals scattered everywhere, and there is romantic music playing ever so softly. It's a warm night, despite summer being on its way out, and there's just enough breeze to make the rose petals dance to the music. Honestly, it's perfect.

'I just...' My voice catches in my throat. I just can't get over someone doing something so sweet, going to so much effort, and then putting themselves out there, popping the question, waiting to see if it all pays off. 'You're amazing, you know that, right?'

I hold my arms out to beckon Ellis in for a hug. Even he looks like he has a tear in his eye as he gives me a squeeze.

'I can't believe we're finally doing this,' he says as we hug. 'And I can't believe we've been able to keep it a secret from Louise for so long either – she's your best friend, I know the two of you usually tell each other everything. It must be strange, lying to—'

'Hello?' a voice calls out from inside the house.

'Shit, it's Lou,' I tell him, letting go of him, practically pushing him back.

'Shit,' he repeats back to me.

'You have to hide,' I say. 'Quick, go hide in the kitchen, I'll go in through the patio doors and distract her.'

Ellis, who looks even more nervous now, runs in through the kitchen door.

Okay, Molly, come on. Game face on.

'Hello,' I say brightly, catching her in the dining room.

'I've been knocking for ages. What are you doing?' Lou replies. Her look instantly shifts to something suspicious. She can read me like a book. 'We're supposed to be going out but... you look weird. What's going on?'

And now would be the time when I say something, anything, to throw her off the scent. Of course, nothing springs to mind in the instant I need it, because I know Lou has a nose like a bloodhound for stuff like this. It really has been so hard, sneaking around behind her back. I'm surprised it's taken her this long to get onto us.

I part my lips, hoping something will fall out, but instead something falls over in the kitchen – well, it's most likely been knocked over, and you can tell from the look in Lou's eyes that she knows someone is in there.

'Is someone else here?' she asks me, her eyes narrowing.

'Nuh... er... uh... ah...'

Come on, Molly, say words. Any words. The sounds are just making you seem more suspicious.

'No?' I eventually say, but it sounds like I don't even believe myself.

Reading my mind, she storms off towards the kitchen, flinging open the door, only to smash it into Ellis, who is hiding behind it.

'Shit,' he cries out in pain.

'Ellis!' Lou blurts. 'What are you doing at my best friend's house?'

Then she turns to me.

'Molly, what is my boyfriend doing at your house?' she asks. '*Hiding* at your house. And you both look guilty as fuck; what the hell is going on?'

The obvious answer (to most people anyway) is surely that we're having an affair, but you can tell by the look on Lou's face that she can't quite bring herself to fully entertain that kind of betrayal.

'All right, look, I'll tell you what's going on,' Ellis says, approaching her with his hands up. When he finally reaches her, he dares to take one of her hands in his. 'Actually, I'll show you. Come outside with me?'

Lou looks at him like he's a grenade with the pin pulled but still she lets him take her out into the back garden. The second she steps outside, her jaw drops. She glances between the lights, the petals, Ellis, me. Her face softens as it slowly dawns on her that whatever it is that is happening, it must be something good.

'Louise Annabelle Spencer, we've been together for three years now and, honestly, they have been the best years of my life,' Ellis tells her, taking both her hands in his. 'I know it's a cliché, but you really do make me a better person, and I can't imagine my life without you. So...'

Ellis roots around in his pocket as he lowers himself down onto one knee.

'Louise,' he says, his voice much steadier now. This is a man who knows what he wants. 'Will you make me the happiest man in the world and... will you marry me?'

Lou claps her hands over her mouth which, hilariously, is the last thing she should be doing right now. She goes to speak without moving them before laughing like a maniac.

'Yes!' she says, as she finally stops smothering herself. 'Yes, yes, yes, yes – a thousand times yes.'

'Yes!' Ellis says victoriously. 'She said yes!'

And that's their cue. Now that they all know it's good news, Lou and Ellis's nearest and dearest all come in through the back gate, where they've been hiding, just waiting for the right moment to pop out and celebrate with the happy couple. Well, there was no chance Lou was going to say no, everyone knows she's head over heels in love with Ellis.

The back garden is a blur of celebration. Hugs, kisses, photos being taken – everyone shuffling around to have their moment with the happy couple.

I take a step back, letting them enjoy their time in the spotlight, before Lou spots me out of the corner of her eye and runs over.

'Oh my God, Molly, I can't... I can't believe it,' she squeaks as she hugs me tightly. 'I can see your fingerprints all over this, as well as Ellis's and… just, wow, thank you. Thank you so much for helping him.'

'And to think you thought we were having an affair,' I tease her.

'I did not,' she insists. 'I knew you were up to something, and I didn't expect it to be this but… oh, I'm so happy it's this.'

'Me too,' I say with a smile. 'Congratulations. I'm so, so happy for you both. And I can't take much credit. It was all Ellis, I just helped him execute it.'

'I feel like the luckiest woman in the world,' she says, smiling wider than I've ever seen her smile before. It's like she's unlocked a new capacity for it.

I smile back. I really, really am happy for her.

'You'll be my bridesmaid, right?' she checks.

'Do you even need to ask?' I reply. 'It would be an honour.'

'You're the best friend a girl could have,' she tells me. 'And you know I'll return the favour when Dean proposes.'

My smile must slip, just a little, because I notice Lou's fade for a moment too.

'He will propose,' she tells me. 'You guys have been together for nearly three years.'

'We're just, I don't know, not on course for that,' I tell her. 'He's got his career, that's his main priority, and I've got my stuff going on and, yeah, we're happy as we are.'

Lou gives me that suspicious look again.

'Like, this evening, he's so busy with work, and he knows I've been busy helping to sort your proposal, but he said he's taking me somewhere special for dinner afterwards,' I say, not intending to sound like I'm making excuses, but I guess I am.

'Wait a sec,' Lou says, the smile creeping back across her lips. 'He knows you've been planning a proposal, you've probably been all excited, and now he's planning a special dinner... you don't think...?'

'No!' I say quickly. 'No, no, no. Unless... do you think?'

'I think, I think,' Lou replies. 'Oh my God, can you imagine, if the two of us got engaged on the same day!'

'Okay, don't get ahead of yourself,' I say with a chuckle.

'Louise, darling, Grandma is finally here,' her mum calls out.

'Go, see your gran,' I tell her.

'I love you,' Lou says, squeezing both of my hands.

'I love you too,' I reply. 'And I can't wait for your wedding.'

As Lou walks off, I finally understand what they mean when they say someone has a spring in their step. She is quite literally bouncing across the lawn, she's that happy. It's nice to see, and I really am so excited for her wedding but, as for Dean proposing to me, well, I think she's way off the mark there. He's not exactly the romantic type and I know that he thinks weddings are kind of lame, and I'm okay with that. Really, I am. I'm going to be a bridesmaid for Lou, which will be great. I can live with being a bridesmaid.

A phrase pops into my head, like an especially mean intrusive thought, almost like my inner monologue is teasing me. And now I can't stop thinking about it which is just – chef's kiss – so, so great.

Do I even need to tell you what it is? You know the one.

Always the bridesmaid...

2

I'm running late – and for a dinner that was booked for late anyway, so hurrying through Leeds city centre at this time just feels all kinds of wrong.

It's almost ten o'clock which, come on, feels more like a getting-home time than a going-out time. It's not that I'm an early sleeper, I'm definitely a night owl, it's more that I think I'm just fully ready to embrace my granny era. I know, I'm only thirty-two, and I'll have plenty of time for that sort of thing later but... I don't know. Is it so bad that I feel so ready now? I work in recruitment, for a big company that makes biscuits, which is more stressful than you might think – although the amount of tea and biscuits we consume on a daily basis is as you would expect, and it's probably the best perk of the job. That said, I'm still knackered, and the early-morning commute isn't for me.

Autumn is pretty much here so all I can really do is just surrender to it, embrace it even. I do really like autumn. I love the colours, the smells, the flavours. I'm all for cosy cardigans, cups of tea, curling up on the sofa underneath a blanket, binge-watching

Netflix while counting down the days until Christmas – which I love. That's what I want.

After that I just have to endure January, February and March, because I hate the cold and dark nights, and then it's spring and summer is on the horizon. And then we do it all again.

I have never been more certain that I was born to hibernate. The nights getting darker earlier and the weather getting colder is only confirming it for me.

Actually, you know what, what I really need is a holiday, more than anything. A proper one. Not a weekend break to London with Dean – which actually just turned out to be for a meeting and to watch the cricket, and it horizontal rained the whole time we were there – but a proper trip to somewhere warm. I need to feel the sun on my skin, for it to warm me through. I need to sit by the pool, sipping cocktails and relaxing. You just can't get that in the UK, even on a nice day, it's not the same.

A cold breeze rushes by me, reminding me that I'm in the UK, and that I should probably hurry up.

Finally arriving at the restaurant, after what I would call some of my best speed-walking, I push my way through the heavy glass doors to find that the place is empty. Have I come to the wrong place? Have I misunderstood the time?

'Molly?' a waiter checks.

'Yes,' I reply.

'This way, please.'

He gestures for me to follow him, so maybe I am in the right place.

I smile when I notice Dean, sitting alone at a table in the middle of an otherwise empty restaurant. We've got the whole place to ourselves.

He looks good in his suit – I don't even think you need an eye for expensive things to tell that his outfit cost a small fortune and that he most definitely works in finance. He's tall with dark hair and blue eyes which is just – the dream, right?

He smiles as he beckons me over.

'Come on, I am starving,' he says playfully. 'Hello.'

'Hi,' I reply, giving him a peck on the lips before I take my seat at the table across from him.

'I ordered us a bottle of wine,' he tells me. 'You okay?'

'I'm great, yeah,' I reply, finally catching my breath. 'How was work?'

'Yeah, it was fine,' he says. 'Well, no, it was stressful, but everyone is richer now, so all is well that ends well.'

He leans back in his chair and grins.

'It all went really well, by the way,' I tell him.

'Good,' he replies. Then he realises he doesn't know what I'm talking about. 'What went well?'

'The proposal,' I remind him.

'Ah, good,' he says simply.

'Ellis was amazing, and Lou was in total shock – over the moon though,' I continue. 'I took some photos, to show you how amazing the garden looked.'

'Great,' he replies.

He's definitely distracted by something, or there's something on his mind, because I don't really feel like he's listening to me.

'She was—'

'I've ordered for us, by the way,' he says, talking over me. 'I thought you'd be starving too.'

'Oh, okay, great,' I reply with a smile. 'It will be a nice surprise then.'

He nods before taking a sip of his wine.

'I just thought, you know, skip that whole step,' he reasons.

'Absolutely,' I reply. 'I really am starving. We only had celebratory drinks and, to be honest, I feel like they've gone to my head a little.'

'Well, weddings are all about getting drunk anyway, right?' he says.

'Yeah, although knowing Lou, you just know it's going to be something super classy – an absolute dream.'

That's just the kind of girl Lou is. If something is worth doing, she does it right.

'So long as you're not the one planning it,' he says with a bit of a laugh. 'You've been so preoccupied with this proposal stuff, I was hoping I might have you back now.'

'I'm sure she can take it from here,' I point out. 'I'll have bridesmaid duties, obviously.'

'Obviously,' he says, rolling his eyes. 'Well, if you're finally all mine again, I was going to ask you...'

Dean pauses to rummage around in his jacket pocket.

Oh... my... God. Is he proposing? Was Lou right? He's got me here, in this restaurant, just the two of us. He's ordered the wine, the food, he's talking about having me all to himself, and now he's going to ask me something. It seems more and more likely by the second, and I can feel the hope rising up through my body, finally reaching my face. I feel my jaw drop slightly in anticipation, I feel like I'm sitting more upright, and my hands have never felt sweatier.

But then he pulls out his phone and my face must fall because Dean looks at me, confused, like he can't work out what has gone wrong.

'What?' he asks me.

'What?' I reply, trying to style it out.

He looks between me and his phone before finally placing it back in his pocket.

'Molly... did you...?'

'Did I...?' I reply, trying to hide my disappointment, but it's not easy.

'Oh my God, you thought I was going to propose, didn't you?' he says, grinning slightly.

'What? No!' I insist.

'You did,' he replies, laughing, shaking his head. 'All of this proposal stuff has turned your brain to mush.'

'Oi, that's not what I thought,' I say, trying not to sound too defensive, but it's not really working. I guess I really did let myself get swept up in the romance.

'Molly, we've been over this countless times,' he says with a sigh.

'I know,' I reply, trying to find my confidence again. 'And I totally get it. You have nothing to worry about.'

'Don't I?' he replies. 'Because it sort of feels like I do. I was just getting my phone out to check if I'd booked an early squash game, because I was going to ask if you wanted to stay at mine tonight, but suddenly it feels like that's never going to be enough for you.'

'It's fine,' I say firmly.

'Is it?' he checks. 'Or are you secretly hoping I'll change my mind?'

I just sigh as I watch Dean knock back the contents of his glass. I need to say something, to smooth this over.

'Dean, honestly, can we just forget about this, please?' I ask. 'I would love to stay at yours tonight. Let's just pretend this didn't happen.'

'Which we could do, but it's only going to come up again,' he says as he rubs the back of his neck.

'Dean, it—'

'No, Molly, come on, I think we need to face the facts,' he says firmly. 'We want totally different things in life. You want a husband and a family and I don—'

He stops mid-word, clearly to change course.

'My work is my life,' he continues. 'It's what I love the most, it's my family – it's my future. And I don't think you fit into that future any more.'

His words feel like a punch to the stomach. I can't believe I actually thought he was going to propose – the only thing he's proposing is that we break up.

I open my mouth to plead or argue or anything to stop the wheels, but they're already in motion and, well, there's no point stopping them now.

I thought Dean and I had a future together, that this was going somewhere whether we made it official with a bit of paper or not, that didn't matter to me. Now I feel like, what, we've just been dating for the best part of three years? I feel so stupid.

I chew my lip for a second. I don't know what the hell I'm supposed to say.

For a moment he just stares at me. Then his expression softens, just a little.

'I think we both know that ending things is the right thing to do,' he says. 'But, look, stay. Have dinner with me. You can even still stay at mine tonight, if you like, but then after that...'

Everything clicks into place for me. Sure, I could have dinner with him, I could even spend the night with him, and maybe, just maybe I could convince him that we can keep things as they are, and that I'll never want more, but this whole embarrassing ordeal has given me a kind of clarity that I didn't have before. I don't want to be with someone who loves their job more than they love me, who will always put me second. Not only that but I was willing to forget about getting married because I loved him, because I didn't care about that, I only cared about him. Surely, if he felt the same, he would be willing to make those sorts of compromises too? If he's not willing to settle then neither am I.

I grab my bag from under the table and stand up.

'You know what? I think I'll give dinner a miss,' I tell him. 'Maybe you could get some work done, while you eat. In fact, maybe you can spend the night in bed with your work. I'm sure the two of you will be very happy together.'

'Molly, you're being daft,' he says, but I don't care. I don't even reply, I just head for the door with my head held high.

I'll show him that I don't need him and I don't want him, and I am totally unbothered. Frankly, I've dodged a bullet.

It feels so much cooler out here, now that I've been inside for a little while, but I'm sure I'll soon warm up as I march home like the strong, independent woman that I am. Home to my home – my home that is still all decked out with pure romance – and I'll walk over the rose petals, go upstairs, get in my bed and then, and only then, will I cry myself to sleep.

Well, just because I know my worth, doesn't mean I'm not totally devastated about it.

3

Puffy eyes, knotted hair, a tea stain right down my white vest – why would any man in his right mind leave me?

I look rough, despite getting my eight hours last night. Then again, it was eight hours of crying, rather than sleeping, so it all checks out.

When I got home last night, I did what any self-respecting woman does after a break-up (and no dinner), I cried my eyes out while I raided my kitchen, eating almost everything I could get my hands on. Then I put on a movie, but not a romcom, like you're supposed to, or even something sad. I watched *I Know What You Did Last Summer* while I shovelled crisps into my mouth and laughed with glee from one murder to the next.

This morning, I feel like I'm hungover. Perhaps I am, just a bit, from the engagement drinks, but I think it's mostly from crying and eating junk before falling asleep flat on the sofa. It feels like some of the crisps are still inside my neck. Wait, scratch that, it's just one smashed one, practically glued to my skin, scratching me. Boys, I'm single again, form a queue.

I grab my phone and notice a text from Lou in the 'Besties'

group chat inviting us all for celebratory brunch in – fuck, in an hour. I need to get ready, asap, but not a regular get ready, the kind that will hide all evidence from last night. I need to sort out my hair, take off last night's make-up, put on some fresh war paint, and I need to do it all right now.

I think when you're like me, and you feel like you're always chasing your tail, and you're always running late, you actually get getting ready in a hurry down to a fine art. I'm like a machine, flying through the motions on autopilot, throwing on clothes, caking on make-up, blasting my hair with enough dry shampoo that it actually looks like I'm ready in an instant, like a magician in a puff of smoke.

Now I just need to get there and, look, I can work miracles with myself, but I have no control over public transport. Luckily, living in Chapel Allerton, a taxi into town is doable. It drops me at the bottom of Greek Street with about thirty seconds to spare. I've done it again.

I spot Lou and the others lingering inside the entrance of the restaurant. Lou notices me and opens the door.

'Molly!' she sings, all smiles, greeting me with a hug.

'Hey, sorry I'm a bit late,' I reply.

'You're not late, we're all early,' she reassures me. 'Come on, let's go take our seats.'

Being a fiancée looks good on Lou. Seriously, the girl is glowing. She always looks pretty flawless, always in that effortless way, but today she's taken it to another level. Her light brown hair has been curled into the softest, bounciest waves, and her make-up is almost invisible, to the point where it looks like nothing but natural beauty. She's wearing a floor-length floral dress with pink and orange detail, and a cropped denim jacket. She looks like she's ready for a photoshoot, and suddenly the rush-job I was so proud I did on myself doesn't feel up to scratch.

A waiter greets the four of us and shows us to our table. There's a seat next to Lou, but Willow practically pushes past me to get there first.

'We can sit together,' Nita tells me, hooking her arm with mine.

'Thanks,' I reply.

Everyone needs a crazy, wild-card friend, and ours is Nita. Even the way I met her is a funny story because, believe it or not, I met Nita on Matcher. Yes, the dating app. I was swiping my way through man after man, feeling completely underwhelmed, when I happened upon her. At first I thought it was some sort of glitch, that I had been served up a woman by mistake (and, to be honest, after all the underwhelming men I'd met, I actually started to wonder whether, if you manage to run out of men, it just starts showing you women instead) until I saw that in her profile picture she was holding a sign that simply said: *stop swiping and read my bio*. Curious, I took a look, only to find this inspiring and hilarious message. I don't remember what it said word for word, but the sentiment of it was: *Are you sick of swiping too? Maybe we don't need to find a man on here to complete us, maybe what we're missing is a fun bunch of girlies to hang out with. Message me, let's hang out.*

I showed the message to Lou and we decided that you can never have too many girlfriends, so we invited her out with us and the rest is history.

Nita is awesome. She looks so cool without ever looking like she has tried. Take the pair of jeans she's wearing right now – I know that she tore the knee by scooting underneath a car to retrieve her phone on a night out, but they actually look like she bought them from some designer shop like that. She's wearing a leather jacket, her long reddish hair pin-straight, and bright red lipstick that I bet she isn't going to get on her cutlery like I would. She looks like a cool, modern Jessica Rabbit.

Finally, we have Willow. Willow is Lou's friend from work and she's fine, I guess, but the two of us just don't seem to get along. We try to make it work, for Lou, but there's just something that isn't quite right between us. We tend to find ourselves on opposite sides of everything – we even look like each other's exact opposite. Willow is short and petite, with a sharp, dark brown long bob – she has that chiselled, smouldering Megan Fox kind of beauty, making her very much the 'girl next door' type. I, on the other hand, am the kind of girl who actually lives next door. I'm tall (but not like a supermodel, just enough to make me stick out like a sore thumb) with green eyes, long blonde hair and a rounded face. I look more… I don't know, lived in? Like I've had a harder life? I know it sounds silly but sometimes it's hard not to feel like Big Bird, when I'm surrounded by brunette bombshells. I feel like Weird Barbie – but I am nowhere near as flexible.

Our waiter appears to take our orders. First our cocktails, then our food. A piña colada is pretty much a smoothie, right? And I can't resist the Nutella pancakes – I'd probably order them even if I wasn't heartbroken but, seeing as though I am, I order the double stack.

'For brunch?' Willow squeaks. 'Surely it's more of a dessert – when it's smaller, of course.'

Oh, of course.

I just shrug my shoulders. She can't shame me into ordering something else, because this is what I want.

'I'll have the breakfast salad, please,' she tells the waiter.

Breakfast. Salad. Honestly, that sounds as vile as it does depressing, but I'm not going to say a word, because I know that grown adults are allowed to eat whatever the hell they want.

I feel Nita nudge me with her knee, under the table, ever so lightly. A silent acknowledgement that she's on my side.

'Okay, girls, so,' Lou begins now that we're alone. 'As I'm sure you've all guessed, the reason I have gathered you here today is to officially ask you all if you would do me the honour of being my bridesmaids.'

'Oh, Louise, it would mean the world to me,' Willow gushes, getting in there first.

'Absolutely,' I add – even though I already said so yesterday, but it hardly feels worth mentioning it just to point score.

'Yeah, count me in,' Nita says. 'Just promise me we can veto any ugly dresses.'

Lou laughs.

'Nita, I know better than to try and tell you what to wear,' Lou replies. 'In fact, I might even let you choose for everyone.'

'Let's not be so hasty,' Willow adds.

Nita shoots her a look.

'Plenty of time to figure it out,' I say tactfully, trying to move things along.

'You say that, but I've put our names on the waiting list for the venue of my dreams,' Lou tells us.

'Oh my God, is it...?' Willow says excitedly.

'It is,' Lou replies in a similar tone.

'Oh my God, where is it?' Nita asks, playfully mocking their enthusiasm.

'La Palacio de la Mar,' Lou replies.

'Where?' I ask, because I'm not even sure what language she's speaking right now.

'You've never heard of La Palacio de la Mar?' Willow says in disbelief.

'No,' I reply, because why would I?

'It's a resort, in Spain,' Lou tells us.

'It's the most exclusive, sought-after wedding venue, favoured by celebrities,' Willow continues. 'Lou and I talk about it all the time at work.'

It definitely feels like Willow is point-scoring, like she's trying to prove to me that she knows Lou better than I do.

'So, all I'm hearing is Spain, and I'm in,' Nita says. 'Imagine the hen do.'

'Well, we'll see if I can even get a booking, but I was thinking maybe somewhere local for the hen party.'

'Hmm, yeah, okay, we'll see,' Nita says mischievously.

Of course, Nita is more excited for the hen party than she is the actual wedding. Love her for that.

The waiter places our food down in front of us and, mmm, it smells so good. I pick up my knife, stab it into the heart of my pancake stack, and then take my fork to cut myself a bite. It's a huge piece, but I can take it.

Lou looks at me with a frown.

'Oh my God, Molly. What's wrong?' she asks.

I just stare at her, my fork hovering in front of my mouth, trying to hide how annoyed I am that she can read my mind.

'Nothing,' I insist. 'I'm just hungry. What are you on about?'

She narrows her eyes at me.

'Did everything go okay with Dean last night?' she asks.

'Of course,' I reply, widening my eyes to hit home my point, but it's too much.

'Molly!' she practically snaps, her voice firm.

She knows. Obviously she knows.

'It's nothing, it's not worth getting into,' I insist.

'It doesn't seem like nothing,' she says. 'Come on, you can tell me, it's okay.'

I sigh as I place down my fork.

'Dean broke up with me,' I blurt.

'No! What?' she replies.

'*He* broke up with *you*?' Nita says in disbelief.

'Dean is single?' Willow adds.

We all turn to face her. Is she serious?

'I just mean, yeah, that's awful,' she says, trying to turn her remark around.

'It's fine,' I reassure them all. 'It's for the best. Really, it is. We both wanted completely different things in life so it was always going to end in tears.'

'Molly, I'm so sorry,' Lou says sincerely. I can tell she feels bad that I'm going through this when she is so deliriously happy. That's why I love her.

'It still sucks, I know, but it's onward and upward from here, right?' I say with a smile.

The only thing to be right now is positive.

'That's my girl,' Nita says, wrapping an arm around me. 'You know what? We can be single girls together, at the wedding. We can pick up a couple of hot groomsmen. And just think how much fun the hen party will be now – especially if we're in Spain.'

'Nita!' Lou says with a laugh. 'It's not going to be abroad.'

'We'll see, we'll see,' Nita jokes. She turns back to me. 'I'm proud of you, Mol. It's all going to be okay.'

I exhale deeply then smile. Yes, this is rubbish, but it's going to be so much easier to get through with my friends by my side.

Well, my friends and Willow.

4

You know what, I'm starting to think a piña colada is not like a smoothie at all, because I've never made a bad decision after a few too many smoothies.

I know it's a bad decision and yet, here I am, doing it anyway, because I am a woman scorned and this is what women scorned do.

Where am I going? I'm going to Dean's apartment. No, I'm not invited. No, I'm not telling him that I'm coming. And yes, I know what you're going to say, that I should turn around, but well, I'm listening to the piña coladas, not common sense.

I'm outside his building, staring up at the city centre highrise, feeling ever so slightly unsteady on my feet. I suppose if I were going to change my mind about doing this then now would be the time, but as I notice someone heading inside, I see this as my only chance to get in through the door without having to buzz upstairs, so I tailgate in. Honestly, it's just too easy to sneak into places like this. I'd be furious if I lived here, but I was never asked to live here, I was invited to stay the night, when it was convenient, and I was allowed to leave a few things here, but not enough to feel like I was putting roots down. Anyway, that's why I'm here, to get my things back. How can I get closure if I still have things here, huh?

Dean's apartment is a total cliché, exactly what you would expect of a bloody banker – something that is tricky not to mispronounce when you've had a few, although misspeaking in the obvious way wouldn't be inaccurate, would it?

He has floor-to-ceiling windows – but naturally he lives high up enough that it isn't a problem for privacy. Inside is your typical bachelor pad. Black leather, wood, sports-y stuff. Completely uninspired. And the whole place is so soulless and clinical. Nothing is ever left out. I used to fantasise about messing the place up sometimes, just to see what it would look like with a thing out of place. It turns out there was something out of place there – me.

Okay, enough of the pity party, I'm outside his door and it's time to take back what's mine.

I knock on the door with my head held high and my speech all planned out, only for the wind to be knocked right out of my sail when a woman answers the door. She's younger than me, prettier if we're being honest, and she's wearing a super-tight, super-short dress. She's a ten, and I'm a drunk.

'Hello?' she says brightly.

'Oh, hello, I, erm...' My voice trails off. 'Are you Dean's girlfriend?'

I shouldn't ask but I can't help myself.

'Oh, no,' she quickly insists.

Oh, man, did I really jump from nought to the worst conclusion? I can't believe I thought he'd dumped me because he had someone else lined up to take my place. I'm so quick to think the worst of him, just because things didn't work out.

'We just met on Matcher. This is actually our first date,' she informs me. 'So here's hoping.'

Oh, that bastard.

'Lovely,' I say. 'Is Dean here?'

'He's just, erm, in the shower,' she says with a smile.

'Well, he said I could drop by and pick up some things, so I'll be in and out,' I tell her, walking in like I own the place, because with confidence you can get away with anything, right?

I march into the bedroom and grab my spare clothes from the drawer where I was allowed to leave a fresh shirt and a pair of knickers. I'm expecting to find the bed a mess but thankfully, for my sanity, it's still made, so I guess they haven't got to that part of the date... yet. The only other thing I have here is a toothbrush. It's just a cheap, disposable one that I got to leave here but, hey, it's mine and I'm taking it.

I walk into the steamy bathroom and grab my toothbrush. I can hear Dean, in the shower, singing to himself. It makes me sick that he's so happy when I'm so cut up. Whether our break-up was for the best or not, surely he should at least be a bit sad? No? Am I crazy?

Flustered, I accidentally knock the bottle of hand soap into the sink.

'Is that you, sexy?' he calls out. 'Decided you want to join me after all, huh?'

I lean against the bathroom doorframe, tapping my toothbrush menacingly against my hand, brandishing it like a weapon.

'Hmm, I don't think so,' I reply. 'I've seen it all before and, trust me, it's not that impressive.'

Dean sticks his head out of the shower door in a flash.

'Molly?' he blurts.

'Hi,' I reply, waving my toothbrush at him.

He just stares at me, his mouth open, water dripping from his jaw and landing on the floor tiles in front of him. It would be a real shame if he were to make the floor slippery, and then fall on it. Suuuuch a shame.

I blow him a kiss goodbye – a sarcastic one – and then head for the door. My work here is done.

The hot redhead is waiting in the hallway, by the open door – she's probably been hoping I would just leave, like a moth who flew into the light and is nothing but an annoyance.

'I have everything I came for,' I tell her. 'Thanks for your help.'

'No, erm, you're welcome,' she replies.

'Can I offer you some advice?' I say. 'You don't have to take it but if I were you, I'd get out of here. Let's just say Dean has some pretty intense stuff going on down there, something that even the antibiotics are struggling with.'

'Oh,' she says. 'Ohhh! Oh, God, thanks for letting me know. Ew.'

'Yeah, big time ew,' I reply. 'Anyway, thanks.'

'Wait up,' she calls after me. 'I'm out of here. I'll head out with you.'

As the woman gets in the lift with me, I smile to myself. I know she's just one girl, and there are thousands more on Matcher, so it's only a small victory but, I don't know, surely he can take the weekend off, right? Then he can shag all the girls he wants, and if he's moving on then I should as well, right? I have two choices right now: I can swear off men forever or I can do what Dean is doing and move on. I know that I want to do the former, to fully embrace granny mode and hide away for the foreseeable, but why should I let him mess up my life? I should do what he's doing and swipe my way through every single person in

Leeds, because what better way to get back on the horse than to, well, get back on the horse?

The thing about Matcher is that it's full of duds – full of Deans – but I could meet someone good, a rare diamond in the rough. Not all men are like Dean, right? I certainly hope not, because the last thing I need is another one of those.

5

EIGHT MONTHS LATER

June. It's supposed to be bloody June, the start of summer, warm weather, and light nights – everything I have been waiting so, so patiently for. Instead, it's been raining nonstop forever (well, at least two weeks), and it's the really grim kind that soaks through anything it touches, gently carries itself under umbrellas, and makes the world look like it has some kind of dystopian filter on it.

Sometimes I feel like Mother Nature is against me. Whether it's having a rain cloud follow me around or sending me my period right before I'm supposed to be going out – Mother Nature is not a girl's girl. Girl code means nothing to her.

I should keep my voice down because I am going out tonight, and she's already sent the rain. I hate going out in weather like this, but I'm meeting Lou for a drink and a catch-up, so I've made an effort. I've curled my hair, winged my eyeliner (perfect, for once – exactly as I intended it, and symmetrical, so of course the rain is going to ruin it) and dressed in my best. If I look like a drowned rat when I arrive, then I do, but know that I did my best before I left my house.

We're meeting at Thin Aire, a swanky rooftop bar in Leeds city centre that we love to visit. You know the type – nondescript, funky ambient music, drinks that cost more than a meal, beautiful people everywhere. It sounds awful, when you put it like that, but when you're raised on a diet of *Sex and the City* and glossy magazines, sitting here (whether you can really afford it or not) gassing with your gal pals actually makes you feel like you've 'made it'.

I'm here – albeit with less impressive eyeliner, and hair that I can practically hear frizzing – and I'm excited for my £18 drink.

With the exception of the doorway, Thin Aire is made entirely of glass, giving you panoramic views of the city... usually. Not today though, thanks to the rain and the dark, it's hazy out there, definitely not a day for sitting on the terrace, but it's lovely and warm inside, with ambient lighting. It's so romantic – not that I'm here for romance.

I smile and wave as I spot Lou, sitting at one of the tables in a great spot by the window. Oh, she has Ellis with her. I thought it was just going to be the two of us.

Actually, now that I'm getting closer, I can see that there's another man at the table too. He isn't anyone I recognise, but he's definitely with them. I smile widely to try and fight off any looks of confusion or disappointment that it isn't going to be just me and Lou.

I wonder who he is, this mystery man. He's tall and broad in a way that is almost intimidating and – look, I love a strong brow – but his thick, close-knit eyebrows make him look permanently angry. He definitely isn't giving welcoming, friendly vibes right now. Then again, neither am I, probably.

'Hello,' I say brightly as I take a seat at the table. 'Sorry I'm a bit late.'

'If you haven't learned by now that the time I give you is always ten minutes before the actual time...' Lou jokes as she leans over to give me a squeeze.

I look between her and the boys expectantly, hoping she'll clue me in on what's going on.

'Ellis and his friend, Mark, just happened to be coming here on their night out too – I bumped into them downstairs, outside the lift,' she *absolutely lies*. 'So I said why not join us for a drink.'

'Oh, okay, cool,' I lie too.

What, so Ellis – her fiancé – and his friend Mark just bumped into her, outside her favourite bar, randomly? I know for a fact that Ellis is more of a pub kind of guy – he hates coming here. Does she really think I'm falling for this? Oh, no, no, no. Lou might be able to read me like a book but I can read her too. Look at her, the look on her face says it all, it's those hopeful doe eyes that are silently telling me to give Mark a chance. This is a set-up – a stitch-up, even.

I notice Ellis give Mark what I think was supposed to be a subtle prompt with his elbow.

Mark clears his throat.

'Mark – Mark Best,' he introduces himself, in a very James Bond sounding way for someone who is not at all James Bond like.

'Molly,' I reply. 'Nice to meet you.'

'Best by name – best man too,' Mark informs me.

'Oh, you're the best man?' I reply.

That's interesting. I would have thought that Rick, the man who I thought was Ellis's best friend, would have been his best man.

'Mark is Ellis's oldest friend, from their school days,' Lou explains. 'He lives in Cornwall now.'

'Devon,' Mark corrects her – you can hear the offence he's taken in his voice. Oh, boy. Would I be that bothered if he thought I was from Lancashire instead of Yorkshire? Absolutely not.

'Sorry, Devon,' Lou corrects herself. 'Mark, Molly is my chief bridesmaid.'

'So, we're sort of a pair, at the wedding,' Mark suggests.

Once again – absolutely not.

'Mark is a plumber,' Lou informs me. 'He has his own business.'

'Impressive,' I say, trying to sound like I mean it, because it is impressive, I'm just not sure what else to say.

'Mark, Molly works in recruitment,' Lou continues, turning to Mark.

'Hmm,' Mark says, rubbing his chin.

'Hmm, what?' I can't help but ask – not that I think I'll like the answer.

'So your job is to find people real jobs,' Mark points out. 'That's not technically a job in itself, is it?'

My polite smile drops from my face.

'It is technically a job,' I inform him. 'It's called recruitment, and it's challenging and rewarding, and I really enjoy it.'

Mark laughs in a way that suggests he thinks I'm taking myself too seriously and it boils my blood.

Part of me thinks that I'm just not giving Mark a chance because I haven't dated a man since *him* (I refuse to even think of my ex's name), and I don't plan on doing so if I can avoid it. Lou, my dear, dear friend Lou, is trying to prevent me from avoiding it by force. But then again, come on, the man is telling me *to my face* that he doesn't think my job is a real job.

'It's just funny to me that your career is, well, getting other people a career,' he persists.

'Anyway, so,' Lou interrupts him, leaning forward in her seat, trying to physically put herself in the middle of our conversation before it's too late. 'Molly, you went to the cinema last night, right? Mark loves to go to the cinema too.'

'I do,' he says, cautiously for some reason.

'You saw that new Will Ferrell movie, right?' Lou adds, working overtime to find some common ground between us.

Mark scoffs.

I pull a face and tilt my head curiously.

'Comedies,' he says, reading my mind.

'What's wrong with comedies?' I ask.

'Nothing – if you like to laugh,' he replies.

Doesn't that just say it all?

'Doesn't everyone like to laugh?' I say.

I can see the look on Lou's face, out of the corner of my eye, and it's one of mild panic, like the situation might be getting away from her.

'I like to watch something with a bit more substance,' he informs me. 'Ellis tells me you've been single for ages – you might need to broaden your horizons.'

I look to Ellis.

'I didn't say that,' Ellis insists. 'I—'

'You're both single,' Lou points out. 'And there's nothing wrong with that.'

'I'm just saying, she might have more luck if she steps out of her comfort zone,' Mark says.

'Me?' I reply. '*I'm* fine. *I* have no trouble dating, thanks.'

'So, you date around?' he says, and there's that tone again.

'I didn't say that,' I clap back.

'It's cool, I respect that different people have different ideas of what is preferable,' he replies.

Just not when it comes to movies, I guess.

'Sometimes, it doesn't have to be a big deal, if two people don't get on, but they have needs, they just want someone to keep them warm at night, or at a wedding...' he continues and, wow.

'Lou, I'm just nipping to the loos, do you want to come?' I ask her, because not only do I need to stop having this conversation, but I need to start having one with her, like: what the hell were you thinking?

'Yeah, okay, I could do with going too,' she replies.

'I'll never understand that about women,' Mark says as we make a move.

I imagine there is a lot he will never understand about women. The man actually has negative game.

Lou hooks her arm with mine as we head for the toilets.

'He's nice, isn't he?' she says optimistically.

I snort with laughter.

'Lou, what are you doing to me?' I cackle. 'That guy? Really?'

She sighs heavily.

'Ellis told me he was great – he's his oldest friend,' she insists.

'That's why Ellis hasn't realised what a tool he is as an adult,' I reply. 'Oh my God, who doesn't like to laugh? And what was all that about – was he suggesting some kind of friends with benefits arrangement?'

'Yeah, that was, well, ew...' Her voice trails off. 'I'm sorry.'

'It's fine,' I reply, holding her arm a little tighter to reassure her. 'But you know that I'm not ready to date anyone, right? Even if he had been a dream date instead of a nightmare, I wouldn't have been interested.'

'It's been eight months, Mol,' she reminds me – as if I need reminding. 'You can't let that clown Dean stop you from living your life.'

I sigh.

'Listen, I know that you mean well, and I know that I shouldn't let Dean ruin all men for me. I'm just not ready right now,' I tell her. 'But I will be, and when I am you will be the third, if not second, person to know.'

'Okay, okay, I am reading you loud and clear but, well, if you let it go on another eight months, let's say we'll have this conversation again?' she suggests.

I laugh.

'Okay, sure,' I reply. 'As far as terms and conditions go, I only have one. Can we go somewhere else?'

'I'll do you one better,' she replies. 'You go join the boys, I'll go grab us some drinks, and you tell Ellis I asked if he'll give me a hand, what I'll actually do is suggest he and Mark go elsewhere. At least that way it won't be awkward.'

'Perfect,' I reply. 'Thanks for trying though – I'm not sure if I've said that already. I love that you never give up on me.'

'Hey, even if you've given up on yourself, I will never give up on you because you're amazing, the best friend a girl could have, and you can do much, much better than Mark. In fact, I'd be surprised if Ellis still thinks he's best man material after this.'

'I mean, don't go changing your wedding plans, just because I think the best man is a bit of a knobhead.'

'Anyone at that table would have thought the same,' she says. 'So go, put the plan in motion, and then we'll have a good night, just the two of us.'

I smile. Now there's an idea of hers I can get behind.

The boys look deep in conversation when I arrive back, just in time for me to catch the tail end of Mark ranting.

'...you never said she was so boring though. I suppose so many girls are, so I wasn't expecting miracles, but I at least thought her dry spell might make her a bit more up for it.

Tonight, at the wedding even, but nope, she's not even up for that.'

I should walk away and pretend I didn't hear that – no, I should say something, because how dare he talk about me like that?

What I actually do is stand there with my jaw dropped. Ellis notices me first, then Mark, whose smile quickly fades when he realises I heard what he just said.

He's going, I know that, so let's just make that happen. I don't want an apology (although what are the chances I would even get one?) and I don't think there is anything I can say to him that will change him.

'What did I miss?' I ask, sitting down with a smile.

Neither of them says a word. They both look embarrassed – Mark because he got caught, Ellis because he brought him here. Ellis is a good guy, there's no way he would've brought Mark here if he knew this was going to be his attitude. Mark might live in Cornwall, or Devon, but the two of them seem worlds apart.

'Ellis, Lou says can you help her with the drinks,' I say.

'Erm, yes,' he replies.

You can tell he's thinking twice about leaving the two of us here alone. It turns out he has nothing to worry about because once he's gone, Mark and I just sit in silence. It's an awkward silence, for him at least, but I'm just glad I'll soon see the back of him.

And this, ladies and gentlemen, is the reason I don't want to date. The world is full of Marks and Deans and I'm just not interested. I'm not saying I want to stay single forever, of course I'm not, but while eight months might seem like ages to Lou, to me it's felt like no time at all. I still find his things in my house – just random things he won't be missing – and I still have tickets for a gig we were going to go to together. It's impossible to feel that closure when the door still feels like it's open, just a little, but I'm getting there. I thought Dean and I were going to spend the rest of our lives together, whether we were married or not, so now, I don't know, I need to figure out what's next, but what I do know is that the last thing I want is a man.

And definitely not one like Mark Best, the *worst* man.

6

Is there a scarier sight than looking at your phone and seeing fourteen missed calls and twenty-seven messages?

My workday has run over slightly (which is funny, given that my job is apparently not a job) because I've been stuck in a meeting for the last two hours. Staff turnover has increased in certain roles, so it was a crisis meeting of sorts. I say this with zero humour intended, so do not laugh, but you'll be amazed how many people in the biscuit factory crumble under the pressure.

Most of the calls are from Lou, apart from a few from Nita, and the main message from Lou, that stands out a mile, reads:

WEDDING EMERGENCY.

Shit, some chief bridesmaid I am, if I'm not around when she needs me.

I grab my bag and head for the door, trying to call Lou as I go, but she isn't picking up.

I drop a message in the group chat saying I'm out of work now, and then try Lou again. Eventually she picks up.

'Lou!' I practically squeak. 'What's going on?'

'Oh my God, Molly!' she replies, sounding as exhausted as she does relieved. 'It's been a whole thing – are you still in town?'

'Yes,' I reply.

'I'm in The Alchemist, with Nita and Willow, can you come and join us?'

'Of course, I'll be right there,' I say.

'Okay, see you soon,' she replies, hanging up before I get a chance to grill her about what the hell has happened.

I head to The Alchemist as fast as my little legs will carry me, almost running out of steam as I pull myself up the steps. But I'm here and I'm ready for... whatever is going on.

I spot Lou, Nita and Willow sitting in the bar. Lou and Willow look quite serious but, to be honest with you, Nita looks like she's trying to stifle a smile.

'Right, fill me in,' I demand, plonking myself down at the table. 'What on earth is happening?'

'Well, you know that hen party in Blackpool that we were planning?' Nita says. 'Well, it's cancelled.'

'Oh no, what happened?' I ask.

And why does Nita look so pleased about it? I know she wanted to do something fancier but, even so, I'm surprised she looks so pleased about it in front of Lou.

'Well, technically it's the wedding that is off, not the hen party,' Lou corrects her.

My breath catches in my throat.

'La Palacio de la Mar called and said something about how they were unfortunately going to have to cancel my wedding – I think they said something about the council and planned work on the drains meaning they were going to have to close, so my wedding couldn't take place. To be honest I was hardly listening at that point, the only words I heard were the ones saying it was cancelled.'

Oh, no, poor Lou. La Palacio de la Mar is her dream venue, she must be gutted.

'So... the wedding is off?' I ask.

'Not exactly,' Lou continues. 'They said they could move it to the next available date... a date in 2029.'

'Shit,' I blurt, the word leaving my lips before I can stop it. That just seems like such a long, long way away.

'But then they said they had one date this year, because they'd had a cancellation...' she continues, and I would swear she was pausing for dramatic effect.

'When?' I ask.

'The end of the month,' Lou says, practically wincing.

'Weeks away?' I check pointlessly.

'Yes!' Nita chimes in excitedly. 'And here's the best part. So Willow and I have checked and pretty much everything is still doable – most of the wedding day stuff is included with the venue anyway – so the show will go on, Lou will get to have her dream wedding at her dream location.'

'My dress will be the only thing I need to sort in a hurry,' Lou adds. 'But, honestly, if I get my dream wedding, in my dream venue, with my dream man, I'll wear a dress off the rack if I have to.'

'Fair enough,' I reply, chuckling through my words, because this is nuts. 'But why do I feel like there's something you haven't told me yet?'

'Because there is something we haven't told you,' Nita replies. 'So, obviously we need to rearrange the hen party, and we need to be in Spain to make sure everything is sorted, and of course every hotel and villa in the area is fully booked for the foreseeable. But, with me being an absolute rockstar – and a luxury travel agent –

I've got it sorted. I called a company in Spain that rents out villas, and it turned out there was this one villa that is under new management, that wasn't listed on the website yet, so they said we can have it. And the best news of all is that it's a two-week minimum booking, so we have to take it for two weeks, so we're going to have a week-long hen holiday, and then when Lou goes off on honeymoon with Ellis, we get to stay for another week, just to make a real holiday of it.'

So that explains why Nita is smiling so widely.

'Wow,' I blurt. 'That's... wow. I'm so glad it's all sorted, and so sorry I wasn't around when you needed me.'

'You weren't needed, it turns out,' Willow chimes in.

Oh, I'll bet she's loving that I didn't answer, that she had to save the day instead.

'I'll tell you what is needed – champagne,' Nita practically sings. 'I'll go grab us some.'

'I'll go to the toilet,' Willow says, obviously eager to get back before the champagne arrives.

Now it's just me and Lou, and I can see the stress in every muscle in her face.

'Are you really okay about all of this?' I check.

'It is what it is,' she says, sighing deeply. 'It was a shock, more than anything, but it's sorted now. I'm lucky to have such wonderful friends and family. There are some things I need to figure out, like finding a hotel further afield for our guests, and booking a coach to take them back and forth between the hotel and the wedding, but it's doable.'

'Well, that's good, so long as you're happy about it,' I reply.

'You'll be happy about it too,' she says. 'Because Mark is on holiday, which means he can't come, which means that Rick will have to be Ellis's best man after all.'

'Oh no,' I say, trying to sound sad, but smiling widely.

'You know, Rick is single,' Lou reminds me. 'Single, eligible, not a total arsehole.'

'The bare minimum – yay,' I joke. 'You need to focus on sorting your own mess, before you stick your nose in mine.'

Lou laughs.

'Okay, okay, I'm just saying,' she replies. Then her face falls. 'Molly, will it all be okay?'

'Of course it will,' I insist. 'We'll make sure it is.'

'I guess a girls' week in Spain won't suck, will it?' she adds. 'It feels like a nice way to say goodbye to singledom.'

'Exactly, focus on the positives,' I tell her.

That's what I need to do to. Focus on the positives. I've been banging on and on about how I'm in desperate need of a holiday – well, one just fell into my lap. I just need to make the most of it.

Finally, something to look forward to. Something that is coming up on the horizon. But now I guess we only have a week or so to get ready for it.

This is going to be fun.

7

Words I never thought would leave my lips: I've had too many biscuits.

I'm not even joking. When I applied for a job here, the free biscuits appealed to me even more than the pension (and, so many things considered, it felt like better value for money too). Truthfully, I have more biscuits than even I can eat – to the point where I'm finding other uses for them these days, like launching a cookie across the office to get the attention of a colleague, or building a house of cards out of chocolate malted milks. Who needs desk toys when you can play with biscuits until you get bored, and eat them? But then, of course, you eat too many, just because they're there, like I have today. I don't know why exactly I thought biscuits would settle my nerves but I do know that they've unsettled my stomach.

The reason I'm all whipped up is because I have a problem. With Lou's hen party and wedding moving to the very imminent future, I'm going to need to take my leave much sooner, and with the biscuit business booming, it's hard to square the time generally – never mind last minute.

Worse still, it's too late in the day to request it via the usual system (where it would be a pop-up that rejected me) which means I'm going to have to ask my boss, Iwan, if I can have the time (and he will have to reject me to my face).

I don't know why I'm so naturally pessimistic – I don't think I've always been this way, and it's definitely gotten worse since… let's just file it under: the events of last year. Perhaps it will be fine. Maybe I'll go in there with my head held high, I'll ask clearly and confidently, and Iwan will just say yes without a second thought. Things have been crazy while we've been looking for a new hire to head up the product development. The company wants to have a big shake-up, to reinvigorate the biscuit biz, and I finally think I have just the person – a recommendation from an old colleague – so maybe if that's covered, they can do without me for a couple of weeks.

I grab my iced coffee and take a sip. My phone vibrating on my desk makes me jump – I'm that edgy today – and it causes my arm to jolt. I don't know how I narrowly avoid pouring my drink over my keyboard but somehow I manage. Thank God – I would've had to try to soak it up with biscuits, given that's basically all I have to hand.

My phone buzzes again but I'm ready for it this time. I pick it up and see a missed call and a message from a number I don't have saved, so I open the message first.

> Hi, it's Dean. Can we meet today?

My blood runs cold. Dean? What the hell does he want? And after all this time too. I would say I've only just stopped thinking about him, had I not thought about him a matter of minutes ago, but I've basically stopped. What is this? Does he want me back? Does he think I'll take him back? Would I…? No. No, of course I wouldn't. In fact, I'm going to show him, right now, that he can't just worm his way back in. Honestly, the cheek of the man, because I blocked his number for a reason. Messaging me from a new number is just so infuriating, like he's found his way around my armour – well, he's in for a shock, because I'm strong enough without it.

> Why don't you piss off, Dean?!

There. That ought to do it. There's no way to read between the lines, there's nothing to misinterpret. Just a good, old-fashioned piss off.

I go back to staring at my screen, looking at the work calendar, willing it to open up, to let me book my holidays, magically defying the laws of how it functions. Surprisingly, it doesn't work.

'Molly, have you got a minute?' I hear Iwan call out.

The autopilot for my breathing switches off all of a sudden as I glance up and see him poking his head out of his office door.

'Sure,' I reply, all high-pitched, clearly overcompensating for the fear I'm feeling right now.

Obviously Iwan can't read my mind, right? Or, more realistic, but still probably impossible, he can't see that I'm trying to book holiday right now? I mean, of course he can't, because the system won't let me, but why do I get the feeling that I'm in trouble?

'What's up?' I ask brightly, taking a seat opposite his desk.

Iwan munches a ginger biscuit before wiping his mouth with the back of his hand. He's a very stressed-out man generally, and he suffers terribly with acid reflux, which he treats with ginger... but in the form of biscuits. I'm starting to think it might be what is causing his acid, because he gets through at least one packet a day, but I'm not going to be the one who tells him, or I'll be needing a recruiter myself.

'What the hell is going on with the new hire?' he asks me.

Wow, his tone is almost angry – he never usually speaks to me like this. I know we're under a lot of pressure, but is there any need to take it out on me?

'I have someone, as I said, someone who seems perfect,' I reply, keeping my composure. 'A friend of a friend has highly recommended him, he's looking for a new opportunity, so I got the impression he was a sure thing...'

'Then why did you tell him to piss off?' Iwan asks, cutting to the chase.

'I... I what?'

I don't understand.

'You told him to piss off – why?'

'I didn't,' I insist. 'I haven't even met him yet... I...'

I don't even know what to say.

Iwan takes another bite of a biscuit before rubbing his temples.

'Then why have I just had a call from someone named Dean Rickitt who says he messaged our recruiter about a potential position, only to be told to piss off?' he asks. 'He *just* called me, saying it had *just* happened.'

The blood surging through my veins runs cold. Oh, God. Ohhh, God. What the hell is wrong with me? I see a message from someone called Dean and I instantly assume it's my ex, begging me to take him back? I don't think it gets much more pathetic than that, does it?

'Ah,' I say simply.

'So you *did*?' Iwan replies in disbelief.

'I can explain,' I insist. 'It was a mistake – a stupid mistake. I went through a bad break-up, relatively recently, and his name was Dean, so when I saw his message about meeting up I just assumed it was from him and... and I'm sorry. I'll call him up, I'll explain, I'll apologise.'

'It's too late for that,' he tells me with a sigh.

'Please don't sack me, it was a silly mistake,' I plead.

My God, I cannot lose my job right now, it's all I have left. I never wanted my work to be my world but throwing myself into it this year is going a long way to keeping me focused.

'Molly, relax,' Iwan insists. 'It's too late because Dean says he's not interested any more. You're not going to lose your job. If it were anyone else sitting here, it might be a possibility, but you're one of my best employees.'

That's some comfort, but not much, and I know things could be worse but he's not exactly going to approve my last-minute holiday now, is he?

'You're good at what you do,' he continues. 'Maybe even too good.'

'Too good?' I reply, even more worried now.

'You've been working so hard, and it sounds like you've been through a lot – have you ever stopped to consider you might need some time away from the job?' he asks.

'Iwan, my job means a lot to me, I can't lose it,' I say, truly unable to hide the panic in my voice.

'Molly, I told you, you're not going to lose your job,' he reminds me. 'When was the last time you took any leave?'

'I took a day, last month—'

'For a funeral,' he interrupts me. 'When was the last time you had a break?'

My silence speaks volumes.

'I think what you need to do – not just for you, but for the company – is take some time off,' he tells me. 'Just a week or two, get yourself sorted out, and then come back ready to find us the person for the job. You're no use to me this stressed out – would you like a biscuit?'

'No, thanks,' I say to the biscuit. 'So, you want me to take some time off?'

'Yes, use some of your holiday,' he says. 'Sooner, rather than later, because I need you back and I need you at one hundred per cent. I know, the voices in your head are telling you to say no, you want to keep working, you want to prove yourself – but prove yourself by taking a break, sorting your head out, and then give me my best employee back. All right?'

'Can I take next week and the week after?' I ask.

He raises his eyebrows, as though he didn't expect it to be that easy to get me to take a break. I mean, I didn't expect it to be that easy to get the time off. It's funny how things work out sometimes.

'Yes, of course,' he says. 'Don't worry, I'll get it sorted in the system. Just figure it all out, okay?'

'I will, I promise,' I tell him. 'Thank you. And, again, I'm so, so sorry.'

'Don't be sorry, be better,' he insists.

It's hard to hide the smile from my face because this couldn't have worked out better for me. Obviously I'm mortified about my mistake, so I don't want him to think I'm not, or that this was all a ploy to get some holiday.

'I will, I'll find someone even better than Dean,' I tell him.

'Dean the chef or Dean your ex?' Iwan jokes.

'Dean the chef, obviously,' I reply quickly.

'Well, don't neglect the other position either,' he tells me. 'I've cut you some slack – I never cut people slack – don't make me regret it. I rarely give a second chance, I never give a third one.'

I nod, my jaw tight as I take in his words.

He's right, he rarely cuts anyone any slack, so it means a lot that he's giving me a second chance here. Telling a potential employee to piss off is a huge, huge deal. Absolutely not acceptable, even if it was a mistake.

I'll take the time off, I'll take the holiday, but I won't take my eye off the prize. I don't care if I have to work every day that I'm in Spain, I will find Iwan the perfect chef to oversee the redevelopment of our products. Like my life depends on it.

8

I'm never sure how I feel about airports. I love them, in theory. If they were just a fun place to hang out, like a trendy bar with a choice of restaurants, shops, and fantastic people-watching opportunities, then I would be all for it. I'd be here every day.

When you're travelling, however, you have that mixture of excitement and stress, both feelings amplifying the other, making everything feel all the more chaotic. I just need to focus on why we're here, we're going on holiday – I haven't been on holiday forever, so it's much needed. Then again, perhaps that's why I feel like I'm under so much pressure, because this is my first holiday in a while, and most likely my last for a while, so I really, really want it to go well. I just need to try to relax.

The airport bar is positively popping off, the kind of buzzing energy you only get from a bunch of excited holiday-goers drinking overpriced cocktails before noon.

I look over at Lou, who's scrolling her phone with one hand, and clutching her cocktail with the other – in a way that suggests she thinks someone might be about to take it from her. I think she's suffering from nervous excitement too, although granted she's got a lot more riding on this week.

Nita is at the bar, sweet-talking the barman to try to get an extra cherry in her Sweet Thing (not a euphemism, that's the name of the cocktail she's drinking, although I wouldn't put it past her if we had time). Then there is Willow, who it turns out doesn't really like flying, so she's knocking back her cocktail a little too keenly.

'I really don't know how she does it,' I whisper to Lou, nodding towards Nita, who is now laughing like she's known the bartender for years.

'It's her superpower,' Lou tells me. 'You could learn a thing or two from her.'

'I generally view Nita's actions as a "what not to do" kind of thing,' I reply. 'Because if I tried to do what she's doing, honestly, it would be a disaster.'

'You never know when you might need to flirt your way out of a situation,' she teases – hard to imagine such a scenario.

'Well, should that ever come up, I guess I'll just have to take my chances,' I reply.

I relax back into my seat, raising my glass to take a sip, when the door swings open, and chaos follows. A group of lads – five of them, loud and clearly already several drinks in by the looks and sounds of it – stumble in.

'Come on, let's squeeze a few more pints in,' one of them bellows, his arms up by his sides confidently, like he's leading his men into war.

'Oh, God,' I say quietly to myself.

'Hello, boys,' Nita says, spinning around on her bar stool to greet them.

'Hello, ladies,' their ringleader says. He walks over to Nina with a genuine swagger. He picks her ticket up from the bar, looks at it, and then gently taps her on the nose with it. 'Looks like we're all getting on the same flight, Nita. Fancy a drink together?'

'Sounds good to me,' she says. 'But only if you get one for my friends too.'

'Then let's merge our groups,' he suggests. 'It'll be more fun as a free-for-all.'

Oh, God, it really, really won't. But before I can say a word, the gang takes a seat at our table, with Nita swiftly joining them.

'Going to Spain for a holiday?' another lad asks Lou.

'We're off to a wedding,' Lou says, ever the polite one, although I notice she doesn't put her phone down.

'A wedding, eh? Great places to pull,' he tells her, nudging the guy next to him. 'We're off on an all-inclusive lads' holiday. Sun, sea, and, well... it's a great place to pull too. Reckon you'll get lucky?'

'I'd hope so,' Lou tells him. 'It's my wedding.'

'Can we get you ladies a drink?' another one pipes up, changing the subject.

'I thought you'd never ask,' Nita says, tilting her head and flashing a smile.

'What would you like?' he asks.

'Surprise us,' she says flirtatiously.

'Four mojitos for the ladies,' he calls out to the barman. 'And five pints for us.'

I can't help but sigh audibly, but I know Nita is already planning how to make this trip start with a bang. I, on the other hand, am trying to work out how we can ditch them.

The boys introduce themselves in a flurry of overlapping chatter. There's Ian, the boyishly charming one; Benny, the loud leader of the pack; Si, the one with the kind eyes who's already blushing at something Nita said; Kev, the one who looks like he's had a ten-pint head start and Johnny, who's got the kind of smirk that makes me think he might be trouble.

'So, what's the wedding situation?' Ian asks, leaning towards Lou. 'Big party? Fancy venue? Have you had your hen do yet?'

'We're having it this week, at a villa,' Lou replies, clearly trying to keep her answers short and uninviting. 'Then, yeah, wedding at a big venue.'

'A villa!' Sam exclaims. 'Nice. Sounds great for a big house party.'

I swear, if Nita invites them for a party...

'It's private,' I add quickly, hoping to steer the conversation away from any ideas of gate-crashing. 'And quiet. And the deposit is huge, so...'

'Maybe we can sit together, if we're on the same flight,' Benny says suddenly, glancing at Nita.

'Yeah, let's have a laugh,' Johnny says. 'It'll make the flight go much faster.'

Will it though?

'Okay, sounds good, we can all sit together,' Nita answers enthusiastically on our behalf.

'Lads, help me grab the drinks,' Benny says, gesturing for his mates to help him carry all the glasses over.

I just blink at Nita for a moment.

'Why are we sitting with them?' I ask her.

'Because it'll be fun,' she says, as if that explains anything. 'And they're fit.'

'They're loud,' I add. 'Lou?'

'I don't mind,' she says with a shrug. 'It could be fun.'

'I guess they are fit,' Willow adds.

Oh, God, I'm alone in this one. Looks like I'm outvoted.

As they join us again, with the drinks, I find myself wedged between Johnny and Si and, genuinely, it's hard to tell which one of them is the loudest. All I know is I get a ringing noise in my ear whenever one of them speaks.

'Oi, mate, can we get some shots?' Benny calls out to the barman. 'Let's really get this party started, and let the good times roll with our new lady friends.'

I cringe and sink deeper into my seat.

'Nervous flyer?' Johnny asks me.

'Nervous sitter,' I tell him.

He laughs like I've just said the funniest thing he's ever heard, then immediately launches into a story about the time he fell off a chair after too many Jägerbombs.

'I think I might go stretch my legs,' I tell him. 'Before the flight.'

I don't get to stroll around for long before it's time for us to board and, would you believe it, we are all getting to sit together. Once we're up in the air, it really does feel like there's no escaping them.

'Ladies and gentlemen, the captain has turned off the seatbelt sign,' comes the announcement overhead.

'Right, now the real fun begins!' Benny shouts, leaping out of his seat like this is one of those zero-gravity flights.

'Sit down!' one of the flight attendants snaps.

He ignores her, of course, as he attempts to rummage around in the overhead storage, obviously looking for something in his bag. God knows what, but I can't imagine anything good that it could be.

A moment later, he pulls out maracas.

'Oh, no,' I say softly.

'Oh, yes!' Nita yells, egging him on.

He barely shakes them before the flight attendants descend on him, threatening to confiscate them if he doesn't keep quiet.

'Let them take them,' he tells us once she's gone. 'I've got castanets too.'

Of course he does.

I can't help but notice that Willow and Si are arguing about chemtrails and turbulence and potential government conspiracies.

'Turbulence is the result of air currents,' she says, glaring at him like he's an idiot. 'Nothing more. You're actually unhinged.'

'Yeah, okay, of course it is,' Si replies sarcastically. 'And the moon landing wasn't filmed in a movie studio.'

I close my eyes, count to ten, and take deep breaths in then out. In then out. This is temporary. A couple more hours, and then it's just us girls, sunshine, and cocktails. Pure relaxation. Absolutely no boys allowed.

'Cheer up, Molly,' Johnny says, clocking the look on my face. 'You're on holiday! You need to let your face know.'

'I'm smiling on the inside,' I assure him seriously.

'Could've fooled me,' he says with a wink.

This is just a temporary blip, a speedbump on the way to paradise. I just need to remind myself that soon enough we'll be in the peaceful cocoon of the villa, in a boy-free zone, and I can finally let my hair down.

That is if the plane isn't forced to touch down somewhere in France, so that Benny can have his maracas forcibly removed.

9

As our taxi bumps down a narrow, dusty road, I can't shake the feeling that our driver may have taken a wrong turn at some point.

We're in the north... somewhere. I know Lou said the resort wasn't in a built-up area, but I wasn't expecting our villa to be somewhere so secluded. We're in a place called Sambuesa, which Nita said she had looked up and it did have a couple of shops and a bar, but I certainly can't see any of them around here. Don't get me wrong, this place is beautiful, with its rolling hills and sunny weather, but even paradise can be kind of unnerving when it feels so remote.

I briefly peer over my sunglasses – as though that's going to give me a better look – before pushing them back up my nose.

'Are you sure there's a wedding venue out here?' I ask.

Lou laughs.

'Yes, somewhere,' she replies. 'See, this is why it's loved by celebs and royals, because it's so remote, so easy to ensure privacy.'

'For you and Ellis?' Nita jokes. 'It's not like someone from

Bacci magazine is going to be parachuting into your wedding to get the exclusive, is it?'

'I'll have you know there was a bidding war, between the glossy mags, for the rights to our wedding,' Lou replies, deadly serious, although obviously kidding. 'But we decided to keep it private.'

'Well, yeah, out here is certainly private,' I reply. 'Are you sure there's even a villa?'

Right on cue, the villa seems to emerge from nowhere, as though it's been carved out of the hills.

Wow, it's beautiful. A stunning stone building perfectly placed in front of a backdrop of green hills and mountains. I don't know if it feels like it's out in the open or tucked away from the world, but it looks so inviting.

The road leads us up a driveway that is lined with olive trees. I feel like I can smell the leaves through the open car window and suddenly I'm absolutely starving.

'I'm so hungry,' I blurt.

'I hadn't realised the shops were going to be so far away,' Nita admits. 'But perhaps if we drop our things off and get changed, then maybe we can head out to explore, buy some food – stock up on a bunch of goodies.'

'Sounds good to me,' Lou says, practically exhaling sunshine and butterflies. She must be so, so happy, and beyond excited. I can't help but wonder if I'll ever get to feel that way but I'm starting to think my butterflies might be dead.

We get out of the car and unload our things before moving our baggage, a bit at a time, to the front door. Nita saunters along behind us, staring at her phone.

'So, they sent me a code for the door, which thankfully I stored in my phone notes because there is zero signal here,' she says.

'No signal?' I say, slightly panicked. 'I need to work while I'm here, I need signal.'

'You absolutely do not need to work while you're here, because you're off work,' she reminds me. 'However, don't freak out, I'm sure they'll have wi-fi. *Everywhere* has wi-fi.'

I exhale heavily. She's right – well, about the wi-fi. Not about me not needing to work though because I absolutely do, I need to find the perfect person to redevelop our products, I need to prove to my boss that I haven't lost my touch, that I'm not a hot mess, that it's all going to be fine.

I also need to prove it to myself.

Nita punches the code in and, as if by magic, the door clicks open.

'Okay, now I finally feel like I can relax,' Lou says. 'We're actually here, it's actually happening.'

'Yeah, unless Ellis doesn't turn up,' Nita dares to joke.

Lou gives her a playful shrug.

We carry our things inside and – wow – this place is unreal. It's funny, because we're only here at this villa because it seemed like everything had gone wrong, but now things just feel… more right? As much as I love Blackpool, this place is something else. Plus, Blackpool would have been a rowdy time, with dicks everywhere – the kind you have at hen parties. I know Nita was going to get dick straws, dick badges, she was even going to get a stripper. Naked men are all well and good but I have to admit, I'm happy there aren't going to be any here. I can't think of anything better than a man-free week, then a wedding, then another man-free week. Sometimes I feel so, so single. It will be nice to exist without that pressure, where there's no boys allowed, where I can just be myself. I don't even need to feel needlessly self-conscious in my bikini, if it's just us, and that is something money can't buy (or I guess it's technically something only money can buy, but you take my point).

The mostly open-plan living space looks like a great spot for socialising. This room has it all – big, inviting-looking sofas, a large dining table, a pool table, a big TV, a stereo. It's almost a shame we're not having a big party. It's also hard to imagine being inside, given how glorious the weather is outside, and I know there's supposed to be a big outdoor area with sun loungers, a firepit, a pool – the works – so I'm imagining myself living out there, even if I do need to work.

'The light in here is just...' Nita pauses to kiss her fingers like a chef would. 'I'm going to take photos of this place until I get cramp in my hand. My Instagram is going to make my followers vomit with jealousy.'

'The goal of any holiday,' I joke.

'Come on,' Willow prompts us. 'Let's see what the kitchen is like.'

See, sometimes we do have things in common.

The kitchen is rustic yet modern. It feels so right for the place, but like it also has everything we could possibly need. Except the food and drink, of course.

'Oh, wow,' Nita says. 'They even left some goodies in the fridge for us – now that's the sign of a good host. It's a shame it's mostly beer and meat, but I guess we are in Spain. It's not like the Lakes, where they leave you teabags, Kendal mint cake and jams.'

'We're not in the Lakes any more,' Lou jokes, with *Wizard of Oz* vibes. I'm not even looking at her and I swear I can hear her smile.

'Oh my God, you know what we should do,' Nita says – and I can already tell by the tone of her voice that I'm not going to like it. 'We should start this holiday off with a bang. We're free – free from life, responsibilities, work...'

She should speak for herself.

'I think we should take all our clothes off, right now, and run out there and jump in the pool. Think of it like a full-body cleanse,' she continues. 'Let's start this trip reborn.'

I'm sure she's being a bit sarcastic, because she's not at all religious, but I take her point.

'Oh my gosh, yes,' Willow replies. 'Let's start as we mean to go on.'

'Naked?' Lou squeaks.

'Having fun!' Nita replies. 'No inhibitions, nothing holding us back. This is your last week as a free woman. Get free.'

'I'll do it,' Lou says, wrestling off her clothes.

'You in, Molly?' Nita asks me.

'I'll catch you up,' I say with a laugh. 'I need to go freshen up first.'

She's kind enough not to push me.

'Okay, well, all the rooms are the same, and each one has its own bathroom, so take any room you like,' she tells me. 'Then catch us up.'

'I will, thanks,' I tell her – I mean, I'll probably catch up in my bikini, but I will join them. I like to think I'm a fairly confident person but there's regular confident and then there is run-naked-and-jump-in-a-pool confident. I guess I'm just regular confident.

I head upstairs, feeling like a bit of a stick in the mud, but I know that my friends won't judge me for it. I'll always judge myself far more harshly than anyone else.

I grab one of my bags – the one I know my bikini is in – and head up the stairs with it. Gosh, it's warm today. I think leaving such underwhelming weather at home has made coming here feel all the more jarring. I think my body was still in winter mode – spring at best.

I pick a door at random, seeing as though all of the rooms are the same, and I'm instantly happy with my choice. It's big, with a massive bed, huge patio doors that are already open, leading out onto a balcony, already trying to tempt me out as the breeze makes the sheer curtains dance.

I'm hoping you'll know what I mean by this, but the place just smells like holidays. I don't know if it's the greenery outside, the stone walls, the faint smell of the pool – everything together just creates the kind of scent that, if it were a diffuser, I could have done with it in my house through the winter to keep my spirits up.

I hear the girls screaming with joy and then a big splash. It makes me smile and pushes me to hurry up, to join them, and to try to force myself to relax. I whip off my dress, stripping down to my underwear, before leaning over my case to dig out my bikini. It's only as I'm bent over, with my bum in the air, that I hear what I assume is the bathroom door click open behind me.

'Oh, hello,' I hear a voice say. It's a man's voice, definitely a Lancashire accent, but a total stranger nonetheless.

I spin around the spot, panicked, my eyes like a deer in the headlights, but he just smiles.

The man, who I'm guessing is in his early thirties, is standing there in his trunks. His head is tipped curiously, like he might be as confused as I am, but obviously being a man he's not as freaked out as me, a woman, in a bedroom with a surprise man.

His dark hair is wet, with the occasional water droplet falling onto his shoulders, before making its way down his body, navigating the contours of his muscles, before hitting the floor below him. He might be a stranger to me but he's obviously no stranger to the gym, and noticing this, as well as his bright blue eyes, gives me a funny feeling in my stomach. It's just fear, surely, because this is a weird situation, and—

I hear my friends' screams rip through the air, but they're not the fun, joyful screams I heard a few seconds ago, it's pure terror this time.

I instinctively run out onto the balcony, to look down at the garden below, to make sure they're okay.

As I look down at the pool, it takes me a moment to realise what I'm looking at, as my friends thrash around in the water, but then I notice that they're not alone either. They're still screaming, clearly freaking out, while the three men in the water with them seem to be taking it more in their stride.

'Friends of yours?' the strange man asks me as he joins me on the balcony.

'Erm, yes,' I reply.

'Should we go down and join them?' he suggests, unable to hide his amusement.

I nod, heading for the door, keen to get out of this room, and to the relative safety of strength in numbers with my friends.

'Erm, one minute,' the man calls after me.

I freeze on the spot for a second, before turning around to face him.

'You, er…'

His voice trails off as he nods towards me, his gaze flickering briefly to my body before moving back up to my eyes.

Oh my God, I'm in my underwear. Shit, right, of course I am. I can feel heat in my cheeks rising to rival the Spanish sun but I try to play it cool.

'Yeah, right, I'll clow some throthes on,' I say, absolutely butchering the sentence. So much for being cool.

He laughs.

'See you in a sec,' he says.

Fuuuuck. What the hell is happening? Naturally I don't put my bikini on, I grab a sundress, and take it into the bathroom with me, locking the door behind me while I get changed. The bathroom, like the kitchen, appears to be fully stocked but, now that I'm looking closely, they're all men's products. Razors, shower gel, deodorant, shampoo – all in the most macho packaging, because God forbid a man wash his hair with a shampoo that came in a pink bottle. Is this his room? The random man's? Have we like, I don't know, rocked up at completely the wrong villa? But, if we had, why did the code work? This is the right place, the right address, it looks exactly as Nita described it. I need to head downstairs and figure it out.

Downstairs, I follow the trail of shoes, dresses and bras until I reach the back door. walking outside, after being slightly cooler inside, feels like walking into a wall of heat. It almost stops me in my tracks.

The trail of clothes is a good indicator of which way to go to find the back door but it's ultimately unnecessary because the sound of screaming and arguing guides me effortlessly to the pool area where I find my friends, in the water, with three other men. Then there's the man I met upstairs just now, sitting on the edge of the pool, his feet in the water to keep him cool, as they all argue amongst themselves.

'Oh my God, Molly, there you are,' Lou calls out when she spots me. Everyone else quietens down for a moment. 'Thank God you're okay.'

'Why wouldn't she be?' one of the men in the pool asks.

'Clearly, none of this is okay,' Nita points out.

'I don't know, you're a bit of all right,' another one of the guys says to her.

She angrily shoves water in his direction, splashing him, but it comes across as vaguely flirty when nothing but a few drops hit him.

Nita puts her hands on her hips, frowning as she pushes air from her cheeks. Thankfully the pool water is protecting her modesty, but only just. It hides the detail, sure, but not the fact that she's naked.

'I just don't understand,' she says, trying to keep her fire under control. 'What are you doing here?'

'We booked this villa,' one of the men in the pool says. 'What are you doing here?'

'*We* booked this villa,' Nita replies. 'For two weeks.'

'No, *we* booked it for two weeks,' the man claps back.

'No, we did,' Nita replies through tightly gritted teeth.

'You can keep saying that, but it won't make it true,' he replies.

He's in the shallow end so he stands on his feet, rather than treading water, which makes him suddenly appear much taller. He's got a bit of a Ben Affleck vibe. Tall, dark, kind of intense. He has a sort of cheeky arrogance (or should that be arrogant cheekiness) that I can see in him already.

'It wasn't even listed when we booked it,' Nita points out. 'So how did you book it?'

'We were told it had new owners, so we booked it through them,' he replies.

'Right, okay, this is nuts, but it's the sort of thing we can only sort out with a phone call,' Lou points out tactfully.

'Exactly,' the Ben-looking man, who appears to be the ringleader, replies. 'So let's do that.'

He sounds confident enough, which worries me.

'Look, I feel like we've got off on the wrong foot,' he says, softening a little. 'My name is Owen.'

Nita narrows her eyes at him.

'We're all friends here. This guy on my left is Harry,' he says, pointing to one of the other blokes in the pool. 'And on my right we have Nolan.'

Harry looks like he would be quite tall. I know, I can't see his entire body, but you can just sort of tell from his torso. He has sandy blond hair and a glimmer in his eye that makes him look like he could be trouble – then again, they all have that look. Nolan has short, light brown hair but it's hard to say what style because they're all soaking wet. His fringe is flat and stuck to his forehead currently.

'And that hunk next to you is Travis,' Owen adds – he's talking to me.

I look at Travis, the man I just met upstairs, and give him a polite smile.

'I'm Nita,' she says, folding her arms angrily under the water. It's almost like she begrudges introducing herself.

'I'm Lou,' she adds, smiling, giving a little wave.

'My name's Willow,' Willow offers up next.

Now all eyes are on me.

'Erm, I'm Molly,' I tell them, for some reason sounding like I'm not quite sure.

'Hi, Molly,' Travis says through a grin. 'It's nice to meet you – properly.'

'You too,' I reply, trying to mask my embarrassment, because of course he saw me in my underwear before he even learned my name.

'Okay, now we're all friends, let's go make some phone calls, clear this whole thing up,' Owen suggests reasonably.

'Yes, let's,' Nita replies.

'After you,' Owen suggests.

'We can't get out first, we're not wearing any clothes!' Lou practically squeaks.

'I know,' Owen replies with a wink.

'Just get out of the fucking pool,' Nita ticks him off.

'All right, all right, I'm only joking,' Owen insists. 'Come on, lads, let's leave them to sort themselves out.'

Owen, Harry and Nolan climb out of the pool, joining Travis

on dry land before the four of them head inside. Honestly, watching them, dripping wet and nearly naked, all laughing and joking together – I feel like I'm tuned in to *Love Island*. They seem like the kind of lads who talk about 'banter' and 'the sesh' and their 'body counts'. I dislike them already, although that could just be me prejudging them unfairly because I'm annoyed about this mess, and embarrassed about my part in it. Still, better to be in my underwear upstairs than down here naked with the others. Now that would've been embarrassing.

'Here,' I say, grabbing hopefully clean towels from the sun loungers. 'Use these.'

The girls take their towels and get out of the pool.

I look at Nita and chew my lip.

'It's going to be okay,' she reassures me. 'We'll get on the phone and we'll sort all this out.'

'Will we?' Lou asks nervously.

'Of course,' I tell her, nodding my head like I mean it, but the problem is I'm not sure I do.

I have no idea how this is going to pan out, but I have this horrible feeling it can't be good.

10

The boys are back outside, sitting around the firepit, huddled around one of their phones which means one of them must be on the wi-fi already. We, on the other hand, are not, so we're being forced to call from the landline in the villa.

Nita is on the phone with the agency we booked the villa through. Lou, Willow and I are sitting next to her on the sofas in the living room, waiting to find out what's going on.

I feel like I'm trapped in a pressure cooker – and not just because it's boiling in here.

The room is pretty much silent other than the occasional sharp intake of breath (I think we're all quite literally holding our breath for the most part) and Nita saying things like 'right' and 'okay' before listening to what the person on the line has to say.

Nita's face is giving nothing away but I don't think that's good news. Nothing that is being said to her is making her smile, nor is it making her show any signs of relief. If anything, I can see her jaw getting tighter. I hope Lou hasn't noticed.

'So, what do you expect us to do?' Nita asks, annoyed.

Yep, this isn't going to be good news.

Lou is fiddling with a decorative tassel on one of the cushions. She always fidgets when she's worried.

I'm trying my best to keep my cool. My tell, when I'm anxious, is to sort of jig my leg, bouncing one up and down on the spot – which Lou knows all too well, so I'm desperately, desperately trying to keep my legs still. I'm pressing down on my knees with my hands, but in a way that is hopefully subtle, and not at all like I'm wrestling an alligator.

'Well, how is that fair?' Nita continues, snapping, startling us a little. I want to say it's her voice that made us jump but, to be honest, I think it's her words. Those don't sound like the words of someone who is happy with the response.

'Right, well, we'll have to consider that,' Nita says. 'But you'll be hearing from our lawyer.'

She hangs up and folds her arms in a strop, flopping back against the sofa.

'We have a lawyer?' I ask.

'We'll get one,' she replies. 'There's... been a mix-up.'

'A mix-up sounds cute and zany,' Lou replies hopefully.

'Then there's been a fuck-up,' Nita corrects herself. 'From what I can gather, this villa belonged to a man who recently passed away. He left it to his son and his daughter, who seem to be at odds over the running of the place, so they've somehow both let it out early, through the same agency, to two groups, at the same time. Us and the boys.'

'What?' Willow replies. 'Can they do that?'

'Obviously not,' Nita says. 'But they have. So we're here and they're here – and the sort of good news is that we're all getting refunds, and that the villa is free for the next two weeks, but the bad news is that we're going to have to decide who gets to stay here.'

'Obviously we need this place,' Lou says, clearly very, very anxious and feeling totally hopeless about it all now. 'My wedding...'

'We can figure it out,' I tell her.

Nita chews her lip for a moment.

'Are we going to address the elephant in the room?' she says.

We all look to her.

'More specifically, the trunks,' she continues. 'These boys – as much as I hate them – are unrealistically hot. All four of them. What's with that?'

'No comment, I'm getting married,' Lou says with a laugh.

'Yeah, I guess they are,' I say, not wanting to give too much away.

'Oh, God, don't tell me you like one of them,' Nita says, reading my mind.

'No, no, no,' I insist. 'I just mean, you're right, I feel like I'm on a reality TV show. Anyway, you started it, by saying they were hot.'

'Yeah but, like, all of them, generally,' she continues. 'Yeah, they're sexually attractive, but only until you hear them speak. Otherwise you'd be looking at one – maybe two – and thinking if you were to—'

'Okaaaay, I think Nita needs to cool down,' I interrupt her.

'Yeah, let's take a breather, think things through, and come up with a plan,' Nita suggests practically, laughing off her outburst of horniness. I'm sure she was joking... at least sort of.

'I'm starving,' Willow adds. 'And I'm guessing all the food belongs to that lot?'

'Why don't we pop to the shop,' Nita says. 'We'll get some food, we'll come up with a plan, and then we can relax – this is just a stumbling block, just a delay on the road to paradise, but it will all be fine, right, everyone?' Nita says, shooting me a look that implores me to agree with her.

'Absolutely,' Willow agrees.

'What do you think, Molly?' Lou asks me. 'Is it really going to be okay?'

I can see her last bit of hope in her eyes as they stare at me, big and round, and ready to burst with tears at the drop of a hat.

'It will be fine,' I tell her. 'Totally fine. Nothing to worry about.'

I say it with confidence, with a big smile, and big sparkling eyes of my own.

Well, I may as well say it with feeling, seeing as though it's going to be the last time I can say it with a straight face.

11

Everything would feel so perfect right now, if it didn't feel so well and truly fucked.

The small town, a short-ish journey from the villa, really is small. That's what you want though, when you go abroad, right? If you're not heading to Spain for sun, sex and sangria on a party island then you're after that authentic experience, seeing the real Spain, and soaking up everything it has to offer.

We're in the one and only local food shop and although it may not be very big, it's got everything.

The terracotta floors are so beautiful, their uneven texture adding charm, and the shelves are packed more than I can even take in. Olives, spices, fresh meats and cheeses, freshly baked breads – and seemingly unlimited snacks like crisps, crackers, chocolates and cakes. And everything just looks so legitimate, you know? I know, I sound silly, but the tomatoes here don't look like the tomatoes back at home, these ones look like actual tomatoes – stock images of tomatoes even. Oh, and the smell, I could eat one right here right now.

The only sight more welcomed than the well-stocked shelves

of delicious food was the small chalkboard on the counter offering Spanish street food to order and eat now, so we all placed orders to be cooking while we filled our bags with shopping for the next few days. Well, even if we don't have our accommodation sorted, we still need to eat, right?

Our food finally ready, we don't waste any time in tucking in, eating just enough to make our hungry brains work before we start chatting, so that we can figure out what the hell we're going to do.

I can't help but let out a little groan as I bite into one of the golden-brown croquetas. Filled with ham and lava-hot béchamel, I can feel my tongue burning, but it's so worth it. We also got enough patatas bravas for the four of us, as well as the Tortilla Española, which is like a potato omelette served in triangles. We also have dips, which I'm eager to try, but we are kind of up against it here, so I'm trying to rein in my enjoyment just a little.

'I need that villa,' Lou says, breaking the silence, waving around her little wooden fork. 'Because it's not just for us, for somewhere to stay, my wedding depends on it. My actual wedding! Because if I'm not here, then how can I get there? And it's been so hard, getting here, and getting there, and...'

Her voice trails off – I imagine because even she is losing track of what she means. I get it though. This is her dream wedding location, which she didn't think she'd get, and then she almost lost it, so I completely understand why she's panicking about having nowhere local to stay. Even the hotel we booked for the guests, which is miles away, is fully booked now, and that would have been far from ideal for her getting ready. No one wants to spend hours on a coach in a wedding dress, with the groom on board too.

'It's going to be okay, Lou,' Nita says – she keeps saying this. Again and again. I wonder if she thinks positive thinking can make a difference. God, I hope it can – not that I would be contributing all that much.

Nita's positivity – or at least the degree to which she is able to fake it – is truly admirable, and I'm sure it's helping Lou, even just a little, so I need to try to do the same.

'Obviously we just need to stay there,' Willow says. 'So, if we just tell the boys that, then it's totally reasonable, right?'

'And what if they don't care?' I dare to ask, knowing that it isn't what anyone wants to hear, but we don't know these boys, which means they don't know us, which means they really might not give a shit.

'Then we give them an incentive,' Nita says through a mouthful of potatoes, licking rogue tomato sauce from her hand.

'What, like we shag them?' Willow replies in disbelief. 'I suppose there are four of them, and four of us...'

Wow, she came around to that idea pretty quickly. There's a beat of stunned silence, where it's almost like no one can actually believe she said that enough to form a reply.

'Willow, what the fuck?' Nita can't help but laugh.

'You know Lou is getting married, right?' I say in disbelief. 'Also, this isn't fucking *Love Island*. There will be no coupling up.'

'Yeah, I mean they are all hot as hell, but even I think that's a terrible idea,' Nita – our resident wild child – points out. 'Not that I don't think it would work, mind you. But, no, I was thinking maybe we could offer them the money we're getting refunded? We'll get to stay there, which we were paying for anyway, so we're no worse off, and they'll have double the money to spend elsewhere. Everyone likes money, right?'

I cock my head curiously. I mean, that could work, if the boys are happy to do it. But would they be happy to do it? I guess Nita is right, everyone does like money.

'I'm happy to do that, if you think it will work?' Lou replies. 'God, I really, really need it to work.'

I take a big bite of my tortilla, buying myself a little time to think before I speak. Yes, Nita is right, money is a language everyone speaks, so the boys might be more than happy to find somewhere else, further afield, with double the dosh. But that would require them to be reasonable and rational and... eesh, I'm not sure they screamed reasonable or rational during my brief interaction with them. I suppose it wasn't a normal first encounter, everyone was confused, the girls were naked – it was a mess. Maybe they'll be cool about it.

'We can give it a try,' I say, giving the project my sign-off.

It's not so much that I think it will work, more that I just really, truly cannot think of a single other option.

12

As the taxi pulls up outside the sun-bleached villa, it's hard to feel as excited this time. Before we had no idea what we were walking into, the possibilities were endless. This time, well, it's the same, but say that exact same sentence in more of a pessimistic tone: we've no idea what we're walking into. The possibilities are endless.

As the sound of crunching gravel stops all at once, we all filter out with our bags of shopping, setting them down on the floor so that the driver can get on his way.

'Are you trying to stock an entire vineyard, Molly?' Willow half-jokes, grabbing one of the bags that is full of bottles – a job I took responsibility for.

'I mean, aside from the absolute nonsense that is suggesting you would stock a vineyard with bottles of wine bought from a shop...' I can't resist pointing that out. '...this is a hen party, you know.'

'So long as we have the actual essentials covered,' Willow says.

'Wine is absolutely an essential,' Lou reminds her. 'But, hey, look how many oranges Nita bought. Five a day covered.'

'Yeah, if you mean five sangrias a day,' Nita says with a chuckle. 'Because that's what I bought them for.'

Nita walks ahead of us, leaving us with the bags so that she can open the door for us.

I watch as she types in the code. Then she tries again. Then again. I swear, each time the keypad flashes red and buzzes in a way that could mean nothing but rejection, my bags get heavier.

'This thing hates me,' she says, frustrated, before trying it again. Once again, the door isn't having it.

'Are you typing it in right?' Willow asks.

'No, I hadn't thought of trying that,' Nita replies sarcastically. 'I'm typing in the same code as I did earlier, but it isn't working.'

'That's because we've changed it.'

It's a man's voice, coming from above.

We all whip our heads up in unison. Standing on the balcony above the front door are the boys – Owen, Travis, Harry and Nolan – leaning casually on the railing like they've been waiting for this exact moment. Smirks all around as they peer down at us.

Owen, the self-appointed leader of the pack, leans casually against the railing, flashing us the kind of smug grin that can only be removed by a slap.

'Hello, ladies,' Owen says, tipping an imaginary hat.

'What the hell is going on?' Nita asks him in a hiss. 'What do you mean, you've changed the code?'

'Well, we've been expecting you,' Owen replies cryptically, doing a bad impression of someone who works for a company that puts on corny murder mysteries.

'You're not a Bond villain, you're a bellend,' Nita reminds him. 'Just tell us what's going on.'

Owen gives Nolan a playful jab with his elbow.

'Nolan here, our resident tech genius, has reset and changed the door code,' Owen says proudly. 'Right, Nolan?'

'Er, yeah,' Nolan replies, in a sort of shy way, but happy to take credit for his handiwork. 'It's super easy, if you know how, you just have to—'

'All right, don't tell them,' Owen reminds him with a laugh.

'Are you even allowed to do that here?' Lou asks.

'I'm not saying we were allowed, I'm just saying that we did,' Owen replies.

Nita looks ready to explode.

'What the hell are you playing at?' she asks.

'We found out all about the double-booking,' Owen explains. 'That this place is basically up for grabs, for free, for the next two weeks. So we're claiming squatters' rights.'

'Aside from how obviously stupid that is,' Nita begins, unable to resist a dig, 'what gives you the right, over us?'

'Yeah, we all booked the place, fair and square, for the same two weeks, so why is it you guys who get to stay here?' I ask, keeping my voice calm and steady.

'Because we got here first,' Travis points out.

His words send a flutter of something through me. It's probably not a nice flutter, right? Just a weird, embarrassing pang left over from our awkward first meeting earlier. Definitely that. Nothing else. It's just that.

'You can't just stop us from coming in!' Lou says, emotion building in her voice.

'Hmm, it's funny you should say that,' Owen replies. 'Because from where I'm standing it looks like we can and we did. You're not getting through this door without the code, and only we know the code.'

'What about the back door?' I think out loud. 'Did you lock that?'

As the four boys exchange panicked looks it becomes glaringly obvious that, caught up in their elaborate plan to change the code to the front door, it didn't occur to any of them to lock the back door that leads out to the pool. The smug looks drain from their faces all at once. At the same time, we know what to do. We need to run, as fast as we can, around to the back of the villa, to get in through the patio doors before the boys have a chance to lock them.

'Go!' Nita yells, her voice sharp and urgent as she tries to motivate us. 'Go, go, go!'

And we're off, moving like we've never moved before (well, I haven't) as the boys scramble to head inside, their footsteps thudding on the balcony as they all try to get in through the door, trying to beat us to the patio doors.

My heart pounds as I run – keeping up the rear, we'll call it, otherwise you would say I'm in last place. I'm powered by a mixture of adrenaline, determination and spite. Who do these boys think they are?

Willow, of course, is the fastest of all of us. She's a sportsy girl, has been her entire life, and has kept it going into adulthood. She runs marathons so I fancy our chances. It's only going to take one of us to get through that door and all of us are in.

Looking ahead, I see her dive in through the open door just as Harry lunges for the handle. Ha. We did it. Well, Willow did it, my stitch has a stitch, but you take my point.

'Too slow,' she tells him triumphantly.

Willow can be so rude but when she's using these powers for good I don't actually mind it. The boys, on the other hand, don't look impressed at all. They're panting, and pouting, like the losing team of a relay race at the Olympics.

'Now then, now that we're all inside, how about we sit down

on the sofas and we sort this out like the grown adults that we are?' Nita suggests, her voice dripping with sarcasm.

'After you,' Owen tells her.

Nita brushes past Owen with a sharp glare and an 'accidental' elbow. He laughs it off as they follow us through to where the sofas are.

'Bring the bag of oranges,' Nita half-jokes to Lou under her breath. 'In case we need a weapon.'

Oh, God, yeah, we're all so mature. This is going to go really well.

'I can't believe they're refusing to acknowledge squatters' rights,' Owen says under his breath to his friends – of course, we hear him.

'I can't believe you think you can say squatters' rights in a situation like this,' I point out. 'You've clearly been learning about the law from clueless people on the internet. You need to get off TikTok, bud.'

'Oh yeah, and what are you, a lawyer?' he replies mockingly.

'No, but I am,' Willow points out. 'What you're talking about is adverse possession, and you can't use that to bagsy a holiday rental for two weeks, so shut up, you're making yourself look dumb.'

Again, not the most polite, but I'm happy when she's directing it at the boys.

Owen leans back against the sofa, folding his arms in a way that flexes his biceps – I swear, he's doing it on purpose.

'Right, so, obviously, we all know the villa's going free for two weeks,' he points out. 'We're all getting a refund, so that's fair – so what we need to work out is who gets this place.'

Lou leans forward in her seat, placing her hands calmly on her lap.

'We're both as entitled as each other to stay here, that's true,' she points out, keeping her voice soft and gentle. I can tell she's about to appeal to their better nature – if they have one. 'But it's very, very important that we stay here. I'm getting married on Sunday, at La Palacio de la Mar. It's one of the most exclusive venues in Spain, and we had to move the wedding at the last minute, which was very stressful, because of a disaster…' She pauses to take a deep breath. 'This was the only place in the area we could find to stay, or we'd have happily gone somewhere else. Honestly, you can have our refund money as a thank you if you'd just let us stay – and you can go anywhere you want.'

Owen sucks air through his teeth like a mechanic about to deliver bad news.

'Oof. Yeah, sorry, no can do,' he says.

'What?' Lou blurts, her eyes widening. 'Why not?'

'Because we're here for a wedding too,' he informs her. 'Also at La Palacio de la Mar. But ours is Saturday.'

'Wait, who's getting married?' Nita asks, her voice overflowing with disbelief, and potentially a little bit of disappointment. I wonder which one it is she fancies…

Owen smiles, pointing a thumb over his shoulder at Nolan, who's suddenly looking like he wants the ground to swallow him whole.

'This guy,' Owen announces.

Nolan waves awkwardly, his cheeks pink. He's clearly not as confident as his friends, not as easy-going with the ladies, although he is getting married so he must have worked his magic on at least one. Maybe he dazzled her with his tech skills. I am annoyingly impressed at what he did with the door – we're so lucky they're ultimately stupid boys, so proud of their handiwork that their egos make them sloppy.

'So, there we have it,' Owen concludes. 'We need this place too, for the same reason as you, just as much as you do –

although probably more so, because our wedding is on Saturday, yours is Sunday. Our wedding is first.'

Travis, who's been quietly scrolling on his phone up until now, looks up.

'I've been checking for other places in the area. Everywhere is full,' he points out.

'Wait, do you have signal? Or are you on the villa's wi-fi?' I can't help but ask.

'There's no signal or wi-fi here,' Harry points out. 'But Nolan brought some fancy modem thing. Works anywhere. Satellite or summat.'

'There's no internet here?' I shriek, the horror sinking in. 'How am I supposed to stay here for two weeks without internet?'

'You're not,' Owen says smugly, as if it's the most obvious thing in the world. 'Because you're not staying here.'

'No, you're not staying here,' Nita says firmly.

Harry visibly relaxes, the very definitely of laid-back, as his lips curve into a teasing smile.

'Oh, yeah? What are you going to do about it? Kick us out?' he says, and I could swear he was flirting with her right now.

'If that's what it takes,' Nita replies slowly, in a breathy voice.

Oh, cool, cool, cool, she's flirting back. That will help.

Harry shrugs, undeterred.

'Who cares? We're boys,' he points out. 'We'll piss in the garden and wash in the pool. And there are four big sofas right here, so that's beds sorted, and the kitchen is only a few steps away...'

'You'll piss outside?' Willow replies in disgusted disbelief. 'What about... about...'

'There's a WC under the stairs,' Travis informs us all. 'We'll use that, not the garden.'

'But you can't wash in a WC,' I point out.

'Like I said, the pool,' Harry says. 'You girls need to chill out – have you thought about a holiday?'

'Plus, the TV and the pool table are down here,' Nolan pipes up before anyone can strangle Harry.

'Yeah, okay,' Travis agrees. 'Downstairs sounds fine to me.'

'Wait, so we have bedrooms, and bathrooms, but you guys have the living rooms, the kitchen, and a loo. You have the TV, the pool table – all the fun stuff,' I can't help but point out. Suddenly this doesn't quite seem fair.

'Yeah, well, that's what you wanted, right?' Travis reminds me, trying to hide his smile.

'I mean, what we want is for you guys to just leave,' I tell him with a smile of my own.

'But with that not happening...' Travis reminds me.

'So, are we including the garden in downstairs?' I ask – because that doesn't seem fair at all.

'Yes,' Owen says quickly.

'No,' Travis says, speaking over him. 'The pool and the gardens are communal areas. We'll share those like we would if this were a resort. That seems fair, right?'

'Not really,' Nita says, huffing as she folds her arms.

'No, that does seem... fairer,' I tell Travis, grateful for small mercies.

'There's no reason we can't make this work, right?' he replies.

'I mean... there's no reason *we* can't make this work,' I agree. 'But we didn't kick off negotiations by locking you boys outside.'

'And for that we're sorry, right, lads?' Travis says, looking to his friends. They don't seem very sorry. 'Lads?' he prompts them again.

'Yeah, sorry,' Harry says, trying to mask a giggle, like a naughty little kid.

'Sorry,' Owen adds. 'But we're all being grown-ups now, right?'

'We will if you do,' Nita says.

Owen claps his hands together, satisfied with the deal we've just done – it feels more like we've been done.

'So, that's settled,' he says. 'Go on then, head upstairs, to your floor, leave our zone. Take your stuff with you, make yourselves at home. Unless...' His smile turns teasing. 'You don't think you can hack it and want to back down?'

'Not a chance,' Nita snaps back, grabbing her bag. 'Come on, girls.'

As we head upstairs, I can't help but feel... I don't know. Like, yay, we're proving a point, we're stronger than the boys – whatever. This sounds like it's going to be hell.

'Come on, we'll show those boys who's boss,' Nita says as we carry our bags across the landing.

Lou exhales, her shoulders dropping a little in relief.

'I'm just glad we can stay,' she replies.

'Me too,' Willow adds. 'And I'm more determined than ever to prove to those boys that we can hack this. They'll be the ones struggling before we do.'

I smile, trying to match their enthusiasm, but really, I'm not so sure. Sure, we've got the better deal with beds and bathrooms, but it's not perfect. The food we need to refrigerate won't last up here. All our drinks will be warm in the Spanish heat, and it's going to suck to rely on dry or long-life snacks for two weeks. It's better than being stuck downstairs without a bed, but only just.

Nita looks ready to go to war, Lou seems like she's willing to do whatever it takes, Willow is Willow, and I'm... I don't even know what I am. Not up for this, that's for sure.

Boys will be boys – and these boys seem like they're going to do whatever they want. Oh, this is going to be fun, and not in the good way.

13

Hilariously, it feels a bit like a sleepover, all of us crammed into one bedroom, sitting on the bed with seemingly endless snacks spread out between us.

We're all in our pyjamas, chatting away about boys – as you would expect at a girly sleepover – but instead of chatting about the boys we like, tonight's conversation revolves around the boys downstairs – the ones we low-key hate right now.

Honestly, everything would be perfect, if they weren't here. This would be fun, this place would be heaven. Instead, it's hell.

We're all in my room – well, with only four identical rooms to hang out in, I guess we'll just take it in turns, to mix things up – hanging out on my bed, eating our way through the food we bought that needs refrigerating. Yes, it did cross our minds that we could ask the boys if we could share the fridge, but there was a worry that they might ask for something in return. Also, Nita is adamant that we need to prove some kind of point to them, so we'll have to see how it goes. For now, it means we get to eat a lot of cheese.

I know it would be great to have access to the living room and the kitchen, but it's hard to feel like we've lost, with bedrooms like these. It's a Mediterranean dream, with rustic décor, crisp white linen, and sheer curtains blowing in the gentle breeze coming in from the balcony doors. Outside the rolling hills are beautifully moonlit and the sky is clear in a way I don't think I've ever seen in England, not even in the depths of the Yorkshire moors.

It's so frustrating, to be so close to serenity, and yet so far away. All of the beauty and the peace is ruined by one thing – well, four things – the boys. I imagine it's so quiet outside, maybe a few relaxing sounds courtesy of nature, but instead, coming from outside we can hear laughter, cheering, chanting – and all so, so loud. I really hope they're going to run out of energy soon.

There might be such a thing as too much cheese, you know, but it's too good to throw away, or to leave to rot on the dressing table in the hope it will be okay for breakfast. Still, it is delicious, so I'll take my chances having a little bit more. I pop a tomato in my mouth at the same time, as though that will automatically transform it into a salad.

'Are we seriously supposed to live off crisps and biscuits for the next two weeks?' Willow asks, looking thoroughly unimpressed.

Nita points at her with a breadstick.

'Look, there was a time, when we were kids, when eating nothing but crisps and biscuits would have been a dream come true,' Nita reminds her. 'So let's just make the most of it.'

Willow wrinkles her nose.

'Not me,' she insists. 'I always preferred things like carrots and celery to chocolate and crisps.'

Nita gasps.

'I don't actually think kid me would have been friends with a kid that preferred to eat celery,' Nita replies with a laugh, but I don't think she's kidding. 'I don't think I would have trusted someone like that.'

Lou laughs.

'I don't care if I have to starve for a week,' she says, smiling widely. 'I'm staying right here. My wedding is on Sunday, I'm right where I need to be, and I'll be damned if I let those boys ruin any of it. As long as I'm here for the big day, nothing else matters.'

You can tell she's trying to stay positive, and that she probably isn't quite as confident as she's making out, but I think given the chaos that we can hear downstairs, and all things considered, she's doing really well to keep it together.

Laughter echoes from the boys gathered by the firepit. Why it is that the sound of other people having fun just pisses you off when you're in a bad mood? If it were us down there, having fun, laughing and drinking, we'd probably be making even more noise than them. But because it's the stupid boys, it's really grating.

'Okay, no one is having that much fun,' Nita says, proving my point.

It does seem like a bit much, like they want the entire villa to know how much fun they're having. I swear I can almost hear the smugness in their laughter.

Willow groans as she throws herself backward onto the bed, covering her eyes with her hands for some reason – I think just to be dramatic.

'They've got to be in their thirties, right?' she points out. 'How are they this immature?'

Lou grabs another slice of ham, shaking her head.

'They do say boys mature slower than girls – it's a scientific fact,' Lou points out. 'I mean come on, the only reason we didn't see them before we jumped into the pool earlier was because they were having a contest to see who could hold their breath the longest.'

'Yeah, and then they just started popping up, one at a time, like hippos,' Nita tells me, seeing as though I missed it.

I can't help but laugh.

'So they're competitive as well as immature,' Lou adds.

'Okay, I get it, boys mature slower than girls do, but that's actual boys,' I point out. 'These boys are actually grown men, who should be fully matured by now. And yet they're not – and someone is actually going to marry one of them!'

It's hard to imagine anyone tying the knot with any of them. On looks, sure, if that's all that matters to you. Every last one of them looks like they would feature as 'man of the month' on a particular kind of calendar, but if you were judging them on their personalities, then you wouldn't give any of them a second look.

'Yeah, Nolan,' Lou says. 'But he's the quiet one. Maybe he's not so bad?'

'So, maybe Nolan is the one we need to get to,' Willow suggests. 'Maybe we can appeal to his better nature?'

I shake my head.

'Honestly? I don't think these boys have better natures to appeal to,' I say. 'That's why I think we only have one option. What we need to do is play dirty.'

Nita sits up straight, her eyes gleaming with excitement.

'I mean, I'm in. But what exactly are we talking about?' she asks.

I love that she's all in, even though she doesn't know what she's agreeing to yet. The best kind of friends are the ones who will do whatever you say, whatever crazy scheme you're cooking up, they are here for it.

'Okay, well, you know when I was with you-know-who,' I start, refusing to say his name. 'Well, there were all of these things that he just hated, most of them irrational, about having a woman or women's things around. Girl chaos was how he referred to my mess, and some things he just couldn't tolerate. What I'm thinking is, if we bring a little of that girl chaos to the villa, I don't know, perhaps we can drive them out? If we're annoying enough, they might beg us to put our offer back on the table, for them to take the money and find somewhere else. If we won't negotiate for things like use of the fridge, then they can't ask for use of the showers – maybe we can break them.'

'Molly, you evil genius,' Nita says. 'This doesn't just sound like a great plan, it sounds like so much fun.'

'It's worth a try,' Lou says through a giggle. 'I know everything I do that drives Ellis crazy – I'll give it a go.'

'Personally, I think I'm a delight to be around,' Willow says, without a hint of sarcasm. 'But sure, I'll give it a go, for the greater good.'

'Great,' I say, letting that one go. 'Now we just need to come up with some ideas.'

'I take it you already have some,' Nita says with a grin.

'Loads,' I reply, smiling back at her like a maniac, the evil side of my brain fully engaged.

Honestly, I remember all too well all of the things Dean hated about having a woman about the house. If we do those, to the extreme, plus anything else we can think of, these boys aren't just going to wish they'd taken our offer to take the money and leave, they're going to wish they were never born.

14

I'm not sure what wakes me up, the noise from the boys who are already having a laugh outside or the knocking on my bedroom door.

'Come in,' I call out groggily.

'Rise and shine,' Nita sings as she walks into the room.

'Morning,' I reply.

Nita looks as bright as the sun outside as she plonks herself down on my bed next to me.

'Someone's in a good mood,' I point out – sounding like someone who's in a bad mood.

'I woke up like this,' she replies, resting her head on my shoulder. 'Something about scheming together, putting the boys in their place – I don't know, it's given me a real spring in my step.'

I laugh.

'I'm excited to see if our late-night mission pays off,' I reply, smiling to myself.

Last night, after the boys went to sleep, we snuck downstairs to put the first step of our master plan into action.

I don't know if we looked as badass as we felt, but truly, I felt like Catwoman in pyjamas, slinking down there, with my little bag of tricks, to put the first pieces of the puzzle in place.

'Do you think they've noticed anything yet?' Nita wonders out loud.

'There's only one way to find out,' I reply. 'Grab the others, I'll throw on something, and we'll go see.'

'We could go have our breakfast by the pool,' she says in a la-di-da voice.

'Yay, our breakfast of biscuits and iced coffees that we hopefully kept cool in a cold bath overnight,' I reply sarcastically.

'We really are living it up,' she says with a cheeky smile as she hops out of bed. 'Don't be long, and don't forget to top your body glitter up.'

I laugh. I won't forget, it's a key part of the plan.

It was funny, creeping down there, with our swag bag, looking like burglars except instead of taking things, we only left things behind. I really can't wait to see if any of the things we left have worked their magic yet so I practically jump from my bed and spring to action.

'It will be nice, to have a day by the pool – relax, scheme, repeat,' Nita jokes. 'Although I suppose we'll need to go buy more food, so that we have stuff we can actually store in our rooms, and we can sneak in a hot meal while we're there.'

'Good idea,' I reply, although I absolutely will have to find a way to get some work done at some point. I've got the product developer of Iwan's dreams to find, lest I find myself stuck in a nightmare.

Nita dashes off to grab the others – and the breakfast – so I start getting ready. I rummage around in my suitcase (because who actually unpacks and hangs up their things in a wardrobe on holiday?).

For a day by the pool and a trip to the (not all that) local shop, all I really need is a bikini and a sundress but – and I'm embarrassed to admit this – something about the boys being here makes me overthink my appearance. Like, if it were just the girls here, I wouldn't even bother with make-up on a day like today, but because the boys are here I feel this pressure to make an effort. It's like it's ingrained in me to 'doll-up' for the men, like it's a reflex, like I want to say fuck it but I can't. I swear, society has done this to me, but I really don't feel like I'll have the confidence I need if I don't do it. It's my war paint and my armour and I won't win without those things. Honestly though, if you have senses, and exist, there's no denying that lots of men (and some women) do treat women differently based on how they look. It's the thing that will make a man hold the door open for one woman, but refuse to give another a refund in a shop. You can be worshipped or dismissed, and I know it's just make-up, it's not a miracle, but the world I live in has me convinced that I will have a nicer time if I conform, and I'll do anything for an easy life.

Of course, the silliest thing in all of this is that I don't under any circumstances want the boys to think I've made any kind of effort for them, which means opting for 'no-make-up' make-up, which I think tends to take me even longer than when I just do my normal day-to-day face. Still, I do it, and then I scrape my long hair to one side and fix it into a loose plait, securing it with a band at the bottom. Then it's just a case of putting on my bikini and grabbing my sundress. Hopefully I look good but casual about it. Effortless, but not without effort, if that makes sense.

Why on earth am I even thinking about this?

I head to Nita's room, the first one at the top of the stairs, where she and the girls are waiting for me. The first thing I notice is that I'm not alone in my thinking, because all three of them have clearly made an effort too, so at least I know it isn't just me who has been damaged by growing up on a diet of glossy magazines with things like 'circles of shame' pointing out flaws, and the size zero culture we all celebrated for a while. Those years and years of shit in my formative years will probably haunt me for the rest of my life. I'll be ninety-eight, in a home, being helped to get changed, and I'll still be needlessly holding my tummy in.

'Breakfast is served,' Lou says with a smile, wiggling an armful of biscuits.

Willow has the allegedly iced coffees, which she's just finished up drying after their cold bath, but it looks like we're ready to head down.

'Okay, let's do it,' I say.

'Yes,' Nita replies excitedly. 'I'll lead the way.'

As we head down the stairs, the sound of the boys laughing and joking by the pool gets louder and louder, echoing in through the open patio doors, rushing through the house like water, flooding it with chaos.

Nita heads out first, followed by Lou and the biscuits, then Willow and the coffees. I'm about to head outside right behind them when I hear a noise coming from behind me.

I turn around and see Travis, closing the kitchen door behind him with one hand, holding his hot coffee in the other. God, it smells good. What I'd give for a hot flat white right now. I know, it's hot outside, and a cold drink should appeal more, but you can't beat a delicious coffee on a morning when you're on holiday, can you?

He gives me a bit of a smile as he stands there, in his trunks, his hair still wet from (I'm assuming) a dip in the pool. Well, it isn't from having a shower, is it?

'Good morning,' I say, trying to muster up a little politeness.

'Morning,' he replies. 'Sleep well?'

'Yes, thanks, the beds are lovely,' I say, not actually intending to rub it in his face, but I don't suppose it can hurt. 'Did you?'

'Surprisingly, yes,' he says, annoyingly sounding like he genuinely means it. 'Those sofas are more comfortable than most of the beds I've slept in on holidays. I woke up feeling great.'

I smile, trying to hide my irritation. Of course they had a lovely night on the sofas, while we were stuck upstairs thinking about all the things we were missing out on.

'We all thought we'd hang out by the pool today,' I tell him, trying to keep the conversation light.

Well, we don't have anywhere else to hang out here, apart from our bedrooms. I suppose the boys are the same, given that the living room is their bedroom, but at least they have a TV and a pool table to keep them amused.

'It's neutral territory,' he says with a playful smile. 'We're doing the same thing.'

As Travis steps closer to me I panic. It's impossible not to notice how smoking hot he is, way hotter than any guy I've ever dated, or known, or double-booked a villa with (although I guess technically this is the first, and hopefully only, time).

He raises a hand, as if he's going to touch me, and it's like I'm frozen in time. I don't know if it's something scary like fear or something even scarier like the fact that I actually do want him to put his hands on me, but it can't be a good look on me.

'Relax,' he says, amused, clearly picking up on my weird vibe as he brushes something off my shoulder. 'You just had a bug on you.'

I giggle like a dork, the tension easing. But then, as Travis looks at his hand, he frowns. 'What the hell is... is that glitter?' he asks as he examines his sparkly fingers.

'Hmm,' I say curiously, like a professor pondering an equation. 'Yes. Yes, that looks like glitter to me.'

'Are you wearing body glitter?' he asks with a surprising level of seriousness.

'Obviously,' I reply, laughing like that's a silly question. 'You know us girlies – we love glitter. We're always covered in the stuff.'

It takes everything in me not to laugh as he wipes his other hand on his abs, leaving a faint shimmer behind on his muscles that actually looks kind of sexy. Sort of like *Twilight* meets *Magic Mike*.

'Well, I guess now I'm wearing it too,' he points out. 'Oh, and it's in my coffee. Great stuff.'

I shrug and laugh, all easy breezy.

'Honestly, that stuff gets everywhere,' I say with a laugh. 'And it, like, really never goes. Not, like, ever.'

I've got my girly-girl level turned up to ten right now.

I don't give him a chance to reply, I quit while I'm ahead, heading outside to join the girls.

Stepping out into the warm sun feels like climbing into a warm bath on a cold day (a better point of reference, if you're from the UK).

Lou is already stretched out on a sun lounger, clearly trying to make the best of her hen week, Willow is on the one next to her, eating biscuits, and Nita is perched on the edge of a chair, looking in my direction, clearly wondering how I got left behind. I notice one of her eyebrows raise as she notices Travis walking out behind me.

The boys are in the pool splashing, throwing things, shouting out what I can only describe as vaguely military terms. I think they're playing army? The grown men in their thirties, pretending to shoot each other, launching grenades – not what I was expecting at all.

'So, this is where the Idiot Army trains their troops,' Nita says under her breath as I sit down next to her. 'Ready for the next part of the plan?'

'Ready,' I say, reaching out for an iced coffee. It might be cold (well, cold-ish) but at least there's no glitter in it. Yet. This stuff really does get everywhere.

'Honestly, my period is brutal right now,' Nita says, loudly, so that the boys can hear. She's styling it out like it's a private conversation, but she's definitely making sure everyone is party to it. 'I'd love to get in the pool but, genuinely, I'd ruin the water for everyone.'

'Don't be daft, you're on holiday,' Lou tells her, joining in.

'I get why she's worried,' I say, playing my part. 'Remember when we went to Italy, and she was swimming in that pool, and it looked like she'd died in the water.'

'It looked like I'd dyed the water,' Nita jokes. 'Everyone around me crossing themselves – it was like a scene from *Jaws*.'

Obviously none of this happened, but if we can put the boys off going in the pool, that's a win for us.

'It's the bullet clots,' Nita says, casually. 'You know the big ones, that fire out?'

Again, not a real thing, but the words have definitely subdued the boys.

'I get the mine clots,' Willow joins in. 'The ones that just go off – and I'm due on in a couple of days. But Lou is right, it's our holiday, we should jump in the pool. Mega clots be damned.'

'Did you say... mega clots?' Harry blurts.

We all turn to face him, all trying to hide our smug grins that we might have finally rattled them.

'Yes,' Willow says simply.

'My sister had trouble with something like that,' he tells us. 'They gave her some tablets for it. Maybe, when you get back home, you should have a chat with your doctor.'

I think his comfort with the subject and the maturity he's showing takes us all aback.

'Oh, okay, thanks,' Willow says, the wind totally knocked out of her sail.

'Yesterday I sneezed and it looked like a crime scene,' Nita informs him, making one last attempt to freak him out. 'I'll ruin the pool.'

'That's what chlorine is for,' he tells her with a shrug.

'No, honestly, it's really, really bad,' she insists.

'If it's that bad, then why did you leave these out for us to play with?' he asks. 'Don't you need them?'

I lean forward to get a better look. Is that... oh my God.

'Why are you throwing tampons around like they're grenades?' Nita asks, clearly unable to believe her eyes.

'Why did you leave them with the pool toys?' Owen replies. 'We just assumed...'

We left them there to try and make the boys feel weird enough to keep away.

'Hey, if you need them, the box is there, take the rest back,' Harry insists.

There's a seriousness and a sincerity to his words but... I don't know... something is off.

'What the hell is going on?' Willow asks in hushed tones as the boys get back to playing.

'They're playing with tampons – that is not normal,' Nita points out through gritted teeth, her smile hiding how she really feels to anyone who can't hear what she's saying.

'I know we have no other choice but, I don't know, I feel a bit uncomfortable here,' Lou adds. 'I have no plan B but, I don't know, we can't stay with them, right? I still haven't told Ellis. I'm sure he'll be fine with it, he'll understand, but...'

'Wait,' I say quickly, also keeping my voice quiet enough for only the girls to hear. 'Something isn't right here and I think I've put my finger on it. Harry mentioned his sister having period problems, and he gave friendly, normal advice. He wasn't grossed out or awkward talking about it.'

'Well, yeah, I'm surprised by that too, but so what?' Nita replies.

'So, all of this, whatever this is, throwing tampons around – it's all an act,' I say.

'Wait, what?' Lou chimes in.

'They're only doing it to mess with us,' I say. 'Think about it. It's the same idea we had, to try and drive them out. They're trying to drive us out by being... whatever this is.'

'Oh, those bastards,' Nita says, still smiling away.

'So, what do we do?' Lou asks.

'Be better at it,' Nita says. She turns to face the pool. 'You know what, boys, you can keep them. I'm just going to let the water take my flow, naturally and peacefully.'

'It'll make our war zone seem more realistic,' Harry jokes.

Oh, okay, they are definitely not only messing with us, but they're onto us, that we're messing with them. I mean, of course we've all had the same idea.

'Yeah, that makes sense,' Willow says, glaring at Harry as he holds a couple of tampons to his ears, like fancy earrings.

'Mad that these things get so big when they're wet,' Owen calls over to us. 'I have so many questions...'

'So, they're trying to mess with us, and we're trying to mess with them,' Lou points out quietly.

'So, this means war,' Nita says simply.

I really think we might actually be stuck here with them, and if we don't all acknowledge that and grow up and play nice together, then it's going to be one hell of a long fortnight.

15

Given the boys' little stunt yesterday, when they changed the code for the front door (and even though they have changed it back), we don't exactly trust them to keep things amicable. So, rather than hope they don't do it again, we've taken custody of one of the back door keys, so we can always let ourselves in and out, whether the boys want us to or not.

Walking through the side gate, into the back garden, it's like walking into another world. Gone is the serene, relaxing beautiful pool and firepit area – the kind that would make even *Love Island* contestants jealous – instead what we're walking into looks more like a scene from *Naked and Afraid* (just thankfully minus the awkward naked people).

'Bloody hell, it looks like a bomb went off,' Nita blurts.

It really does. There's just crap everywhere. There's stuff floating in the pool, litter, garden cushions scattered around, chairs turned over.

'What is wrong with them?' Lou asks no one in particular.

'It's such a mess,' Willow says with a sigh.

'I think it's called a disaster zone,' Lou replies flatly, gently moving an overturned chair with the tip of her flip-flop. 'How does this even happen? It's been, what, two hours?'

'They're like toddlers,' Nita says, shaking her head. 'Drunk, unsupervised toddlers who need a timeout.'

I can't help but smile, because I see what they're doing here, and it's kind of brilliant – but completely annoying for us.

'It's about as trashed as it can get without anything being ruined,' I point out. 'It's the perfect mess – too perfect. They've done this to try to rattle us. I mean, come on, there are tampons everywhere, but we left them out. This is a retaliation.'

'Okay, so what do we do?' Nita asks.

'We trash the kitchen,' Willow suggests.

'No, let's not trash anything,' I say quickly. 'Let's just do the last thing they will expect. Let's just go and talk to them. Calm and rational. Reasonable. We're adults, we shouldn't be making messes in communal spaces.'

'I mean, that sounds very reasonable and rational,' Lou replies. 'I'm just not sure what you're expecting to get out of a group of lads who have decorated a palm tree with tampons.'

I can't help but snort with laugher.

'They've only done that because we left them out, in their way, to try and bother them,' I say again. 'We've hit the ball to them, they've hit it right back.'

'I still think we should hit them,' Willow says.

'I could actually be on board for trying violence,' Nita (presumably – hopefully, even) jokes.

'Molly is right,' Lou says as we walk towards the villa. 'The mess is too perfect, too curated. The way the bag of crisps has been poured out artfully on the floor, like an abstract painting.'

'Right?' I reply. 'They've tried too hard.'

'Did they have to burst the flamingo float?' Nita says, clearly disappointed, as she picks up the remains of a pool inflatable from the floor, holding it up next to her like a dead animal carcass.

'They've probably just let the air out of it,' I reassure her.

'Then let's go and let the air out of them,' she replies.

This seemingly dead flamingo is an act of aggression – the modern-day holiday, very specific to our exact situation equivalent of a head on a spike – and we're not going to take it. I don't know why they can't just be normal. Okay, sure, we left some girly stuff around, but they locked us out. I really think we just need to call it quits and get on now.

'I hate them,' Nita announces. 'I hate every single one of them.'

'We all do,' Willow adds.

'So, let's go in there, talk rationally, kill them with kindness even,' I suggest. 'Because they're clearly not responding well to games, and we don't want them upping the ante.'

'Fair,' Lou says. 'Okay, let's do it.'

'Allow me to take the lead,' Nita suggests, which is fine, but she does have a tendency to go into some situations kind of hot.

I step over an empty bag like it's a landmine, terrified of what might be inside it, but I'm certain this mess is all show. Staged to perfection.

We all head for the patio doors, to head inside. I can see the anger in Nita's walk. Whatever the boys are up to, they're about to get an earful.

The boys are all still in their trunks, and the room stinks of chlorine, but they're all dry, hanging out, playing pool.

In here – which is essentially their bedroom and living space – isn't messy at all.

'What on earth happened out there?' Nita asks them, going in a little gentler than I expected her to.

They glance up at us, totally unbothered, like we're interrupting an Olympic final and not a casual game being played by a bunch of dickheads who are essentially in their underwear.

'What?' Owen asks, leaning casually on his cue.

'What?' Willow repeats back to him, irritated. 'The back garden is a disaster, that's what's up.'

'Is it?' Owen replies. 'I mean, we were out there earlier, having a laugh, but I didn't notice any excessive mess, did you, boys?'

He turns to the others who all just shrug, straight-faced, but you don't have to look too closely to see eyes narrowing and the corners of mouths twitching.

'I mean, if you girls are so passionate about tidiness, you're welcome to go out there and clean up,' Harry suggests.

Oh, he did not just say that.

'Because we're women?' Nita asks angrily.

'Because you're bothered,' Harry replies. 'Just think how fast you'd do it, as a team.'

You can tell by his smirk that he probably isn't actually a raging sexist, he's just trying to annoy us.

Still, the audacity hits Willow like a slap across the face.

'What the hell?' she blurts.

Nita places a hand on her shoulder as she takes a deep breath, composing herself, before she speaks.

'Okay, let's just cut the shit, shall we?' she says, stepping forwards, picking up a couple of pool balls from the table, rolling them around in her hand. 'I think we all know what's going on here. You're trying to make life difficult for us, and yeah, we're not exactly making it easy for you. The fact of the matter is that we both need this villa for the week, both weddings are this weekend, we all need to be here for them.'

The boys exchange glances but don't say a word.

'We just need to get along, for one week, to make space for

each other,' I point out. 'Surely we're all adults, capable of treating each other with dignity and respect?'

I can hear myself saying the words, and they should be true, but I'm not even convincing myself.

'And then the second week?' Harry asks.

'One week, two weeks – it's the same thing, right?' Travis says tactfully.

'Except none of us actually has to be here next week,' Harry points out. 'Our groom and their bride will be off on their honeymoons. There's no reason to share the place for the second week.'

'Which is why we're thinking – not that we're usually ones to give second chances, so keep that in mind – that we do the adult thing, we share the place for a week, and then you guys accept our very kind offer of taking our refund money, adding it to yours, and finding yourselves somewhere even better for next week,' Nita suggest hopefully.

Owen tilts his head, still clearly not at all taken with the suggestion. I'm wondering, at this point, if it's nothing but a matter of principle, or because they can – whatever it is, these boys aren't budging.

Nolan seems quiet, and not all that unreasonable, but he's definitely a follower and I'm sure he would do whatever the others told him to. Travis seems sort of decent... maybe?... although I do kind of fancy him, so that can't be helping my judgement. I do hear these fleeting bursts of sanity from him though. It seems like it's Owen and Harry who are the instigators, the ringleaders, the ones we're going to need to convince.

'I'm trying to be reasonable here,' Nita adds, clearly sensing that they're thinking the opposite.

'See, that doesn't sound reasonable to me at all,' Owen replies. 'How is that reasonable? You girls get to stay, we have to leave and find somewhere else...'

'With double the money,' Lou reminds him.

'We have money,' Owen tells her. 'I just don't see why we should leave. Why don't you leave? We can give you our money.'

'Because we're the ones being mature,' Nita points out.

'And because we asked you first,' Willow adds.

Owen laughs.

'Oh, yeah, you sound so mature, saying things like that,' he replies.

I can feel my jaw tightening to the point where my temples ache. This is getting us nowhere.

'Because we're the ones trying to compromise,' I say. 'We're just trying to think of something that works.'

'And we can do that too, right?' Travis says to his mates. 'There's got to be something we can do. A fair way to decide who gets to stay here the second week.'

See, this is what we need, a calm, considerate voice on the other side. Someone to make them see reason.

'Travis is right,' Harry says – much to my surprise. Wow, has that actually worked? 'We just need a fair way to decide who gets to stay here the second week. How about we fight for it?'

'As much as I'd love to punch you in the face...' Nita jokes, laughing it off. Then she realises he isn't joking. 'Sorry – what?'

'Not a fistfight – although great to know where you stand,' Harry replies playfully – flirtatiously even.

I'm getting the strong feeling that Harry is their Nita – if that makes sense. The fun, chaotic, cheeky friend. Owen seems more like the sort of boss of the group, which would tend to be Lou in our group (only in that she's organised, happy to lead, and stuff like that – which she's usually great at, when it isn't her wedding on the line). Nolan, hmm, I guess he's a bit of a Willow. She may have more confidence than he does but they're both sort of happily different to their friends. That just leaves me and Travis and I wonder, are we similar? We're both trying to keep the peace, both shying away from the scrappiness. Or maybe I'm just over-simplifying things. Or maybe I'm trying to work out who should take on who in a fight. They're clearly gym boys. The only 'gym' I've anything to do with is Jim, the barman at Thin Aire in Leeds, who always chats to us while he mixes our cocktails.

'I mean a competition,' Harry clarifies. 'We do something, this week, to determine who gets to stay for week two and who has to pack their bags and go as soon as the weddings are over.'

'Like what?' I can't help but ask, my imagination going into overdrive.

'We could agree on that,' Owen chimes in, clearly into the idea. 'It could be a few rounds, of a few things, and whoever has the highest score at the end of the week gets to stay.'

'But who decides on the rounds?' Willow asks. 'Obviously it's not fair, if you get to pick. I could thrash you at chess but if it's something silly, like football...'

'I mean, football isn't silly,' Harry insists defensively. 'But I take your point.'

Travis puffs air from his cheeks, almost like he can't quite believe he's engaging with this.

'I suppose, if we get to pick an activity each, even if we all pick something that plays to our strengths, it should all balance out,' he suggests.

It's like someone has switched a light on in Owen's eyes. Like he's just won some kind of all-inclusive, fun package holiday with an access-all-areas pass to a theme park, with unlimited rides.

'You know, I was worried this villa might be boring,' he says – which begs the question why he agreed to book it in the first place. 'But this sounds like it could actually be fun.'

'And fair,' Travis says. 'I guess?'

'I suppose it's one way to settle things,' Nita says. 'But we get to pick whatever activities we want, and you have to compete, no questions asked?'

'Yes, but the same goes for you,' Harry practically warns her. 'What do you say?'

Nita turns to face us.

'I'm in if you girls are,' she announces.

I look to Lou, our beacon of sanity (plus, it's her wedding week) to see what she's got to say, aka how she's going to shut this down.

'I mean, we're stuck together for a week anyway, and it beats arguing,' she replies.

Wait, what? Lou is up for this?

'I guess, we might as well, if we're going to be fighting all week anyway – we may as well get a say in how,' Willow adds.

So they're all in? Really? I mean, yeah, okay, I don't see too many other options for us. The boys won't leave. We can't leave. We have to share the space. Even if we agree to be the ones to be the grown-ups, and say we'll forgo the second week so that the boys can stay, that doesn't help us this week. They're still going to be difficult, and we're all still stuck here. At least if they think they're getting the opportunity to kick us out through sportsmanship, perhaps they'll be better this week? No more trying to torture us out, no more silly games. Just actual games instead. God, sounds exhausting, when I was hoping for a mixture of relaxing and working. But I suppose everyone is right, what choice do we really have?

'Yeah, okay,' I say – well, I don't know what else to say.

'We're all down, right, lads?' Owen asks. 'Harry, obviously. Nolan? Travis?'

'Yeah, I'm in,' Nolan says. 'I already know what I'm going to pick.'

Travis laughs for a second.

'Yeah, count me in – if everyone else is in, I can't exactly sit and watch, can I?'

Well, that's what I was hoping for.

'Great,' Owen says, clapping his hands together loudly. 'But let's keep this fight clean, okay? Anything is fair game, but we get to pick the same number of activities, and we'll keep score, and whoever wins, wins, no questions asked.'

'What if we're tied?' Nita asks.

'Then I'll be shocked,' Harry says with a snort.

'Then we do something simple,' Travis suggests. 'Like picking the highest card of a deck of cards, or Rock, Paper, Scissors. Something down to chance.'

'Sounds good to me,' Owen says.

'Yeah, okay, fine, that works for us,' Lou says.

'Not that it will come to that,' Owen points out. 'You girls are going down – I'd start packing those bags now.'

'We're not packing your bags for you,' Nita replies. 'You know, when you all have to leave, next week, first.'

'Game on,' Harry tells her.

'Come on, girls, let's take our shopping up to our rooms,' Nita says, scowling at the boys before turning on her heel.

'We've been wondering what you're eating, with no access to a fridge or anything to cook with,' Harry calls after her.

'Mind your own business,' she replies.

'We don't mind sharing. We're having paella tonight,' he tells her. She turns around to look at him, the word 'paella' clearly ringing in her ears. 'But, when I say we don't mind sharing, I mean we don't mind sharing the information, of what we'll be eating. Sorry, silly me, it sounded like I meant we'd share our food.'

'You're a dick,' Nita tells him. 'You're all dicks. And you're going down.'

'Bring it on,' Owen calls after her.

I can't believe it. Lou – lovely, easy-going, proudly quiet Lou – has somehow ended up with a hen party week that has turned into chaos. We all knew it was never going to be all that messy, that no one was going to get too drunk, or hit in the face by a stripper's appendage, or chained to a lamppost, or put on a boat to Prague (which, yes, I know is landlocked, but that's what makes it so crazy).

Suddenly it's like we're in some kind of trashy reality TV show. It's boys vs girls. Fighting for a holiday in a luxury villa. Bloody hell, it's like something I'd watch, but never, ever take part in. And yet here I am, living it, for the next week, when I have so much other stuff going on.

'This is so not how I saw my hen party week playing out,' Lou says as we walk up the stairs.

I think we're all in agreement on that one. But really, truly, what choice do we have?

I just really, really hope we win. Because if we don't, God, imagine how insufferable the boys will be then – and the holiday will be over, that's for sure.

16

The villa is quiet – almost too quiet, suspiciously quiet even, but it's the kind of peaceful stillness that you can only really experience at this late hour on a hot summer's eve.

I step outside to the pool area (keeping my wits about me, because I've seen too many horror movies). The cool tiles beneath my bare feet send a small shiver up my spine – not that they're all that cold, I think my body was just expecting them to be hot, like they were earlier. It's strange how much worse something can feel when you're not braced for it – like, you know, cold tiles, or the man you thought you were going to spend the rest of your life with dumping you.

The air feels softer, cleaner even, for not carrying that faint scent of chlorine that comes from the water being heated up by the midday sun. I think without the boys here too, it just feels less suffocating. Less intense. Being out here at night is like a snapshot of what this villa could be like if the boys weren't here, and if that isn't motivation to win this silly competition then nothing is.

The space has transformed into something serene, something almost magical. I could be tempted to sit out here for a bit.

The pool glimmers under the dim outdoor lights, its surface smooth and perfectly flat, like a mirror, reflecting the starry sky above.

I'm here to look for my book; I think I left it out here earlier. Well, initially I'd tried to get some work done out here, but there's no bloody wi-fi which made it impossible, so then I tried to relax instead, by reading my book, but the boys were too loud, shouting at each other over whatever game they were playing in the pool. This time I don't think they were doing it to be dicks, I think boys are just boys sometimes, and they were having fun. My kind of fun just happens to have a much lower volume, so I gave up.

I weave between the sun loungers, scanning the area for my book. It's still a bit messy out here. Abandoned bottles and cans clutter the tables, their contents long since drunk or evaporated, and a few damp towels are still draped half-heartedly over the chairs. I wonder if we might need to agree on some sort of cleaning schedule, or to just really drive home that if this is going to work everyone needs to clean up after themselves. Perhaps we'll see how the first round of the competition goes, before we start trying to be 'reasonable' again.

It's funny, really, how quickly things change. One minute, we're all excited about our girls-only getaway, lounging by the pool, drinking cocktails, and having a chilled-out time. And the next, we're having to work out how to share the villa with them, a bunch of guys – and a really annoying bunch of guys at that.

I just... I didn't sign up for this. I mean, I did, but not like this. Suddenly I feel more like I'm on an adventure holiday, like sharing the villa with four boys is some kind of adrenaline junkie sport – it certainly feels that way.

I'm trying to stay calm about it. I mean, it's only for a week, right? We can survive a week. I'll just pretend I'm in prison, or something, serving a sentence (although God knows what I would have done to have this as a punishment), one that will soon be over. And then I can get back to my life, rehabilitated, careful to never land myself in a situation like this again.

Finally, I clap eyes on it, on the floor, next to where I was sitting. I really did just give up and abandon it. At least now I can take it to the peace and quiet of my bedroom, and get lost in a few chapters before a sleep.

I'm currently reading (or trying to read, at least) the latest Mia Valentina romcom – although it's optimistic of me to think I can take my mind off my current situation, which is a lot like one of Mia's plots, by reading a book called *Love at First Fight*. Still, a bit of good, light-hearted fun is just what I need right now. Nothing stressful, nothing scary, nothing that's going to send me into an existential crisis. Just good, clean—

'Hi.'

A man's voice snaps me from my thoughts, making me jump.

'Shit, sorry, I didn't mean to scare you,' he says.

It's Owen. He's lying on one of the sun loungers, alone, in total silence.

'No, sorry, it's not your fault,' I insist. 'I didn't realise anyone was out here.'

'I didn't realise you were here either – until I did,' he adds with a smile. 'Looking for something?'

'Just my book,' I tell him, holding it up as evidence.

He pulls a face.

'I didn't think you would have been the type for girly romantic comedies,' he says, like he knows me.

'What are you doing out here, alone, at this time?' I ask, ignoring him.

I don't mean it to sound as accusatory as it does, I'm just

curious really, why he would be out here, in the dark, doing nothing.

He makes himself comfortable, leaning back on his hands again, gazing upward.

'I was just looking at this,' he says.

'At what?' I reply. 'There's nothing here.'

'Yes, there is,' he insists. 'Lie down, have a look.'

My curiosity gets the better of me so I lie down on the sun lounger next to him and stare up at the sky. It takes my eyes a second or two to adjust but then...

'Wow,' I blurt.

'See,' he replies.

I'd noticed that there were stars in the clear sky, sure, but it's only when you take a moment to look up that you realise that you almost can't even focus on the black of night, you can't find a space without stars in it, the sky is full.

'So, you're just out here admiring the sky?' I say – I don't know why, I don't have him for the type.

'Yeah,' he says. 'Don't sound so surprised. I'm fascinated by it. Okay, I don't know much about it. I can't point out any constellations or planets or owt like that, but I love to see it. I like to think about what's out there, what's going on that's bigger than us—'

'If your real parents might come back for you, to take you back to your home planet,' I add, daring to tease him.

Owen laughs.

'Make fun of me all you want, I love this stuff,' he replies.

I exhale slowly and deeply for a moment, trying to make sense of the layers and layers of stars.

'You know, I do get it,' I tell him. 'A few months ago I was at my parents' house, in the back garden, letting their dog out one night after dinner, and I saw this thing...'

'Was it a UFO?' he says in a silly voice. 'Come on, you can quit mocking me.'

'No, I'm being serious,' I insist. 'I saw this thing – at first I thought it was a firework, but it was silent, and it wasn't going in any sort of direction that made sense for a firework. It burned through the sky, so brightly, leaving a trail for a few seconds and then it was gone. I went in and told my dad and he told me I'd seen a meteorite. He went on social media and searched it – loads of people had seen it all over the UK.'

'That's incredible,' Owen replies. 'I'm so jealous.'

'It was incredible,' I admit. 'It was beautiful and remarkable and fascinating but, more than anything, it made me think. Not about space or aliens or anything like that. More about, I don't know, fate maybe, or luck, even? I just couldn't believe that I was outside, looking up, at that exact part of the sky, at that exact moment in time. It was just a thin line, over a few seconds, and I happened to be in the right place at the right time to get to experience something so magical.'

I catch myself for a moment. Why am I telling him this? Why am I chatting with the enemy not only generally, but almost intimately?

'See, it makes you think,' he replies. 'Not only that there's so much out there, so much beyond us, but also that sometimes life finds a way to put us in the right place, at the right time, for the right thing to happen to us when we need it the most. Everything happens for a reason, right?'

'Oh, what, like us turning up here at the same time?' I ask, pulling a face at him.

'Maybe,' he suggests. 'You guys are from, where? Yorkshire?'

'Leeds,' I tell him – that seems broad enough that it's not like he'll be able to pop over the Pennines and find me. 'You?'

'Manchester,' he says, confirming my suspicions. To anyone

much further north or south from us, we probably sound exactly the same, but a Yorkshire lass knows a Lancashire lad when she hears one. We're practically in *Romeo and Juliet* territory.

'We live about an hour's drive from each other,' he points out. 'And yet we met here, in Spain, at this villa, through some booking error. What if we were supposed to meet?'

'If we were supposed to meet, and we weren't supposed to kill each other, I imagine it would have been in better circumstances?'

'Better circumstances and being in a swimming pool when a bunch of naked women jumped in?' he jokes. 'I notice you didn't join in, which kind of ruins the sexy magic of the whole situation…'

'Well, I needed a wee,' I tell him, playfully but purposefully trying to well and truly murder the 'sexy magic'.

All of a sudden it feels like the air has changed between us. It feels harder to breathe, like it's thick with something.

'Think about it like it's your meteor,' he suggests. 'If you hadn't been looking up, you would have missed it. You could have missed having one of those romantic comedy interactions with your dream man, the kind that always happens in the books you read, because you were having a wee.'

'Somehow I seriously doubt my dream man is the kind of guy who would lock me out of a villa, in a foreign country, with nowhere else to go,' I point out.

'And yet somehow, I doubt any girl who would take time to rub glitter into hers and her friends' bodies, just to prove a point to us, would be doing so if she wasn't at least a little bit interested in… getting a rise out of us,' he replies, oh-so slowly and breathy.

'I have no interest in getting a rise out of any of you,' I tell him – mirroring his almost flirtatious tone. I'm not even sure why, it just feels… competitive? Competitive flirting, that's a first. 'You think the universe has a plan for me. I know that plan doesn't involve anything but kicking your arse in this competition.'

'I don't think the universe works like that,' he replies.

'Are you always this philosophical?' I ask.

'Only when I'm trying to impress someone,' he replies. 'Or push their buttons. Or both.'

I notice the corners of his mouth being tugged at. He's trying to fight it, to keep himself from smiling, but he's fighting in vain. He's enjoying this. Our little back and forth.

'I'm not that easily impressed,' I tell him.

'I like a challenge,' he replies.

'Then save it for the competition,' I insist. 'I'm telling you, you're going to need it.'

'Then may the best man win,' he says simply.

'The best woman will win,' I correct him.

'That second week belongs to the boys,' he tells me. 'The sooner you accept that, the easier it will be for you.'

'Sorry, am I supposed to feel threatened by the boys who threw tampons around like grenades?' I ask in disbelief. Okay, I'll admit it, I'm enjoying this a bit too much. 'That doesn't exactly scream "winners" to me.'

'Don't underestimate us,' he replies. 'We won't be the ones at a Spanish shop, with no signal to use an online translator, desperately trying to mime what tampons are because we wasted ours trying to upset a bunch of grown men, who have all had girlfriends, who all know what periods are, with them.'

Shit. He might have won that one.

'Well, then you'll know how much fun it will be to share a villa with us, when that happens, won't you?' I reply. 'All those hormones flying around.'

'They'll keep the pheromones company,' he jokes. 'I'm starting to think there's a lot of those in the air…'

Before I can say anything in reply to that, a voice calls out from above.

'Molly!' Nita's sharp tone breaks the tension.

I look up to see her leaning over her balcony railing slightly. Her room is next to mine, so we both share the balcony that looks over the pool area.

'Hi,' I blurt, trying not to sound like I've just been caught out doing something I shouldn't. I wasn't doing anything, just talking, so I don't know why I sound so guilty.

'Have you got a minute?' she asks me. It doesn't sound optional.

'Sounds like your friend needs you,' Owen says with a smile, looking at me briefly before turning his attention back to the sky. 'Good night.'

'Night,' I reply simply before getting up and heading back indoors.

I head upstairs, trying to shake off my conversation with Owen. I'm not usually so competitive but, I don't know, something about his tone, it makes me want to win.

By the time I get to Nita's room, it's clear she isn't messing around. Lou and Willow are already here too, sitting cross-legged on the bed in their pyjamas. Willow looks like she's just woken up. Why do I feel like I've been summoned?

'Emergency girls' meeting,' Nita announces as I sit down on the bed with the others. Okay, so I have been summoned.

Nita is pacing back and forth, her hands on her hips, like she's clearly worked up about something.

'What's going on?' I ask, setting my book to one side, making myself more comfortable.

Nita narrows her eyes at me.

'What were you doing out there with Owen?' she asks suspiciously.

I blink, part taken aback, part feeling like I've been caught red-handed. But I wasn't actually doing anything. I haven't been caught doing a single thing wrong.

'What? I wasn't... I just went to grab my book,' I insist. 'He was out there, looking at the stars, and we got talking. That's it.'

Her arms fold tighter across her chest, squashing her boobs so hard one almost pops out of her vest.

'Talking, eh?' she replies. 'Because it looked a lot more like flirting, from where I was standing.'

'You were standing on the balcony,' I remind her. 'You can't have seen or heard anything. We were out there in the dark, talking quietly while we looked up at the stars. That's all.'

'That's flirting,' she corrects me. 'Talking quietly, in the dark, star gazing. That is so flirting. Dream flirting, even!'

I scoff.

'We weren't flirting,' I insist. 'Well, I definitely wasn't.'

'But you think he was?' she asks, curiously, like she might be onto something.

Lou's eyebrows shoot up, and even Willow perks up a bit.

'You think Owen was flirting with you?' Lou asks, her voice a mix of teasing and surprise.

'No,' I insist. 'No, no. I don't think so... no?'

'Oh, because I was going to say we could use that to our advantage,' Lou says.

'And I was going to say perhaps that is what Owen is doing with Molly,' Nita points out. 'Maybe he's flirting with her, to get her guard down, to give him an advantage in the competition.'

'Ohhh, that does make more sense,' Willow adds.

I shoot her a filthy look.

'It was just silly banter,' I tell them all firmly.

'Banter is flirting, Molly,' Nita points out. 'I know you refuse to date, but you must remember that? Either way, we can't afford it.'

'We can't afford it?' I repeat back to her.

'No, we can't, not if we want to win,' she replies. 'These boys think they've got this competition in the bag, they'll do anything to win, and we're not having it. So, no fraternising with the boys. No getting along with them. No flirting. Absolutely no hooking up under any circumstances. We don't know these boys – they're strangers, we know next to nothing about them, apart from that they're clearly playing to win. Any friendliness, any slip-up, gives them an advantage.'

'Nita, I love you, but you're taking this a little too seriously,' I point out with a friendly giggle.

'Or you're not taking this seriously enough,' she replies. 'We're doing this to win. We're doing it for us, for feminism even. To wipe the smiles off those boys' stupid faces. So are you all with me or not?'

Willow groans and rubs her face.

'Nita, it's late. Do we really need to make a whole thing out of this right now?' she asks.

I don't think she's on my side, I think she's just tired.

'Yes,' Nita says firmly, glaring at each of us in turn. 'We're making a pact, right now. No one fraternises with the boys. No talking, no flirting, and absolutely no hooking up. Deal?'

'Hooking up?' Lou repeats back to her, unable to hide her amusement. 'You know I'm here to get married, right?'

'I'm not worried about you, I'm worried about Sister Molly here,' Nita points out. 'It's a been a minute since she had a man.'

'Oi,' I insist, laughing it off, because I know she's joking. 'You're the one who pulls everywhere we go.'

'Right, so I must be taking this seriously,' she replies. 'I just really, really want to win this holiday. We get fuck all holiday and we're here and it's amazing. So, please?'

'Okay, fine, you have my word,' I tell her.

'Obviously mine too,' Lou adds pointlessly.

'Yeah, all right, if I can go back to bed,' Willow moans.

'Yeah, okay, meeting dismissed,' Nita says. 'I'm just thinking of us all.'

'You must be, if you're saying you won't be flirting with a bunch of hotties like we've got downstairs,' Lou jokes.

'Well, we can where it's strategic,' she replies. 'But only if we don't mean it.'

'Okay, Mum,' I tease her. 'Strategic flirting only. Good night, see you in the morning.'

Nita laughs. It's all light-hearted and good fun but, wow, you can tell she really does want to win. But she's right, we don't get much holiday, especially not together, and it would be a shame to leave without getting to properly enjoy the place.

'Glad we're all on the same page,' she calls after us as we all head back to our rooms.

Finally back in my room, I lie down on my bed, setting my book to one side again (it hardly seems worth the bother of going to find it), because I don't really need to read now, not when my own imagination is running wild.

Tomorrow is going to be interesting...

17

I'm up, sure, but I wouldn't exactly say I was 'at 'em'.

I was kind of hoping that, after a night of sleeping on it, enough people would see sense, or have a change of heart, or something to put the silly idea of having a competition to bed. But no, it seems like everyone is raring to go. Like they all don't just think it's a good idea, but they're actually looking forward to it too. Am I mad? Because it feels like I'm the only one who just wants to have a nice, peaceful, normal time. Not a battle of the sexes.

The boys are already outside by the firepit, looking bright-eyed, sounding loud, and clearly ready for action. Their energy is like a punch to the face, which is usually the first thing I feel like doing when I look at them.

Nita is raring to go, looking alarmingly perky as she practically marches towards the boys, leading the way for the rest of us to follow.

'I can't believe we're doing this,' I say to no one in particular.

'Chillax,' Willow tells me – I hate the word chillax.

'Yeah, honestly, we've got this,' Nita reminds me.

We've been talking all morning about what we should do and how exactly we're going to win this thing. We have a plan but, I don't know, I'm just so nervous about it all, and nowhere near as excited as anyone else.

In a way, I get it. There's not much else to do here. Relaxing would be lovely if it were possible, but it isn't because of the constant chaos from the boys. Working would also be good, but I can't work, because I don't have wi-fi, and I can't imagine the boys agreeing to let me use theirs, because they won't even let us use the fridge.

I just need to look at this competition as something to do, a distraction from everything else, and try not to worry about what happens if we lose, because that would mean going home early, and I really don't want that. I know Lou will be jetting off on her honeymoon after she and Ellis tie the knot, but staying here with Nita and Willow – without the boys – sounds like heaven. Hot coffee on a morning, quiet lazy days by the pool, chilling by the firepit on an evening, warm food. I want it, I need it, I'm going to psych myself up so that we stand a better chance of winning it.

However, looking at the boys, practically vibrating with competitive glee, I'm guessing it isn't going to be easy as just having a positive mental attitude and hoping for the best. I need to take this seriously – ah, why not, eh? If there's nothing else to do…

Owen, Travis, Harry and Nolan are all sitting around the (obviously unlit) firepit. They're loud, cocky, and clearly ready to go. And I can't shake the feeling they might actually be good at whatever we throw at them, because there's always a chance that our strengths are also theirs. On the flipside though, we could share their strengths too. Stay positive, Molly, stay positive!

'We're feeling generous,' Owen says as we approach them, 'so you girls get to pick the first round.'

'Flags,' Nita says simply, cutting to the chase.

'Flags?' Harry repeats back to her, a mixture of disbelief and disgust. 'Sorry, I thought this was supposed to be fun.'

'Flags are fun if you're not thick,' Nita shoots back with a jarringly angry smile. 'Plus, you said we could pick anything. No questions asked.'

'It wasn't a question, it was a statement,' Harry replies. Honestly, the sexual tension between the two of them is not going unnoticed. 'So, what, do you just carry flags around with you, like a dork, ready for a situation like this?'

'No,' Nita says simply. 'But there's this magical thing, called the internet.'

'At least there should be,' I can't help but say under my breath.

'We can use that thing.' Nita points at Nolan, who looks up and realises she's talking about his iPad. 'We can load a quiz up, that way it's all fair, and random, and no one can cheat.'

Nolan looks at her, then the iPad, like he's just been asked to give up state secrets. After a pause, he sighs.

'Yeah, okay, I'll find one,' he says.

'Identifying tiny flags on a screen sounds so painfully boring,' Harry says, folding his arms across his bare chest, emphasising his pecs in a way that I'm sure is entirely deliberate.

'We did say they could choose anything,' Owen points out. 'Just like we will, when it's our turn.'

I'm not sure I like the sound of that.

'Fine,' Harry says, exhaling deeply and dramatically. 'But if I fall asleep halfway through, go on without me.'

Flags on the agenda or not, it's nice to be out here, with something to do, knowing that there's a ceasefire with the boys (for the time being, at least).

The sun is getting high in the sky now, shining down on us, making everything scorching hot – including our drinks. You can't beat a cold can on a hot day, but all we have are warm-ish cans, with contents that are only getting warmer. A hot Coke doesn't quite hit the spot in the same way as an ice-cool one, but it's all we've got.

It's frustrating to be staying in a luxury villa, and to not only be without all of the luxuries that should be included, but without basic necessities like a fridge.

'I'm going to need a beer for this,' Harry says, despite it not being midday yet.

'I'm a bit hungry,' Travis says. 'Shall we go grab some stuff, before we start?'

'Yeah, come on,' Owen says.

The four of them head inside, to their lovely kitchen, to get their ice-cold drinks and their properly stored snacks.

Travis gives me a bit of a smile as he passes me. He reminds me of me, in that he generally keeps his head down and his mouth shut – although, if he's really like me, he's probably thinking a lot more in his head than he's saying out loud. I'm curious about him, for some reason. I want to know more about him, about what he's thinking... I'm not sure why though.

Lou is fanning herself with one of the cork coasters that are laid out around the firepit.

'My gosh, it's warm,' she says.

'Isn't it,' Nita replies, smiling joyfully, like the sun is her own personal energy source.

I'm slathered in factor 50 and wondering how hard it would be to drag one of the parasols over here, so I'm with Lou on this one. The cold pool looks so inviting right now. That's exactly where I'd be if I didn't have to do... this.

'Is it weird that I'm nervous?' Lou says.

'You shouldn't be with this round, this is my round, I've got us,' Nita replies. 'One of the benefits of being a luxury travel agent is knowing flags. They're everywhere – brochures, websites, client forms. You learn them. I know my Barbados from my Bahamas, trust me.'

'Well, that, plus how competitive you are – I'm hoping it will serve us well,' Willow replies.

'Good, because I don't know my Buenos Aires from my El Salvador,' I joke.

'Buenos Aires is a city,' Nita corrects me seriously.

'I know, I was making a jo… you know what, never mind,' I reply, laughing it off. 'Wow, you really are competitive today.'

'I'm only in it to win it,' she replies.

The boys return in a chorus of laughter, clutching their beers. I don't even like beer but I bet one would be so cooling right now. The condensation glistens on the glass bottles, mocking our warm cans of pop.

The four of them saunter back towards the firepit, looking like a low-budget *Reservoir Dogs*, thinking they're oh-so cool. Owen gives me a wink as he sets the iPad in the middle of the group, between our two teams.

We sit on one side, the boys on the other, almost like we're squaring off, like boxers meeting before a fight, or like we're in some kind of Western standoff.

Nita rubs her hands together in delight as the first flag lights up the screen. Here we go.

The iPad screen glows with the first flag: green, white, and red.

'Italy,' Nita says, almost bored. 'Easy peasy.'

The boys collectively groan, with Owen offering a slow, sarcastic clap.

'Wow, amazing, you're killing it,' he teases.

I think we all knew that one.

Next up it's the boys.

I bite back a grin as the next flag pops up – a tricolour of blue, yellow, and some kind of symbol in the middle. Nita's smile sharpens which makes me think this is a harder one.

'Moldova,' Nolan says, without missing a beat.

Owen keys in the answer for him and it's right.

As his teammates cheer him, I can't help but cock my head curiously. I guess they have a friend who is good at geography too. Typical.

My eyes flick to Nita, whose confident expression falters for just a second. I don't think she thought they were going to get that one.

The next flag appears – a yellow cross on a blue background. Nita doesn't miss a beat. 'Sweden,' she says, and the iPad confirms it. We're in the lead again.

It's the boys' turn again, and their flag is green, then white, then green again.

'Nigeria,' Harry says confidently.

'Yeah, definitely Nigeria,' Travis adds.

I tighten my grip on my warm can, just a little, because I had no idea on that one, but these boys are on it.

Owen keys their answer in, given that he's the closest, and it's correct. Again. How are they this good? I exchange a puzzled look with Lou. Nita being a flag expert makes sense, it's her job, but it's like all four of the boys are good at this. What are the chances?

The iPad flashes up another flag: it's white, with red sort of triangles, with a blue edge... honestly? I feel like I'm seeing it for the first time in my life.

'Nepal,' Nita says confidently, like she could do this in her sleep.

Of course, it's right.

The boys' turn comes up again. This time, it's a red, white, and blue horizontal tricolour. Owen leans forward, scratching his jaw theatrically before saying, 'The Netherlands.'

He's correct, and the boys erupt into cheers again. Nolan claps Owen on the back. 'Masterclass,' Harry tells him.

Oh, please.

The next flag for us is a green field with a crescent moon and star in white.

'Pakistan,' Nita says without hesitation.

Correct.

Another one for the boys.

'Argentina,' Harry and Travis both say at the same time.

Correct.

'We should do this like pens,' Owen suggests.

'Pens?' Lou repeats back to him.

'Penalties,' Owen says ever so slowly. 'Like football. We'll be doing this all day otherwise. So if you get one wrong, and we get one right, we win. If you get yours right, but we get ours wrong, you win. We both get them right or we both get them wrong, we do another round.'

'Sounds good to me,' Nita says. 'It's just too easy.'

I'm impressed by how good she is at this. I mean, I'm hopeless. I knew Italy, and Sweden – although that's probably just because of Ikea. But I can tell by the look on Nita's face that she has known them all so far. Long may it continue.

Our turn again – well, Nita's turn at least.

I'm not even expecting to know them now so, when the flag pops up, showing green, red, and yellow stripes, along with a central yellow star, I'm not even bothered about being clueless. After the first couple, I felt like it was a weakness of mine, and something I could work on. Now I've realised that the flags that I don't recognise far outnumber the ones I do, meh, what's the point? We all have our strengths, and I don't think geography will ever be one of mine.

'Senegal,' Nita says. 'Final answer.'

I don't think anyone is more surprised than she is to see that it's the wrong answer.

'Nope, it's Cameroon,' Harry informs her – and he's not at all unhappy about delivering the news, he can hardly contain the smile on his face.

'What?' Nita says, leaning forward in her seat. 'But it's... oh, fuck. It's the colours. It's the same flag, but with different colours.'

'Unlucky,' Owen says, though he doesn't even try to hide his smirk. 'If we get this one, we win.'

Oh, God, here's hoping they don't. If Nita can't get them all then the boys can't, surely?

'And if you lose, we go again,' Willow reminds him.

'Then let's not lose,' Harry says.

The flag appears on the screen: a striking diagonal red stripe cutting through a black background, bordered by white. I squint at it, as though getting a clearer look at it is going to make me suddenly an expert in flags of the world. I have no idea. I look to Nita who is smiling slightly now, which makes me think she knows it, and that she thinks there's a chance the boys might not.

'No way,' she mouths at me.

But Nolan leans forward, his grin spreading across his face once again.

'Trinidad and Tobago,' he declares confidently.

And... it's right. Shit, it's right.

The boys roar in triumph, but Nita looks like she's just lost her life savings.

'How the hell do you know that?' she demands. 'Are you cheating?'

Nolan shrugs, still smiling.

'Dwight Yorke. Legend – he's from Trinidad and Tobago,' he points out.

Lou's brow furrows.

'Katie Price's ex?' she says, confused.

Harry rolls his eyes.

'Er, yeah, he's also known for playing football,' Harry says sarcastically.

Nita sits back, arms crossed, visibly fuming, sick to her core.

'This doesn't make sense. How are you all so good at this?' she asks.

'Football,' Harry says simply, as though it's the most obvious thing in the world.

Ugh. Football.

'Or Football Manager,' Nolan adds – whatever that is. 'You learn where all the players are from when you're scouting them.'

Owen claps his hands together victoriously, clearly beaming with pride at his boys' efforts.

'Amazing. We're starting as we mean to go on,' he announces. 'Victory jump in the pool?'

He takes off towards the water, the rest of the boys whooping and following him.

Travis lingers behind for a moment, giving us an awkward shrug and an apologetic laugh. 'We got lucky, with the football crossover,' he says.

'Thanks,' Nita replies, though the tightness in her voice suggests otherwise.

Travis jogs off to join the others, who are already splashing around.

'Shit, sorry, girls,' Nita says.

'Oh my God, don't be daft,' I insist. 'I think I knew two.'

'Yeah, you did far better than any of us could have done,' Lou reassures her.

The boys climb back out of the pool, dripping water all over the paving stones. It's no sooner landed when it looks like it's drying from the heat of the sun.

'Well, lads, I think we should celebrate,' Harry announces, loud enough for us to hear, as he shakes water from his hair. 'Why don't we get ready and head to the nearest bar, have a few drinks with the locals, meet some ladies who appreciate real winners.'

Nita can't resist taking the bait.

'Well, good luck impressing any woman with a sense of smell,' she replies. 'You all absolutely reek of chlorine.'

'Whatever,' Harry replies to her. 'Later, losers.'

The pack head inside, leaving us with the pool area to ourselves for a bit.

'I hate them,' Nita says simply.

'We all do,' Willow agrees. 'We need to beat them, we really do.'

'I'm sure we can,' I say optimistically. 'Today was just…'

'…bad luck,' Lou says, finishing my sentence. 'They only did well because football has taught them so much about world geography.'

'Yeah, we're going to have to be smarter, moving forward, to make sure they don't catch us out again,' Nita says, folding her arms, and slumping back in her seat.

We really will, because I never want to see them this smug again. I'm all in now. This means war.

18

Is it a secret garden if everyone knows where it is?

Just off the main outdoor area is a walled garden, hidden away behind a gate, but the fact that it's listed as a feature of the place kind of kills the idea of it being hidden. Plus, with there being eight of us here, and all of us knowing about it, it's not much of an escape. Still, it feels like the only place to wander off for a breather right now, without leaving the villa grounds. Well, I'm always in my bedroom (or one of the other, identical bedrooms) or out in the pool area. The not-so-secret garden feels like the only place I can get some time to myself, without staring at the same four walls. Plus, you know, there's a chance there might be signal here.

Hedges, flowers, trees – this place somehow looks completely wild, and yet perfectly manicured. I don't know enough about flowers (so I won't be choosing anything to do with that as a round for the competition) but I feel like I can smell each one as I stroll by. I lightly brush the petals with my hands, unable to resist touching them for some reason.

As I walk further, the main path splits, one side curving back towards the villa while the other dips into a shadowy archway of trees. I choose the shadows, the air is so much cooler and quieter here, the light filtering through the canopy of the trees in scattered golden patches. It's a welcome break from the heat, that's for sure.

My footsteps crunch softly on the gravel, until I find a shadowy clearing, with a bench right in the middle of it, the perfect place for some time alone.

'Molly, have you got a minute,' a voice calls after me.

So much for time on my own.

I turn around and see that it's Travis. I feel weirdly pleased to see him, in a way that I can't quite put my finger on. I suppose I'd just rather it was him than any of the others. Well, I'm on a flirting ban with Owen, Harry seems like a bit of a dick, and I'm not sure how much I have to talk to Nolan about – seeing as though I know nothing about football, or Football Manager.

Travis, who is much taller than me, ducks under a branch to join me. His hair is still damp, and a little messy, like he's just rolled out of a nap or broke free from a headlock one of the other boys had him in. There's a casual energy about him that always makes him look so at ease, like he's just sort of wandered into his life and decided he'll stay.

'I wanted to pull you for a chat,' he says, flashing me a cheeky smile.

'Did you just make a *Love Island* reference?' I ask in disbelief.

'Yeah, the villa pool area kind of reminds me of it,' he says. 'Plus, with us being sort of boys together, girls together – from what I've seen, it's just like it.'

'From what you've seen?' I reply through a knowing smile.

'Bits and bobs,' he says. 'Anyway, I found you.'

'In the middle of a secret garden – I want my money back,' I reply.

'You have your money back,' he points out, sitting down on the bench next to me. 'Anyway, I saw you heading through the gate, so I followed you.'

'That's kind of creepy,' I tell him, powerless to stop myself mirroring his smile.

'So creepy,' he jokes.

'Well, it's like a maze in here, so you're lucky you found me,' I point out.

'I figured you would be where the chaos wasn't,' he replies.

'And I figured you'd be hosing your friends down, ahead of your big night out,' I joke. 'I'm sure there's one here somewhere.'

Travis laughs.

'I didn't know this was here, you know,' he says. 'I assumed the gate just went out of the garden, into the countryside around us.'

My eyebrows shoot up.

'So, it really is a secret garden,' I say. 'Well, it was until you stalked me into it. I guess the secret is out now.'

'Nah, your secret is safe with me, I won't tell the others you're in here,' he replies. 'You need somewhere to retreat to.'

'Good to know, I wouldn't want this being the area for your next wrestling match,' I say, laughing it off, but that is actually very good of him.

'Not a chance – the plants would get in the way,' he replies with a smile.

'So, you're the ringleader of your lot, hmm?' I say.

'I do my best,' he replies. 'I try to wrangle them, where I can. I've noticed you're a bit of a peacekeeper too – what's your secret?'

'Oh, I don't know, keeping everyone calm, putting things into perspective – bribery as a last resort.'

'You have a very calming vibe,' he says. There's something

warm in his voice that makes me feel relaxed and, I don't know, noticed maybe? 'That's why I wanted to talk to you, actually.'

From relaxed to nervous again. Travis wants to talk to me about something? It's ironic, that he says I have a calming vibe, because while I'm okay at calming other people, I'm generally always quite stressed myself. And, come on, who doesn't panic when they learn someone wants to talk to them?

He turns his head to look me in the eye for a moment. God, his eyes are gorgeous. Deep, dreamy – the kind of eyelashes that make you mad, because you'd pay a fortune to have them, and it turns out boys were at the front of the queue when they were being handed out.

'You're pretty quiet when everyone's scrapping,' he points out, his tone light but observant. 'It makes me wonder if you think this whole competition thing is as daft as I think it is...'

I glance at him, a little caught off guard by the honesty.

'Well, yeah, I don't think it's the best idea anyone has ever had,' I reply. 'But mostly I just worry about it all spiralling out of control. It's not that I don't think it will be fun, it's just...'

'Sort of dangerous?' he replies, finishing my sentence for me.

'Exactly,' I reply. 'It's all fun and games, until someone gets hurt.'

'I thought this holiday was going to be a chilled one – lord knows I need one – so I wasn't exactly down for...' He gestures vaguely, like he can't even find the right words for this particular brand of chaos. '...but now I'm thinking all I can do is roll with it.'

'Exactly!' I reply, a little overexcited because he just gets it. 'I don't think we have any choice but to play along.'

'Which is why I thought I'd come to you, to say look, let's do our best to keep things vaguely amicable,' he replies.

'I thought I was going to have a nice, chilled-out break too,' I confess. 'I didn't think I'd be wrangling my friends but, you're right, if we do our best, this might be okay. It might even be fun.'

'So we keep things from blowing up,' he says simply. 'You keep an eye on the girls, I'll handle the lads.'

'I mean, that sounds good to me,' I tell him. 'But... I thought we were supposed to be enemies?'

I raise an eyebrow suspiciously, only semi-serious, but I'm not wrong, we are supposed to be enemies right now.

'Oh, no, we are,' he says, his smile turning mischievous. 'And just because I want to keep the peace, make no mistake about it, I'm Team Lads. We're still rivals, and we're still all playing to win. So, don't get too comfortable. I'd still keep sleeping with one eye open if I were you. You never know what's coming next.'

I laugh, shaking my head.

'Well, I'll be keeping an extra-close eye on you, then,' I tell him. 'Your boys are playing checkers, but I think you might be playing chess.'

He purses his lips and smiles with his eyes.

'You're definitely not playing poker,' I point out with a laugh.

'Or I've always had a good poker face,' he replies. 'I'll be keeping you on your toes.'

There's something in his voice, something playful but charged, that lingers in the air.

'And I'll be putting you on your back,' I tell him, but trying to match his vibe makes what was supposed to be playfully violent come across as aggressively sexual.

Thankfully he laughs it off.

'Well, I'll leave you to your secret garden, and go get ready to go out,' he tells me. 'You sure we can't use your bathroom?'

'What do you think?' I reply with a smile. 'You want me to keep the peace. If I tell Nita you said that, it'll be blood that needs cleaning up, not chlorine.'

'Well, luckily there are period products everywhere,' he jokes. 'You know we've all had girlfriends, some of us have sisters, mums – you're not going to freak us out with stuff like that.'

'And we've all had boyfriends, dads, brothers,' I reply.

'You've had dads and brothers?' he replies with a grin designed to tease me over my wording. 'Anyway, see you later.'

'Not if I see you first,' I call after him, because of course I do.

I watch him go, feeling a little better than I did before we spoke. This competition might be a bit mad, and I know I just talked to Travis about keeping the peace but, I don't know, it feels like there's something between us now, a one-on-one rivalry, something to play for...

Maybe a week at odds with the boys might not be so bad after all.

19

It's so nice out here, without the boys. Things are just so peaceful, without the distractions they bring to the table, and I find myself noticing and appreciating so much more about where we are and what's around us.

The afternoon sun hangs perfectly in the sky – it's almost like a stock photo of the sun because it just looks and feels exactly as you would hope on holiday. I know, it's the same sun we see back in Leeds, but I'll bet it's hiding behind a cloud over Chapel Allerton today.

The pool is sparkling, looking so inviting, but it would almost be a shame to disturb the water. It's moving slightly in the breeze, causing these little twinkles that keep catching my eye, like someone has scattered the surface with diamonds.

I'm just lying here, taking it all in, watching the world go by (or not go by, as the case may be), listening to the gentle wind rustling through the trees. It's a glimpse of what it would be like if we were here alone (like we were supposed to be!), and it's heaven.

Nita is settled on her lounger, her face buried in a glossy

magazine that occasionally gets suspiciously close to her face. You can't see, because of her oversized sunglasses, but I think she might be snoozing on and off.

Lou is next to her, reading a book, and then there's Willow who is sitting on the edge of the pool. She dips her foot into the water, destroying the stillness, and moves her leg from side to side. The ripples and gentle splashing sound almost like white noise, the kind of perfect ambience you usually get from an app, which just adds to the rustling of the wind and the occasional chirp from a bird. It's pure paradise.

Lou sets her book down and lies back on her cushioned lounger, cradling a can of lukewarm lemonade, its citrusy scent wafting through the air as she takes slow, thoughtful sips. Everything is so delicious here, even though we're limited, but it would be so nice to have an actually cold drink for once. Maybe we should take another trip to the shop tomorrow, get some more hot street food, and a drink from the fridge. I swear, I appreciate them all the more, for not having such easy access to them. I never thought I took things for granted, but I have a whole new level of appreciation for hot food and cold drinks.

As is always the case when you find yourself beginning to relax, I notice Harry and Nolan stride out from the villa, out of the corner of my eye, with an exaggerated casualness that just pisses me off for some reason. They're always all so easy breezy.

They're still in their trunks – and Harry is wearing that trademark cocky smile of his. I thought they were supposed to be going out. Then again, how much getting ready can you even do without a bathroom? I wouldn't be surprised if they just threw on T-shirts and shoes.

'Ladies,' Harry starts, his tone light as a feather as the two of them pitch up in front of us. 'Can we have a quick chat?'

'You're already having it,' Nita replies flatly, flipping a page in her magazine without so much as a glance in their direction. The sound of the page-turning feels more defiant than dismissive.

Harry is unfazed, his smile still plastered on his face.

'Right. Well, look. We've been thinking – not just us, the other lads too – and we just wanted to say... wouldn't it make more sense for you guys to bow out now? Save yourselves the time, the effort. We're already in the lead. We all know how this competition is going to end.'

Willow snorts, twisting her body around to shoot them a dirty look.

'You have one point out of a possible one point,' she reminds them.

'And how exactly is it going to end?' Nita asks.

'Well, with us winning, obviously,' Nolan says bravely, nodding as if he'd just explained the most obvious thing in the world.

'There is absolutely no shame in bowing out,' Harry adds. 'We won't think any less of you – we couldn't. We don't want any trouble.'

Lou raises an eyebrow, her arms crossed tightly in front of her.

'What trouble?' she asks, looking back and forth between them.

'Trouble for you,' Harry says.

This is... I don't know, weird?

'Girls are supposed to be the mature ones, right?' Harry continues. 'Graceful, practical, poised – you could just sack it off and enjoy the rest of the week. No need to drag this whole competition out.'

Nita finally lowers her sunglasses, clearly wanting them to see something in her eyes.

'Harry, are you allergic to reading the room, or are you doing this on purpose?' she asks him. 'Because you're coming across as chauvinistic. You think our collective poise means we should let you win the competition?'

'All right, take it easy, Nita. Don't cancel me,' Harry replies with mock innocence, feigning a wounded expression. He's so obnoxious. 'We're just trying to be helpful.'

I exchange a glance with Lou, who rolls her eyes so hard I'm surprised they find their way back.

'Try being quiet instead,' Nita suggests.

'The competition is figured out, we're happy to do it,' I tell them, trying to keep my voice steady, though a hint of agitation creeps in. 'Let's just leave it at that.'

'We just figured it was worth asking,' Nolan interjects, a hint of defensiveness creeping into his voice. 'You know, in case you wanted to avoid the embarrassment later.'

'Thanks for the concern,' Willow says dryly, crossing her arms as if to shield herself from their insufferable smugness. 'But we'll take our chances.'

Harry grins again, clearly enjoying himself, taking pleasure in pushing our buttons. 'Okay, okay. Just thought we'd offer. But don't say we didn't warn you.'

'Noted,' Nita replies, her voice cool and dismissive. 'Are we done here? I thought you were going out…'

'We are,' Harry tells her. 'Have fun while we're gone. We'd better go get ready. Big night ahead.'

As they walk away, Nita mutters something under her breath that I can't quite catch, but it sounds a lot like a four-letter word that springs to my mind too.

I take a sip of my drink. Ugh, it's even warmer now, and suddenly it's annoying me all the more. Who do these boys think they are? They're seriously underestimating us. Well, fine, let them. Let them think we're pushovers – they're in for an unpleasant surprise. The lingering tension hangs in the air, heavier than the humidity around us. Why did they have to come out here and whip us up before going out? We were actually having a nice time for once, making the most of what we've got.

I can see Nita's jaw tense, a sign that she's not willing to take this lying down.

'They really think they can just waltz out here and say whatever they want,' she says, her voice edged with disbelief. 'No one tells me what to do.'

'We didn't come all this way to back down now. We're not giving them the satisfaction,' Willow tells her.

'They've got another thing coming,' Lou agrees. 'But you sure put them in their place, Nita. I don't think they'll come out here and try that again.'

Right on cue, Owen and Travis walk out of the villa, pitching up in front of us like a couple of *Dragon's Den* hopefuls. Their business? Pissing people off, clearly.

The two of them look dressed to impress – they've scrubbed up well, given their limited facilities, and it annoys me because I know how much I'd be struggling to look half decent in their situation.

Owen's shirt is crisp, his hair perfectly styled, while Travis somehow makes casual look effortlessly cool with his rolled-up sleeves and easy confidence to pull it off.

The late-afternoon sun casts a warm glow over them, illuminating them, giving them a glow and a tan – and even more reason to piss us off.

'Ladies,' Owen pipes up, his tone smoother than it has any right to be. 'Mind if we interrupt for a moment?'

'Depends,' Nita says, squinting up at them with a hint of suspicion. 'Is this going to be as pointless as the last interruption?'

Travis smiles, casually tucking his hands into his pockets.

'You mean Harry and Nolan didn't soften you up for us?' he dares to joke.

'Is that what that was?' I reply.

'Obviously they're not as charming as us,' Travis points out.

Infuriatingly he is really fucking charming, but I'm not about to let him know that.

'If this is another pitch for us to leave, save your breath,' Nita says, cutting to the chase. 'We've just been through this with your minions.'

You can tell the boys want to laugh. I think they like the idea of Harry and Nolan being their minions. Still, they're obviously here for something, so they're not about to let their masks slip.

'Look,' Owen says, raising his hands peacefully, as if he's trying to calm a pack of wolves. 'We're just saying what we said from the start – why put yourselves through all of this? Why not just call it now? You're supposed to be on holiday, relaxing. It'll save a lot of time and trouble...'

I can't help but laugh. What on earth are they playing at? Do they really think they can pester us into backing down?

'You do realise we've just been through this with the other two, right?' I point out. 'Seconds ago. The answer is still no. It's not going to change because you guys dressed up nice to ask.'

Travis chuckles, his grin widening.

'You think we look nice?' he asks, teasing me.

'That's not what I said,' I protest.

'You did,' Owen points out.

'Then it's not what I meant,' I say firmly.

'I think we'll take the compliment anyway, if you don't mind,' Travis says.

'I mind,' I insist.

'Look, we just thought we'd try asking too,' Owen says. 'You can't blame us for trying, can you?'

'I think I could blame you for anything,' Nita points out. 'Definitely wasting our time. Run along now.'

'Okay, well, we tried,' Owen says.

'You tried our patience,' Nita adds.

'We're reasonable people,' Owen tells us.

'Oh yeah?' Nita replies. She has a smile on her face that I know is not her smile, so it's kind of unnerving. 'So, how about you let us use the kitchen while you're out?'

'You didn't offer to let us use your bathrooms,' he replies. 'Luckily, it's an old door, it has this metal key in it, so we thought we'd best lock it while we're out, for safety.'

It did cross my mind that we might be able to sneak in there, and use the kitchen, while they were out. I don't know why I thought it would be that easy.

'You said it's an old door,' Lou replies. 'What if the key doesn't work? What if it breaks? You'll be locked out too.'

'That's a risk we're willing to take,' Owen says. 'We like to live dangerously.'

'I hear drinking and driving is fun for that,' Nita jokes. She would never normally make such a dark joke, they must be really pushing her buttons.

They just laugh.

'Don't wait up,' Owen tells us. 'Although, I guess your bedrooms are the only place you have to go so…'

He lets his voice trail off as he heads back to the house.

'What do you think that's in aid of?' I ask the others.

'I'm not sure,' Nita says. 'Odd though.'

'Maybe it was just an excuse to rub it in, to tell us to stay out of the kitchen, or to psych us out for tomorrow,' Lou suggests.

'Yeah, maybe,' Willow says. 'Still really bloody weird though.'

'I hope they do lock themselves out of the kitchen too, the idiots,' Lou says. 'It's no skin off our nose.'

We all laugh together for a moment. That's a really good point – in fact, if we were more like them, we'd probably go and mess with the lock.

'So, are we going to try to break into the kitchen?' Willow asks.

'Nah,' Nita replies, putting her sunglasses on, lying back on her lounger. 'Let's just enjoy the peace and quiet without them.'

That's not a bad idea at all, because it really is quiet without them, and they'll be back before we know it.

20

Dressing for dinner feels utterly pointless, and kind of sarcastic, when dinner consists of crackers, crisps, and tinned olives, but here I am, decked out in my 'going-out' dress – for a night in.

My red dress is short and glitzy, and my heels are high – the kind that would be suited for a trendy bar or a club. To be honest, shoes like these aren't great on an actual night out, because they always leave you with burning, aching feet. At least here I can just kick them off.

That said, I do wish I was going out for dinner and drinks, rather than just sitting here eating bar snacks.

We're eating around the firepit this eve because, well, it's that or the bedroom. I follow the glow of light and the smell of the fire until I find Lou sitting there alone.

'Well, look at you, all dressed up with nowhere to go,' I joke as I approach her.

She's wearing a green dress – one that she bought and then customised herself, Lou loves sewing – with silver sequins that reflect the flames in front of her.

'Looking good,' she tells me. 'Although you'll never shimmy in through the kitchen window wearing that.'

'Then I guess espionage, breaking and entering, and theft are off the menu tonight,' I reply, feigning disappointment.

'There's always tomorrow,' she says, patting the seat next to her, welcoming me.

'And, truly, why not look fancy when you're eating olives from a tin?' I reply.

'Well, exactly,' she agrees. 'We'll make anything five-star. Here, let me pour you a glass.'

Lou pours me some Prosecco.

'I managed to get it pretty cold in the bath,' she tells me.

'Delightful,' I say with a laugh. 'Thank you.'

Lou hands me a glass of bouncing bubbles. I can smell the sweetness in the air.

'To... whatever this is,' Lou says, making the toast.

'To whatever this is,' I agree, clinking my glass with hers.

Lou shifts in her seat, her gaze glued to the flickering flames in the firepit. There's a tension in her smile that makes me wonder if she's got something on her mind – more than just, you know, this entire shit show.

'You doing okay?' I ask, giving her a nudge with my elbow, keeping my tone light.

'I'm just trying to keep myself focused on the wedding,' she replies. 'That's what all of this is for, right? I just need to keep reminding myself that.'

'What did you tell Ellis in the end?' I ask, my curiosity piqued.

I feel like I can see the gears turning in her head. She glances at me, and her lips twitch as if she's holding back a secret.

'Not everything,' she confesses. 'Just that we're double-booked and sharing with another group. I left out the fact that it's all boys, and they're being difficult.'

'Ah,' I say simply.

Lou shrugs, suddenly looking a bit sheepish.

'You know what Ellis is like,' she replies. 'He trusts me; he didn't ask, and honestly, I don't want to worry him with it. I'll tell him after we're married, when we can find it funny. Right now he'll only feel sorry for me or he'll turn up, which would be even worse. I just want everything to go to plan.'

'You know best,' I reassure her. 'I wonder if Nolan has told his fiancée about us.'

'I doubt it,' Lou says. 'He probably doesn't want to stress her out either – I feel like a woman would take this sort of revelation badly. I know I wouldn't like the idea of Ellis sharing a house with a bunch of girls on his stag week. I know, that's hypocritical of me...'

'You don't need to explain yourself to me, I get it,' I reassure her. 'It's not that you don't trust Ellis, it's just that you know you trust yourself. And also it doesn't hurt that these boys in particular are completely unlovable.'

'Oh, completely,' she echoes.

I do get where she's coming from. No one would be happy about this – no one *is* happy about this – but we're just making the best of a bad situation.

She exhales a deep breath, her expression softening as she leans back, her shoulders relaxing a bit.

'All I care about is getting to the wedding on time, marrying Ellis, and then jetting off to Sydney for our honeymoon,' she says. 'Sometimes it feels like it just isn't going to happen. Like something is going to go wrong, or the boys are going to make something go wrong.'

'I won't let that happen,' I promise her. 'None of us will, we've all got your back. This whole competition is just a bit of fun. It's just daft. It's only to see who gets the second week – you'll be off on honeymoon either way. If we have to go home, we have to go home.'

I smile to let her know that I mean it.

'It's oddly fun, right?' she says, in a significantly lower voice, like she shouldn't really be saying it. 'A wild last hurrah of single-girl craziness before I officially shift into married life.'

I can't help but smile back at her, although there's a tiny pang of something in my stomach that I hadn't anticipated. Lou's moving forward, taking the plunge into her new life with Ellis, leaving little old me all alone, stuck in single-girl craziness, navigating it on my own from this day forward (well, from Sunday forward).

'Okay, enough moping. Spill,' Lou suddenly says, her voice playful but piercing through my thoughts. 'Do you like any of them? You can tell me, I won't say anything to the others.'

Caught off guard, I laugh nervously.

'Oh my God, you do, you're into one of them,' she says. 'Come on, you have to tell me now. Quick, before Nita and Willow get here.'

'All right, fine, I guess Travis seems kind of nice,' I confess, trying to sound all cool and casual about it.

'Oh,' she says simply.

I look at her, surprised. Does she know something I don't about him? Has she noticed something?

'You don't like him?' I reply.

'I don't like any of them,' she says with a laugh. 'He's definitely cute though. I just thought it was Owen who you liked – that's what Nita said.'

I roll my eyes.

'Honestly, since she caught me talking to him, once, she's off on one,' I reply. 'No. It's definitely Travis.'

'Definitely, hmm?' Lou teases, her eyebrows dancing knowingly.

'Hey,' Willow says as she approaches us, putting an end to our conversation – probably for the best.

She sits down at the firepit next to us.

'Love the dress,' Lou tells her.

'All dressed up with nowhere to go,' Willow jokes, although there's a slight edge to her voice that makes me think she might actually be mad about it.

Willow has also opted for a sparkly dress – also in red. So that's me, her and… oh, and Nita's face. She looks furious as she marches over to join us.

Her eyes are wide, her hands gripping what looks like a… a bottle of shampoo?

'Unbelievable!' she practically spits, holding it up as though she's just won an Academy award. 'This is custom-made. £140 a bottle! And it smells like mangoes – because I love mangoes!'

'Nita,' I say cautiously, raising a hand in a futile attempt to signal peace. 'Calm down. Slow down. Sit down, and just tell us what's going on.'

Nita ignores me entirely and starts pacing – well, technically it's pacing, but in her head, I think she thinks she's circling her prey.

She stops on the spot suddenly, as though a thought had just occurred to her, and then she starts sniffing us, one after the other, kind of aggressively, like a dog at an airport.

'Nita!' I squeak, laughter bubbling at the sheer absurdity of the situation. 'What are you doing? Are you actually sniffing us?'

She stops in front of me, her face dead serious.

'It's half empty!' she declares, shaking the bottle to emphasise the fact – not that it makes a sound, it's shampoo. 'Half. Empty.

Do you have any idea how much shampoo that is? Do you know what it takes to make this?'

Her voice rises with every word, echoing through the hills that surround us.

Lou leans forward, eyebrows drawn together in confusion.

'What are you saying? Someone used it?' Lou asks. 'Obviously it wasn't one of us. We have our own shampoo.'

Nita laughs. Slowly and softly at first, but then it turns into a cackle.

'Oh, not someone,' Nita replies darkly, her gaze narrowing like a laser beam. 'The bloody boys. It has to be them. Who else?'

I think for a moment. The boys? When could they have... oh!

'Earlier, when they came to talk to us, two at a time, I think they were keeping us distracted,' I say. 'That's why it was so weird, so out of character, so repetitive. They needed to keep us here while they snuck into our bathrooms.'

'They probably all used Nita's, because it's the first one at the top of the stairs,' Lou adds, almost excitedly, happy to have cracked the case but then furious that they've got one over on us.

'The idiots weren't even smart enough to use different bathrooms,' Willow points out. 'They all used your shampoo, that's why it went down so quickly.'

'Eww, I hope they didn't all use my towel,' she says. 'I thought it felt a little damp when I used it.'

'I'm sure they took their own towels,' I reassure her. 'But it's a boundary cross either way. And to think, they had the cheek to lock the kitchen! It's because they judged us by their standards.'

'Bastards!' Nita blurts, finally taking a seat.

She reaches out, grabs the bottle of Prosecco and takes a big swig.

'So, what do we do?' Lou asks.

'We're going to have to start locking our rooms,' Nita declares.

'If they can lock the kitchen, we can lock our bedrooms. It's only fair. And we have to smell them, obviously.'

'Obviously,' I joke. 'But why?'

'We have to call them out,' she says, her voice sharp with determination as she stands tall again.

'They'll just lie. What's the point?' Willow replies. 'If they deny it...'

'Because we're going to have them banged to rights,' Nita insists. 'We smell them before they get chance to deny it. If they smell like mangoes, they can't actually deny it.'

'The proof is in them smelling like pudding,' Lou jokes.

'Exactly,' Nita replies. 'But we have to think fast and do it before they get in the pool again, or the evidence will be washed away.'

'But what's the point?' Willow says again. 'It won't bring your shampoo back.'

'Leverage,' I chime in. 'If we catch them, and there's proof, then they'll owe us. They'll have to even the score, if they want to be fair. We might even be able to wangle an evening in the kitchen.'

'Exactly,' Nita says. 'We're being cool about the competition, honouring the rules. They'll owe us, but we have to smell them before they can destroy the evidence.'

'I don't think the kind of men who are dishonourable enough to sneak use of the bathroom and liberally use your shampoo are going to be honourable enough do the right thing,' Lou points out.

'Nah, if we smell it on them, there's nothing they can do but make it up to us,' Nita replies. 'This competition means a lot to them. I think they'd be gutted, if we said we weren't playing any more.'

'Hmm, she might have a point there,' I tell the others.

'But if they can get away with it, they will, so what we need to do is take a boy each, and focus on them – and smell them.'

Nita says this like it's the most normal thing in the world.

'I'll take Harry,' she suggests. 'We really push each other's buttons, I think I can get to him.'

'Fine. I'll take Nolan,' Willow replies. 'He's the quiet one, I'm the quiet one – maybe he won't bolt the second I try to sniff him.'

I'm not sure she's the quiet one but she's welcome to tackle Nolan.

Nita's gaze drifts over to Lou and me as she waits to hear what we're bringing to the sniffing mission.

'Molly should take Travis,' Lou says, before I get the chance to say a word. 'I'll handle Owen.'

'Good idea! Keep Molly and Owen apart, so he doesn't wrap her around his little finger again,' Nita suggests.

My cheeks burn as I look to Lou. She gives me a completely innocent look, but I know exactly what she's doing. She's giving me the chance to spend time with Travis.

'So, what's the plan?' Willow asks, her tone a mix of curiosity and doubt. 'How do we do this?'

'We seduce them,' Nita says through a smirk.

Lou chokes on her drink, practically spraying it across the fire.

'I'm sorry, what?' she shrieks. 'I don't know why I have to keep reminding you, but I'm engaged. We're here for my wedding! This week!'

Lou gestures dramatically at her engagement ring, like she's an extra in a Beyoncé video.

'Lou, relax,' Nita says, rolling her eyes with exaggerated annoyance. 'No one's asking you to cheat. Just... offer Owen a shoulder rub or something. Tell him there's a bee on him. I don't know, just think of something.'

'You know Nolan's engaged too, right?' Willow points out. 'I can't seduce him.'

'Can't or won't?' Nita replies. 'I'm just saying get close to him. Molly and I will do the heavy lifting, won't we, Mol?'

'It's a bit... extreme,' I point out. 'Will it even work?'

'Molly, come on. We've all seen how Travis looks at you,' she replies. 'Seduce him – or at least pretend to. Sniff him, get him banged to rights, and it's done.'

'Okay, fine, fine, I'll do my best,' I tell her.

'Good,' Nita says, sitting down again. 'Need any pointers? It's been a minute, hasn't it?'

'Cheeky cow,' I reply, rolling my eyes with faux annoyance.

She means well, and I know she's only trying to use humour to point out the obvious, but Nita always finds a way to slip in these digs about my non-existent love life.

Still, part of me wonders – maybe this could be good practice? Seducing someone, even if it's just a joke, or a scam, or whatever, is a no-pressure way to not quite jump back in the deep end, but paddle in the shallow end. I wonder if I'm even capable of seducing anyone any more? The art of flirting is a skill, a dance I haven't done in a long time, and if all I have to do is give a man a big sniff, then there's no pressure. Practice makes perfect, so I'll use this as an exercise. It will come in handy when there's someone I really do want to seduce.

But that's not Travis... right? Which makes him all the better for practising on.

21

'Okay, girls,' Nita begins as we all gather on one of the front, upstairs balconies. 'Let's talk strategy.'

Nita pauses for dramatic effect – well, everything has to be dramatic with Nita, but that's why we love her.

'So, the mango shampoo smell might have faded if they've been out, being boys, getting sweaty and gross. But...' She raises a finger, like she's a scientist, delivering an important keynote speech. '...a point-blank sniff should still reveal the scent.'

'A point-blank sniff,' I repeat back to her, so she can hear how absurd that sounds, but she doesn't even flinch.

'Can you hear yourself?' Lou says.

Nita just shrugs.

'What? It's a good plan, it's going to work,' she insists.

We can't help but dissolve into giggles – I mean, come on, a point-blank sniff! But before any of us can say another word, Nita's eyes widen. She gasps, ducking down quickly.

'Quick! They're here!' She crawls back into the bedroom. 'Places, everyone! Places!'

I peek outside and, sure enough, the boys are stepping out of a taxi at the gate. Their laughter drifts towards us, carefree and oblivious. God, if only they knew what was about to happen to them. They'd probably willingly turn around, leave, and never come back.

'Lou,' Nita barks, spinning around to face us, 'you're on Owen. Catch him as he heads to the kitchen, I'm sure he'll be keen to unlock it. Willow, Nolan's yours. Get him alone.'

Willow straightens her shoulders and tucks her hair behind her ear.

'I'll do my best,' she says.

'Me too,' Lou adds. 'This is weirdly, oddly, strangely fun… in a bananas sort of way.'

'I'll catch Harry by the pool,' Nita continues. 'I'll handle him, no problem. Molly, you've got Travis, yeah? Just, get him alone – is there anywhere else you can take him?'

'There's the secret garden,' I reply. 'He knows I like it there. I'll quite literally lead him up the garden path.'

'That's my girl,' Nita says with a laugh. 'Now, quick, come on.'

Shit, we're actually doing it. I think I'm probably more nervous than I would be if I really were just actually trying to seduce someone. At least that way, if they knocked me back, it would all be over. Sniffing is a little too close to first base for my liking.

Well, there's no time to second-guess my life choices because I'm downstairs and heading for the garden as they sound like they're approaching the side gate, their voices getting louder as they approach.

I duck behind the garden gate, my heart pounding in time with their laughter. They're clearly in good spirits (or should that be they clearly have good spirits in them?) as they get louder and louder until I hear Nita greet them.

As predicted, Owen makes a beeline for the kitchen, and it sounds like Nolan heads inside too.

'Harry, can I talk to you?' Nita asks him. 'Just you.'

'Er, yeah, okay,' he replies.

'I'll just, erm...' Travis babbles, sensing he should make himself scarce.

'I think Molly is in the garden,' Nita tells him. 'She's on her own – probably lost track of time.'

'I'll go get her then,' Travis says.

'You're a doll,' Nita tells him.

That's my cue to take off, deeper into the garden, so that Travis can come in and find me and I can... and I can 'point-blank sniff' him. It never sounds any less ludicrous.

I take a deep breath as I head deeper into the garden, trying to retrace my steps from earlier.

The garden is even prettier at night, the spotlights casting soft shadows on the path and the scent of night-blooming flowers mingling with the faint trickle of the fountains. It's so romantic – aggressively so, even. I wouldn't describe myself as a sexy person, unlike Nita who just oozes sex appeal, but I'm hoping the location will do a lot of the heavy lifting for me. The ambient sound, the dim lighting, the water features – all I really need to do is get close enough to him to give him a sniff. It's a tale as old as time.

I find the clearing, the one I was in earlier, and sit myself down on the bench. Then I steady my breathing, to seem more relaxed, like I've been here for a while.

'Molly?' Travis's voice startles me, even though I was expecting him, and knew he was hot on my heels. 'What are you doing out here?'

I force a casual smile, trying to ignore the way my pulse kicks up.

'Just enjoying the garden,' I say, gesturing vaguely at the trees like a crazy person. 'I told you, this is my safe space.'

'Even at night?' he asks, stepping closer. 'Mind if I join you?'

'Of course. And I just love it here. Especially at night,' I reply. 'Everything smells so different at night.'

'Okay,' he says with a laugh, sitting down next to me.

One – I'm going to retreat on making myself out to be some kind of smell enthusiast, because that's making me seem a little mad. Two – he has sat himself down a respectful distance from me, so not point-blank sniffing range at all.

I take another deep breath, trying to summon some of Nita's trademark confidence. If I'm going to pull this off, I need to get closer. No, even closer than that.

I can practically hear Nita's voice in my head: *Seduce him, Molly. Or at least pretend to.*

I mean, you've got to wonder if this is about more than just shampoo, or if the shampoo is just one more thing on an already long list of things that the boys have done to piss us off. Still, it clearly means a lot to her, and it's not like there's anything else to do around here. Bold of her to think that I could match her perfect timing and her sultry glances. I'm more of a comedy meet-cute kind of gal. Not so much 'accidentally' grazing their arm, more inadvertently spilling a drink down them.

What I really need is a plan B. A way to get close to him, or to have him get closer to me, that doesn't rely on me having any sex appeal at all.

'I... I think I hurt my ankle,' I blurt. 'That's why I'm still here, because my ankle is hurting.'

'Did you injure it?' he asks with genuine concern.

'Yes, I mean no, I mean... I think it might just be cramp,' I tell him, making it up as I go along. Wait, this could work. 'In fact, could you rub it for me, please? I think that might be all it needs.'

'Yeah, of course,' he replies.

And then he drops to his knees. To. His. Knees. In front of me. Why was that so sexy?

'So,' I say, my voice slightly higher than usual as he slowly removes my shoe, 'did you guys have a good night?'

'Yeah,' he replies, sliding my heel off with the kind of gentleness that is frankly disarming. 'We went to the little bar, in the local town. It was quiet. We're a long way from Ibiza – even though we're much closer than we would be in Manchester.'

I laugh as I raise my foot a little, so that he can get a better grip on it, and in doing so I swipe my foot over his leg, grazing his inner thigh, accidentally on purpose.

He freezes, for a millisecond – just long enough for me to internally combust – before he takes my foot in his hands, politely carrying on like nothing has happened.

Of course, now that my foot is elevated, I'm dangerously close to recreating my own *Basic Instinct* moment. I don't think Sharon Stone-ing him right now is going to get me any closer to him – if anything it's going to scare him away – so I lean forwards, resting on my elbows, but protecting my modesty and allowing me to lean a little closer, because all the better to smell you with, my dear.

Shit. It's just still not close enough.

Travis starts massaging my ankle, and oh my God. His hands are warm and firm, and I have to subtly bite my lip to keep from making any embarrassing noises. Honestly, it's like he's the one seducing me.

A breathy little sound escapes me before I can stop it. Travis glances up, one brow arched, a sly smile playing on his lips.

'Feeling any better?' he asks. I don't know if it's true or if I'm just letting my imagination run away with me, but his voice seems much lower and softer all of a sudden.

'Much,' I reply, sounding like I've got a frog in my throat.

'So, what have you and the girls been up to?' he asks, his fingers still working magic on my ankle. It feels so good, even if there was nothing wrong with it in the first place.

'Nothing!' I blurt, far too defensively. 'Why?'

He blinks at me.

'I mean to hurt your ankle,' he clarifies. 'Swimming, walking, dancing...'

'Oh, right, no, nothing,' I insist. 'Just... chilling too hard.'

Travis stifles a smile. If I had to call it right now, and say if I were successfully seducing him, I would have to say no.

I can't start worrying about my game (or lack thereof) right now, I've got bigger things to worry about – how to sniff this man's head without looking like a complete lunatic.

I'm overthinking this – I just need to go for it.

I steady myself, trying to ignore the throbbing panic in my chest. I just need to sniff him, I just need to sniff him – and it doesn't matter how many times I say that to myself, it doesn't sound normal.

His head is right there, his glossy hair catching the faint moonlight (which is definitely a telltale sign of expensive shampoo), so close I can almost smell it. Almost. All I have to do is lean in. Just a little closer...

Travis is staring at me now, his brows slightly furrowed, but there's something else in his expression. A flicker of surprise, or curiosity, or something... Oh, no. Oh, no. He thinks I'm going to kiss him. Abort the mission! Except I can't really stop now. I'm so close. So, so close.

The tension between us is practically choking me. Travis's eyes flicker down to my lips, then back up, and it's like time slows down. Is he leaning in? Is he actually going to let this happen? For one glorious, ridiculous second, I think he might.

Ugh, but I'm not here for that. I'm not here for him. I'm here for evidence and evidence alone, for my friends, for girl code, for use of the kitchen.

For God's sake, Molly, just sniff the man!

I make my move – quick, decisive, and nose-first, completely bypassing his lips.

The next thing I know, I'm flat on my back, the breath sucked out of me as Travis pins me to the ground. His hands grip my wrists, holding them down above my head with an ease that's frankly offensive (and incredibly sexy), as his face hovers inches above mine, his mouth open in disbelief.

'Did you... did you just attack me?' he asks, laughing incredulously.

'No!' I blurt, feeling the intense fire burning away under my cheeks. 'Did you just... do martial arts on me?'

'It was self-defence,' he insists. 'Were you... trying to kiss me?'

'No, absolutely not,' I insist, and it's true, but he's definitely picking up on something, because I'm not being completely honest, am I?

'It kind of seemed like you were leaning in to kiss me,' he points out, still holding me in place on the floor. 'You definitely leaned in, like you...'

Now would be the time to tell him that I was trying to kiss him, because that's maybe less awkward (but definitely not less weird) than trying give him a big old sniff, but he can't find that out.

He pauses for a second and I can see the cogs turning in his brain before realisation hits him like lightning.

'Molly, were you trying to sniff me?' he asks, like it's a normal question.

Oh shit, he knows.

His eyes widen as the puzzle pieces slot into place. He knows what he did, so he knows what I'm doing, and judging by the slow, smug grin spreading across his face, he knows why.

For a second, I just freeze, caught in his gaze like a rabbit in headlights. But then I remember what's at stake. He's onto me, which means there's no point in playing coy any more. I just need confirmation. I just need to fucking sniff his dreamy hair and be done with it.

Travis's grin widens. It's like we're in a sort of standoff – although admittedly he has the upper hand. We both know something is going to happen, that one of us needs to make the first move, so I'm going to make sure it's me.

I wriggle under the weight of his body, twisting and squirming to free myself from his grip – while, confusingly, still trying to lean in closer to his head. He has me pinned tight but I'm powered by sheer petty determination right now, and this is all just so stupid that it would almost be worse not to see it through.

Yeah, you're right, maybe I did get too much sun today…

'Would you stop fighting me?' Travis laughs, but he's struggling now, his grip loosening just enough for me to break free. I make a desperate (in more ways than one) lunge, aiming my nose towards his head, but he flips us both over with ease, pinning me again, this time with a knee pressed to the ground and his hands bracketing my wrists. Honestly, it's the way he's being so forceful, and yet so gentle, laughing as he does that makes this oh-so excruciatingly horny. Every receptor my body has is sounding every alarm bell to let me know that I am into this. It's been so long since a man got my blood pumping through any other method than sheer rage. It's making me feel dizzy – but I can't let myself get distracted. I'm not giving up. Not now.

With a twist, I roll us over again, and for a split second, I'm on top, straddling him. It's almost comical – almost, because again, it's just red hot. Where my body is touching his I can feel a heartbeat. I'm not sure if it's mine or his or a bit of both but it is racing.

His hands find my waist as he tries to throw me off, but I cling to him like I might never let him go, wrapping my arms and legs around him as he rolls over and he tries to crawl away.

'Oh my God, Molly, give it up!' he groans, laughing through his protests as he drags me across the path, my dead weight doing nothing to slow him down.

'Not until you stay still!' I reply, trying to climb my way up his back like some kind of crazy, sparkly spider monkey. His hair is right there, tantalisingly close, but every time I reach for it, he ducks or swerves. 'This will be over in a second, if you just...'

'I can't believe you're doing this,' he says, shaking his head, but his tone is full of amusement. He's clearly enjoying this just as much as I am. I swear, he's going easy on me, letting me get some kind of advantage now and then, just enough to make sure it doesn't end.

And then, before I can make one final attempt, he shakes me off a little. I cling tighter, but he's too strong. He drags himself along on his arms, dragging me (hanging off his waist) with him, as he makes a play for one of the water features.

'No!' I shout, because I know what he's about to do, but it's too late. With a triumphant grin, he plunges his head under the flowing water, letting the fountain cascade over him and effectively washing away any trace of evidence.

Defeated, I slump to the ground, collapsing onto my back in the grass. Travis joins me a moment later, flopping down beside me, his chest heaving with exertion.

'Did you just waterboard yourself to destroy evidence?' I ask, panting between words.

'A question you probably should have asked me while I was doing it,' he jokes. 'Allegedly.'

We lie there for a moment, catching our breath, the cool night air soothing our warm bodies. I glance at him, his damp hair glinting under the faint light, and I can't help but laugh.

'You're crazy, you know that, right?' he tells me.

'It's been said before,' I reply simply. 'But, hey, so are you, if you think I was going to kiss you.'

'Yeah, I don't know what I was thinking,' he replies. 'Wrestling me, trying to sniff me – far more common.'

'I should think it is, for you,' I joke.

He just laughs.

We lie there on the floor, just a little longer. Travis reaches out slowly next to him, finding my hand, taking it in his. He gives mine a few gentle, playful shakes before settling down on the ground again.

I don't know if he's shaking my hand to say good game, holding it to say no hard feelings, something more, or all of the above.

Whatever it was, my God, that was exhilarating. I don't think I've ever felt so alive.

22

We're back in the bedroom, sprawled across the bed and the floor like defeated war heroes after what turned out to be a totally embarrassing battle.

The ceiling fan whirls rhythmically above us, but it's doing little to cool us down, and it's not even helping to dry Nita off one bit.

My hair, which I'd curled earlier, is now a frizzy mess, full of leaves and twigs and God knows what else. I noticed, as I passed the mirror, that my mascara was smeared all over my face, but honestly I got off lightly.

Willow and Lou are unscathed – physically, at least – but Nita is soaking wet, from head to toe.

'You're actually dripping,' I say, pointing at Nita, who is sitting cross-legged on the floor, sulking into her own puddle.

She lets out a dramatic sigh and wrings out a section of her hair onto the towel on her lap.

'Yeah, well, being rugby tackled into a swimming pool will do that to a girl,' she says. 'Harry didn't even hesitate. I'm not sure if he even knows whether or not I can swim. I was halfway through putting my best moves on him, I got closer, and then he was onto me; he grabbed me and launched us both into the pool, like a kind of hostage situation.'

Willow snorts from her spot on the bed.

'To be fair, you were trying to smell the man – it turns out men get really freaked out when you try to smell them,' she points out.

'Especially when they've done something wrong, and they know you're onto them,' Lou adds.

'Honestly, a loser like Harry should count himself lucky to be sniffed by a babe like me,' Nita says – half joking, I assume.

I bury my face in my hands to stop myself from laughing because, honestly, I didn't actually come out of this situation much better myself.

'Come on then, Willow,' Nita prompts her. 'How did your plan go? You were supposed to get Nolan…'

'I don't know what happened,' she says. 'He went into the bathroom, and I thought, fine, I'll just… wait. Except I panicked and started interrogating him through the door.'

'What did you say?' Lou asks.

Willow shrugs.

'Stuff like, I don't know, how do you get such nice hair? What shampoo do you use?' Willow admits.

I wince.

'Not very subtle,' Nita tells her.

'Yeah,' she agrees. 'So, anyway, by the time he came out of the bathroom his hair was soaking wet. He must have dipped it in the sink.'

'That's what Owen did,' Lou adds. 'Although, to be fair, I did such a terrible job. I just thought, fuck it, honesty is the best policy, so I just asked. He had his hair under that kitchen tap like a shot.'

'They're not as stupid as we think they are, are they?' Nita says begrudgingly. 'Okay, Mol, come on, how did it go for you?'

'I tried being flirty, I really did, but it just wasn't working... I don't think. I think he thought something was wrong with me,' I confess. 'And then he thought I was going to kiss him, which is when I tried to smell him, and then we just sort of ended up wrestling on the floor.'

'Which explains why you've got half the garden in your hair,' Nita points out. 'So, not a sniff?'

I shake my head.

'But not through lack of trying,' I tell her. 'I hung from his waist as he crawled through the dirt. But he managed to stick his head underneath a fountain before I could work my way up his body.'

'So, we blew it?' Willow says.

'We didn't get them this time, but they know that we're onto them,' Nita says. 'So they won't think about doing it again. At least there's that – not that it puts the shampoo back in my bottle. But, mark my words, we'll get our revenge on these silly boys.'

'What are you planning, Nita?'

'I'm thinking...' Nita starts with a frankly menacing grin, 'that we take all of this pent-up frustration – all of our bruised egos, our dented pride, our soggy clothes – and we channel it into beating the boys at the competition. Forget the battle, let's win the war.'

'Yes!' Willow says, clapping her hands excitedly. 'No more flirting. No more seduction. Just total annihilation.'

Lou laughs, shaking her head.

'Okay, sure, if we can't have their nice-smelling heads on spikes, then thrashing them at the competition will have to do,' she says.

'Why not?' I chime in. 'Now it's personal.'

For a moment, we all sit there in our damp, messy, slightly pathetic states, and laugh.

We might not have them banged to rights with Shampoo Gate, but the war isn't over yet. Not by a long shot.

'I hope they're ready for what's coming their way,' Lou says.

'Not a chance,' Nita replies. 'Let's get them.'

23

I love how quiet the villa is on a morning. I know, it's the calm before the storm, but it really is peaceful.

I tiptoe downstairs, mindful that you could hear a pin drop right now. The girls are asleep, and it sounds like the boys are still asleep too – well, I can't hear a thing coming from their room at least. If they were awake, I'd hear something.

Clutching my laptop, and my sad little breakfast that consists of a warm-ish can of lemonade and a packet of biscuits, I head outside, pausing briefly in the doorway to check for signs of life, because if any of the boys were out here I think I'd go right back upstairs, only to return once I had backup.

But no, there's no one, it's like the villa is holding its breath.

I walk across the garden, to the sun loungers by the pool. The paving flags are already so warm and the sun isn't even in full swing yet.

I set my breakfast down on the table next to me and pull out my laptop. I really, really need to work. I'm finding it slipping my mind more and more, but without an internet connection, what can I actually do?

I can see Nolan's special satellite (or whatever it is) network on the list – the only network on the list – but it's password protected. I wonder if I could guess his password. Something like 'ILoveFootball' or 'ImADick' or 'MeAndMyMatesStealGirlsShampoo'. Jokes aside, the chances of my guessing his password seem pretty slim, because you know a tech guy like Nolan isn't just using his pet's name as his password, he probably generates passwords with a computer program that spits out strings of random nonsense – letters and numbers mixed together in a way that would take an equally smart computer program a million years to guess.

With a resigned sigh, I close my laptop and sink into the sun lounger, letting the warmth wash over me like a cosy blanket. At this time of day, when it's not too hot, it's just what I need to warm up, so I'm enjoying it while I can before it feels like something that needs escaping.

'Good morning!' A familiar voice snaps me from my thoughts.

It makes me jump, only because I thought everyone else was still asleep.

Travis walks towards me, a cup of coffee in one hand, a plate in the other.

He sits himself down on the lounger next to mine, before placing his breakfast alongside mine too.

Oh... my... God. A perfectly golden bagel, piled high with scrambled eggs and smoked salmon. It looks like something out of a magazine.

'Morning!' I reply, trying to sound nonchalant, although I'm talking to his breakfast, rather than his face. 'What's on the menu today?'

I look to him as he flashes a grin that makes me equal parts angry and doe-eyed.

'It's just a bagel with scrambled eggs, smoked salmon, and

chopped chives,' he says – just a bagel. When you're as hungry for something real as I am, just the chives would feel like a big deal.

'It looks like a work of art,' I can't help but admit, my stomach growling (it might even be moaning) at the sight.

'Thank you.' He laughs. 'How are you feeling after our little brawl yesterday?'

'Oh, I'm okay – I thought I did okay, considering I've never physically fought anyone before,' I confess, laughing so he knows that I know we weren't actually fighting. I mean, for me, it was closer to sex than it was a fight, but that really might just be me, and I should probably keep that to myself.

'That said, if I wasn't so malnourished from having no access to the kitchen or real food, I might've put up more of a fight,' I point out – obviously food is on my mind right now, because I'm looking at the breakfast of my dreams.

'Lucky for me you're starving, then,' he jokes.

'Speaking of the competition...' I start, trying to pull my gaze from his food. It doesn't help that I can smell his coffee too. 'It's your turn to choose what we do for the competition today. Please tell me it's not going to be awful.'

'Well, Owen and Harry were cooking something up last night,' Travis replies. 'But they hadn't decided yet.'

'Oh my God, you torturer,' I clap back. 'Don't say cooking up, you know I'm starving.'

'Sorry, sorry,' he insists, laughing it off.

He rubs his chin for a second, clearly thinking something over.

'You know what, I don't think I fancy a bagel any more,' he announces. 'I think I want something else so... I guess I'll just throw this in the bin.'

'You wouldn't!' I blurt.

'Oh, I would,' he replies.

Is he really so cruel that he would throw away something so delicious just to mess with me?

'But I'm too hungry to throw it away first,' he continues as he stands up. 'So, I guess I'll go make something else and I suppose I'll just leave this here… unattended, until I've got time to throw it away. I just hope no birds swoop down and snatch it while I'm inside. I might come back out here only to find that it's gone but, you know, I'm just so hungry so, yeah, see you later.'

With a smile that confirms exactly what I think he's doing here, he casually heads back towards the villa. I stare after him, completely stunned, wondering if he really just did that, but he couldn't have been more clear about it, without stating the absolute obvious.

The moment he disappears from view, I fully become the bird that swoops down and steals the bagel. I grab it with both hands, taking a huge bite, more than I can comfortably fit in my mouth. Oh God. Oh my God, is this the best thing I've ever eaten or am I just starving? Truly, I think it's both. Travis knows what he's doing with a bagel. The eggs are creamy, the salmon seasoned to perfection, and the chives are a perfect touch. I could take down ten of these without batting an eye.

I reach for his warm coffee next, washing the heavenly bagel down with a sip. It's glorious. Warm coffee! It feels like it's been forever. I feel like someone just gave me a shot of adrenaline. I don't think there's any round of any competition I couldn't win now.

Now that my desperate hunger has been taken care of, I can sit back, slow down, and think straight.

Travis didn't have to do that. That was so generous of him, to break the rules, just so that I could have something good – something great – to eat. I'll have to keep this from the guys, and the girls, all in the name of keeping the peace, and not just because

I'm hoping he'll keep sneaking me things. Perhaps he could start sneaking things for the other girls too – but I don't want to push my luck.

Maybe – just maybe – there is actually more to Travis than meets the eye. Maybe he's not so bad after all.

24

The sun blazes down over us as we all gather in the empty field next to the villa.

It's one of those perfect days where the breeze not only feels good but it smells amazing too. It almost makes it feel worth it, being out here with a bunch of annoying boys who clearly have no idea about the concept of boundaries and just general human decency.

It is, unfortunately, their turn to pick a round of the competition, and whatever they have chosen is currently being hidden behind Owen's back. God only knows what it's going to be. Oh, no, wait a minute, it's golf. I can see a golf club. Ugh, I almost preferred not knowing, because I am not a sporty girl at all. I could probably throw the club further than I could hit the ball.

Owen and Harry are radiating the kind of smugness that only comes from someone who knows they've got the upper hand. Owen adjusts the brim of his cap, looking every bit the part of a golf pro – or a wannabe pro, at least – while Harry starts lining up invisible shots, with an invisible club, except he looks more like he's auditioning for *Happy Gilmore 2* than he does a serious player. It's a truly ridiculous sight, and yet I can't enjoy it, because I am going to suck at this.

'Right,' Owen says, clapping his hands together with the authority of a self-appointed... referee? Umpire? What do they even have in golf?

'Today's round is simple: we're doing a driving competition. Whoever hits the ball the furthest wins. Easy.'

Harry steps forward to take a club and a ball, and he has the kind of smug grin on his face that kind of makes you want to pick up a club and wrap it around him.

'Okay, ladies, I'll give you a quick demo so you know what you're up against,' he tells us 'kindly'.

He drops the ball down and pretends to swing at it, to show us how it's done.

'Wow, thanks, Harry,' Nita says sarcastically. 'We'd be lost without your expertise. Please, tell us more about how to dramatically swing a club and miss the ball entirely.'

Harry just winks at her.

'I bet they're not half as good as they think they are,' Nita whispers to me.

Here's hoping.

Owen, raring to go, ignores her sassiness as he lines up golf balls on the grass.

'To minimise the embarrassment, each team gets four shots, but you can choose which person or people take them,' he explains. 'Whoever has the team member that drives the ball the longest distance wins the round. Simple. Fair. Let's do it!'

My teammates don't look so jazzed... except Willow. I can already see the cogs turning in Willow's head, like she might have an idea.

'I'll take all four shots for us,' she suggests. 'There's no point in us all doing it.'

'Fair enough,' Owen says with a laugh.

'Well, I'm shit at golf, so I'm happy to give up my shot,' Travis says.

'Yeah, I'll spectate too,' Nolan adds.

'But can you guys go first?' Willow asks. 'So I can at least watch you, to learn how it's done. I've never played golf before.'

Harry shrugs.

'Why not,' he says. 'Owen and I are actually getting really into golf so, when we saw the clubs in the shed, we knew it would be an easy win. Just watch how it's done.'

Owen and Harry step up, their swagger unbearable. Owen goes first, his stance looking almost ridiculously professional, like this is the PGA Tour, and this could be his winning shot. He takes his swing, and the ball flies cleanly through the air, landing impressively (to me, at least) far, at the other side of the field.

'Is that any good?' I ask cheekily.

'Is that good?' Owen replies, almost offended. 'Er, yeah, that's good.'

'This will be better,' Harry says, like he's Tiger Woods or something.

He hits his ball as hard as he can and, while it veers significantly to the left, it does still go quite far.

'That still counts as a good shot,' he assures us. 'And they were just our warm-up shots. These next two are the winners.'

Sure enough, they hit their second shots further than their first ones. Well, who didn't see that coming?

'Right, your turn,' Owen tells Willow, looking far too pleased with himself. 'If you even make contact with the ball we'll be impressed. Honestly, don't sweat it.'

Willow steps up, grabbing a club, lining up her shot, and exhaling deeply.

'Here we go,' she says.

The boys all snigger behind her, kind of rudely, but as soon as she swings their laughter disappears almost as fast as the ball does.

It soars through the air like it's got a rocket attached to it, sailing past Owen's ball – the furthest for the boys' team.

'What the...' Owen's voice trails off in disbelief, his jaw hanging ever so slightly.

'You expect us to believe that's beginner's luck?' Harry says quickly, but his voice is shaky, and definitely loaded with accusation.

Willow doesn't even acknowledge them; she's already setting up her next shot.

'Obviously you've won, and you don't need to hit any more,' Owen points out, thoroughly annoyed.

'Oh, I know, it's just fun,' she tells them. 'And I really haven't ever played before.'

Nita bursts out laughing, clapping her hands together like she's in the front row of a concert.

'Willow, you're amazing!' she tells her. 'How? How are you so amazing?'

'I know,' Willow replies with a smile, curtseying playfully. 'I played hockey in school. I was really good at it – they called me Willow Tree, because I was so freakishly strong. I still love any sport where you get to hit things.'

She smiles at the boys.

Nita grins.

'I feel similarly... around certain people,' she adds, flashing Harry a smug yet dirty look.

'So you played hockey?' Owen says. 'I mean, you should have disclosed that. That's not fair.'

'You never mentioned that you played golf,' I point out.

'Yeah but, I guess, in the spirit of the competition, we're all going to pick the things we're good at, right?' Travis points out. 'So we probably would have picked something else, if we'd known.'

'Well, isn't that just tough luck,' I reply. 'Better luck next time.'

He smiles at me. I think he's enjoying the playful sparring.

'Sorry,' Willow says, without a hint of sincerity. 'I guess it just never came up.'

'So that's 1-1,' Lou says, grinning wider than I've seen in ages. 'Looks like this competition just got interesting.'

'Yeah,' Owen replies, looking back and forth between Willow and where her ball landed. 'We'll just have to up our game.'

'Loser has to get the balls,' Nita says. 'Owen, Harry, I guess that's you two.'

As we all head back to the villa, Travis and Nolan walk with us. Nolan dares to reach out, to grab Willow's bicep. He gives a squeeze.

'Amazing,' he says. 'You'd never know they were so powerful.'

'Careful,' Travis warns him. 'She could launch you into the pool from here.'

As we near the gate to the villa, I notice Travis hang back a little, slowing down, almost like he's trying to synchronise his walking pace with mine.

'I wonder if we'll have to go head to head on anything,' he says.

'Well, I'm glad it won't be golf, because I wouldn't have been able to compete,' I reply.

'Nah, me neither,' he says. 'More of a football guy – watching it, mainly.'

'And yet that somehow makes you marginally more athletic than me, so congrats,' I tell him with a laugh.

'Oi,' Nita ticks me off. 'No fraternising with the enemy.'

'Sorry, my mum says I have to go in now,' I joke.

'Well, we wouldn't want to get you in trouble with your mum,' he replies through a smile.

25

It wouldn't be so bad, if we could store and cook food at the villa. Seeing as though we can't, we have to trek to the shop for hot food. Honestly, I don't think we'll ever financially recover from the taxi journeys, but they're worth it, because the street food here is to die for.

'We need an intervention,' Willow says. 'We need real food, every day, not just junk food. We'll die.'

'Don't take it up with me, take it up with the boys,' Nita tells her. 'They're the ones being unreasonable.'

'We're all being unreasonable,' I point out.

'Yeah, but they deserve it,' Nita adds.

She grins, but I can see the exhaustion in her eyes.

'I can't believe we're still here, putting up with them,' Lou says as she eats. 'If it weren't for the wedding, we'd have run a mile by now.'

'Well, that should show you how much we love you,' I point out.

'You really must,' she replies. 'Thank you. Needless to say, when any of you get married, you'll get the same energy back from me.'

I don't doubt that for a second.

'You're not worried about the wedding, are you?' Nita asks her.

'Honestly, I think we're all good,' Lou replies, her voice unusually calm given the situation. Her eyes shine with a little more excitement than I've seen in a while. I'm so glad she isn't letting it bother her. 'I mean, we've got everything we need for the big day. My dress is here, the venue's stunning, and the cake is set to arrive on time. I guess, after the craziness of the last few days, I'm really excited now. It's almost over. I'm getting married! It feels... surreal.'

'Surreal, yes,' Nita agrees. 'But also exhausting. We didn't need the boys making it harder.'

'We didn't, but it's not going to be a problem,' I say, making sure Lou feels reassured. 'Plus, after living with guys like these, your new husband is going to seem like a dream.'

'Any man would seem like a dream after these tools,' Nita replies. 'Even...'

Her voice trails off. I wonder if she was going to say Dean...

'What do you think the boys are up to right now, while we're out?' Nita says, changing the subject. 'Telling each other how big their muscles are is my guess.'

Lou laughs.

'Probably. They're all so... suspiciously buff,' she points out.

'I bet they're not real muscles,' Willow says.

'What else would they be?' I ask with a laugh. 'Inflatable suits?'

'No, obviously they're real, but, like, can't boys work out in a way that gives them muscles that look like muscles, but aren't actually strong?' she replies.

'I don't know about that one,' Nita says. 'But, real or not, they think it makes them so hot. Muscles aren't for everyone – someone should tell them.'

'You can do that,' Lou tells her.

'Yeah, well, I will, when we win this competition, and we're waving them goodbye,' she replies. But then her confidence fades a little. 'God, I really hope we win. I really want us to stay. I want that second week for us, girls.'

'We'll do our best,' I tell her. 'And we'll make the most of this week.'

'Here's hoping,' she says. 'Now, does anyone want any more hot food, because it's crisps and biscuits for the rest of the day…'

'Yes, please,' I say in an instant.

'Absolutely,' Lou adds.

'Yeah, me too,' Willow agrees.

'I'll get us another round,' Nita tells us.

You're supposed to have drinks in rounds on holiday, not food, but we're just working with the hand we've been dealt.

I just hope things don't get worse, because we've got a wedding to stick around for.

But what happens after that? All bets are off.

26

It's a nice night to be sitting outside. The heat from the firepit is wrapping around me like a cosy blanket, taking the chill out of the air that comes when the sun disappears for the night.

We've got drinks, snacks – and we've all dressed up, not that it really matters but, hey, if they do it on *Love Island*, we can do it here, in our own 'pull for a chat' area.

'Yo, yo, yo,' a male voice calls out.

Did I say it was a nice night to be sitting outside? It was – but probably not any more, now that the boys have turned up.

'Oi, you've nicked our spot!' Harry's voice breaks through the calm atmosphere like a box of fireworks with a lit match dropped into the mix.

He, and his crew, are carrying armfuls of beer bottles, clearly ready to make a night of it.

'We were here first,' Nita tells him.

'No, you weren't, we were here at three,' Owen replies.

'That was this afternoon, this is this evening,' Lou points out. 'You weren't here first, you were here earlier.'

'It's a communal area either way,' Travis points out. 'So, why don't we join you?'

'Can we actually say no?' I ask no one in particular.

'Not really,' he reminds me.

Now we're all sitting around the firepit, all eight of us, like we're at an awkward school disco. Honestly, I wish someone would put the 'Cha Cha Slide' on, so that we can disperse.

The guys take one side, making themselves at home with their beers, while we manoeuvre ourselves to the other side with our wine.

The flames flicker and crackle between us, giving the boys a warm but almost creepy glow about them. Well, they've definitely been giving off satanic vibes so far.

'So,' Lou begins, trying to make the best of the situation, if we're going to have to play nice with them. 'Where are you lot from?'

'Manchester,' Owen says, cracking open a beer. 'Lancashire born and bred, the lot of us.'

'Proper northern lads,' Harry jokes. 'Manchester is the best city in the north.'

'Is that so?' Nita replies.

'Go on then, where are you from?' Harry asks. 'Don't think we haven't clocked those accents.'

'Leeds,' Nita tells them.

Owen playfully spits into the fire, in disgust.

'So, what do you do?' she asks. 'When you're not stealing villas from people – presumably you all have jobs?'

'We didn't steal anything,' Harry reminds her. 'We booked the villa fair and square, just like you.'

'I'm a builder,' Harry says, moving things along. 'Big strong lad like me, what else is there to do to put my skills to good use?'

'You know those labs, where they test products on animals?' Nita pipes up.

'Yeah – is that where you work?' Harry replies, raising an eyebrow.

'No, I just meant that, well, given your skills, that's another job you could do,' she replies.

'A scientist?' he asks.

'One of the animals who gets tested on,' she claps back.

Harry frowns at her.

'I'm in marketing,' Owen tells us. 'Same agency as Nolan – he's a backend developer.'

'What about you?' Travis asks, shifting his focus to me. Suddenly he seems like he needs to know. 'What do you do, Molly?'

'I work in recruitment,' I tell him.

'That's a job finding jobs?' Harry teases.

Why does everyone get so hung up on that?

Our conversation drifts from work to travel, to who has the superior accent, to how to make the best cup of tea. We weave in and out of hostile territory. Sometimes it feels like we're getting on, but then someone inevitably has a dig at someone else, and suddenly we're not playing nice any more.

'Anyone fancy playing Truth or Dare?' Harry asks. 'Unless you're too scared.'

Absolutely not.

'We'd love to,' Nita replies.

Would we though?

I shoot her a look that mixes horror and excitement. Yeah, sure, this could be a fun game, but it could also be a car crash.

'All right,' Harry says, leaning forward, a grin playing on his lips. 'Nita. Truth or dare?'

'Truth,' she replies.

'Boring!' he heckles her. 'But, okay, who's the worst shag you've ever had?'

'Easy,' Nita replies. 'Guy called Paddy. Small, quick, zero effort – I thought I was going to have to fake it, just to get it over with but, no, he got it over with pretty quickly on his own.'

'Gutted for you, Paddy,' Harry says with a laugh.

'Harry,' Nita says, wasting no time in retaliating. 'Truth or dare?'

'Dare, because I'm not a chicken,' he replies.

'Give a sexy lap dance,' Nita tells him.

'Not a problem,' he replies.

'To Owen,' she adds.

He stares at her for a moment.

'Give Owen a sexy lap dance,' she says again.

Owen narrows his eyes at Harry.

'I can't back down, can I, mate?' he says to him quietly.

'Just get it over with, will you?' Owen replies through gritted teeth.

You've got to give Harry credit where it's due, because he takes off his shirt and throws it at Owen before placing a leg up on the bench where Owen is sitting, and gyrating inches away from his face.

Owen looks horrified. The other boys are in stitches. As are we.

Harry turns around and starts wiggling his bum at Owen.

'All right, enough,' Owen says, shoving him away.

Harry laughs to himself as he sits back down.

'My turn again,' Harry says as he scans the crowed. 'Hmm... I'll choose... Nita.'

Oh God, it's going to be like this, is it?

'And I guess you have to choose dare, because you can't pick truth twice in a row,' he tells her.

'Erm, that's not a real rule,' I point out. 'I don't know how you play in Lancashire, but in the rest of the world that's not a real rule.'

'Ah, it's fine,' Nita reassures me. 'He lacks the creative intellect to come up with anything that would bother me.'

'Kiss one of your friends,' he tells her.

I mean, who didn't see that one coming?

Nita scans the three of us.

'Molly?' she says.

I mean, what a double-edged sword, because as she was looking between the three of us, working out who she wanted to kiss the most, part of me was hoping she would pick anyone but me, while the other part of me was panicking about overthinking why wouldn't she pick me? What do the other girls have that I don't, besides generally better lives and prospects?

'Me?' I squeak.

'Yeah, you lucky lady, come here,' she says.

Nita shuffles closer to me, takes my face in her hands, and plants a long, lingering peck on my lips. I mean, it's nothing, we peck each other all the time – we're friends. However, something about doing it for an audience makes it feel kind of... I don't know. I feel like the boys should be paying per view.

As Nita releases me, and we both look over at the boys, for the first time since we arrived I think they might actually be stunned into silence. Travis is staring at me, his jaw almost in the fire.

'Need a hand picking that up, Travis?' Nita jokes. 'In fact, Travis, truth or dare?'

'Er... dare,' he says, instantly looking like he wishes he hadn't.

'Okay, I dare you, for the rest of the game, to sit with Molly on your knee,' she tells him.

'What?' he and I both blurt at the same time.

'Is that a dare for him or for me?' I ask.

'For him,' Nita replies.

I wince slightly. Do I really have to do this? Nita gives me a look that says... something. I don't know. I think she's doing something. I'll just have to go along with it.

'Erm, okay,' I say, making the short journey to Travis, before sitting down on his lap.

I feel his body tense up a little, as I sit down on him. I sit sort of sideways, so that I'm comfortable, and stable, and not putting too much weight on his knees.

'Erm, hi,' he says with a cute laugh.

'Hello,' I reply.

'Don't worry, Molly, I know self-defence, so if he tries anything, I'll put him on his back,' Nita says before downing the last of her wine.

'Okay, I guess it's me,' Travis says as he puts his hands on my hips to support me. It feels... weirdly good, but don't tell anyone I said that. 'Nita, truth or dare?'

We really are just retaliating at this point.

'Dare,' she says. 'And keep in mind, you can't repeat any of the dares we've had so far. I can make up rules too.'

'Fair enough,' Travis says with a chuckle. 'I dare you to – how did you say it? – put Harry on his back.'

'What?' she replies.

'You said you knew self-defence, and that you could put me on my back, so I want you to do it to Harry,' he says. 'Flip him, or whatever.'

'Mate, she can't flip me, I'm too jacked,' Harry points out.

'I absolutely can flip you,' Nita tells him. 'They taught us how to use people's strength against them.'

'Okay, little lady, this I've got to see,' he replies, and you can see it winding her up. I wouldn't like to be in his shoes right now.

To be honest, I can't think of anywhere I'd rather be – maybe it's the wine talking.

Harry stands in a clear area. He puffs up his chest and smirks at Nita as she approaches him, and then it all happens in an instant, she flips him, but she doesn't put him on his back, she puts him on his front. Face down, on the flags.

'Fuck,' he says as he rolls over.

As he does, blood flows from his nose. Oh boy, that's a lot of blood.

'You psycho,' he tells her. 'You've broken my nose.'

'It's okay, calm down, I know first aid,' Lou tells him. 'Let me have a look. Nolan, grab some tissues.'

'Okay,' he says, before dashing off.

Lou examines Harry's nose for a few seconds.

'I don't think it's broken,' she tells him. 'There are no signs of any real injury, I think you've just got a nosebleed, from the impact.'

Nolan appears with tissues.

'Here,' Lou tells him. 'Pinch the bridge of your nose and keep your head upright, don't tip it back. It will stop soon.'

Harry holds his bloody nose in a wad full of tissue. He looks up at Nita.

'What?' she replies. 'I just did what I was dared to do, like everyone else.'

'Maybe we should stop playing,' I suggest. 'Maybe that's enough excitement for one night.'

'I'm going in,' Harry says.

'Right behind you, mate,' Owen replies.

Travis hangs back for a moment.

'Sorry, Nita, that was my fault,' he tells her. 'I didn't think he'd go down so easily.'

'They always do,' she says with a smile. 'Sorry I cut short your time with Molly sitting on you.'

'Oi,' I reply. Her teasing him makes me feel sort of embarrassed.

'I'd better go help them out,' he says. 'Sorry again.'

'Well, that went well,' I say, when it's just the four of us again.

'Yeah, I don't think they're going to want to hang out with us tomorrow night,' Lou adds.

'I don't know about that, I reckon they will,' Nita says.

'Anyway, why did you have me sit on Travis?' I ask her.

'Just to confirm something,' she says with a smile.

'What?' I ask.

'Something I'm cooking up – you'll see tomorrow,' she tells me. 'But I think it's going to win us the next round of the competition.'

Oh, great. I'm sure I'll sleep real easy with that on my mind all night...

27

The sun isn't messing around today. It's not even midday yet and it's boiling, the kind of weather that makes you want to jump in the ice-cold pool – although you know you should probably be indoors or in the shade until it lets up a little.

Of course, we can't do that, because we've got a competition to participate in, and if we can just win then next week we'll get the nice, relaxing holiday we should have had this week. Speculate to accumulate – or something like that.

One thing I know for sure is that my hangover, from last night's antics, really isn't helping. I can actually feel my head throbbing. I'm sure everyone else feels the same, so at least it levels the playing field, but still. I'd rather not.

I practically chug water from my bottle, sucking it down for dear life, hoping it will fix me. Sadly, it's just water, not a miracle hangover cure, but I know that my body needs it right now, even if what I would prefer is a strong coffee.

Lou, Nita and Willow – who, don't get me wrong, are my friends, so I say this as kindly as I can – look like they've been dragged through a hedge backwards. The boys, on the other hand, are sitting across the firepit from us looking as fresh as daisies. I know they must be hungover though, they must be. They just wear it a lot better.

The show – or the competition rather – must go on. It's our turn to choose an activity and Nita says she has it covered. She hasn't told me what it is, but it's something, so I guess we're all going to find out together.

'So, what's the plan?' I ask, leaning in close.

'You'll see,' she practically warns me. 'I'm having to make part of it up as I go along.'

'Because that's not terrifying at all,' I whisper back.

She just smiles.

I look to Lou, who just about caught our conversation, and she shrugs.

The problem with Nita going rogue like this is that you really, really don't know what crazy idea she's cooked up. It could be anything – like seducing one of the boys. Thank God that one is out of the way now. I wasn't exactly great at it, it turned into a bloody wrestling match, for crying out loud.

'Come on then, don't keep us in suspense,' Harry prompts.

I secretly suspect he's about to topple over – he must be, after the amount I saw him drink, but it's well hidden behind his armour.

'Yeah. We're raring to go,' Owen insists.

The only thing I'm raring for is a coffee, maybe a slice of toast, and a nap.

'It's a test of endurance,' Nita announces, gesturing towards the pool like a glamorous assistant on an old game show. 'See that thing in the middle of the pool, where the fountain sprays out? We're turning off the fountain so that one boy and one girl can stand on the podium together. The last one standing wins!'

We all glance over at the small podium-type structure in the middle of the pool and there isn't a ton of room for one person, never mind two. Is she serious right now?

The boys laugh, because of course they do, stupid ideas are their favourite kind.

'Is that it?' Harry asks in disbelief. 'Because that would be an embarrassingly easy win for us.'

'Yep, that's it,' Nita says simply. 'So, who will it be?'

'I'll do it,' Travis suggests, holding up his hand.

'Fab,' she replies, still cool as a cucumber. 'Molly will be doing it for us.'

It takes every facial muscle I have to stop my eyebrows from shooting up. Me? I'd love to know the thought process behind choosing me for something that requires endurance and balance – the same me who manages to trip over a perfectly flat surface and then instinctively apologises to it.

Travis smiles at me – it's that relaxed, charming, infuriating, gorgeous grin of this that makes me think I probably shouldn't be the person to do this with him.

'Come on, lads, let's prep Travis,' Owen suggests, leading the pack indoors.

God knows what prepping him involves. Oh, God, I hope they're not going to, like, smear him in something stinky, like onions from the kitchen, or some sweaty clothes they've had rotting on the floor for a couple of days.

'Nita, what the hell?' I blurt as soon as it's just us girls. 'Me? You chose this and you chose me for it? Could we not just have, I don't know, had a competition to see who can contour a face the best? Granted, I'm not the best, but I've got to be better than the boys – they probably don't even know what that means.'

'Okay, first of all, I don't even know how anyone could win that competition, because who would judge it? You've not thought that through,' Nita points out.

'You've not thought yours through!' I snap back.

'I have, because, look, the second point I was going to make is that we clearly get under the boys' skin, all of them, in one way or another, so forcing one of them to be in close quarters with us is a guaranteed win,' she replies. 'Look what happened when we were trying to work out if they stole my shampoo. They went nuts. So I thought, well, let's see who they choose, and then select the best one of us to psych them out. They chose Travis so obviously we choose you – we all see how he looks at you.'

'Nita, I'm not going to get a chance to psych him out, because I'll probably fall first,' I tell her.

'Looks more like he's fallen first,' Lou jokes quietly.

I shoot her a look.

'Girls, this is ridiculous,' I tell them, unable to silently go with the flow this time.

'It's perfect,' Nita corrects me. 'He likes you – he might even let you win. If he puts up a fight, well, just push his buttons like you did the other night. Flirt with him – grind on him if you have to.'

Oh, wow, so she really is suggesting I try to seduce someone again, because it went so well last time.

'Be a team player, Molly,' Willow prompts me.

'Erm, I'll remind you that you said that when Nita has you lap dancing one of them for a cold drink,' I half joke, because that might have happened already if Nita had thought of it first.

'So the big plan is I fail to seduce Travis again?' I check.

'If it ain't broke, don't fix it,' Nita replies.

'It absolutely is broke,' I correct her. 'But, fine, if you want me to make a fool of myself, and you want us to lose, then I'll do it. I'll do it with bells on!'

'That's the spirit,' Nita replies.

I don't think it's that she isn't detecting my sarcasm, I think more likely that she's just ignoring it.

'I'd go for a wee, if I were you,' Lou suggests. 'You don't know how long he'll last up there, but I wouldn't put it past any of those boys to not just pee in the pool.'

'It would psych him out if you did that,' Nita points out.

'More like gross him out,' Willow adds, pulling a face.

'Erm, if boys can do it, girls can do it,' I inform her – and that's got to be the weirdest act of feminism I've ever performed. 'But, yeah, I think I'll just nip to the bathroom. I'll top my sun cream up too.'

'Great idea,' Lou replies. 'You'll burn to a crisp if you don't.'

As I head to my room, the sheer absurdity of the situation swirls around in my head, making me feel a little dizzy – which is not good for balance at all.

Standing on a tiny podium in the middle of the pool, trying to outlast Travis, all while flirting to psych him out? I am so not the woman for the job here. It's the kind of thing that, if it were Nita and Harry up there, would play out exactly as expected, but I can't see me and Travis being anything but awkward. It won't be a case of who falls first, it will be who jumps in to escape the uncomfortableness.

In the bathroom, I splash some water on my face, trying to shake off the lingering grogginess from last night. Then I take my sun cream and cover every inch of my skin that isn't covered by my bikini. But then, as I look myself up and down in the full-length mirror, I suffer with what can only be described as a moment of madness because... am I really going to do this? In a similar moment of madness, when I was shopping for the trip, I bought myself one of those silly, tiny bikinis that you see the girls on *Love Island* wear so effortlessly, but always wonder to yourself how you would keep all your various bits and pieces in them. Yes,

I saw them, had those thoughts, bought one anyway, packed it and – and had no intention of wearing it until right now. Maybe Nita is right, maybe all I do need to do is psych him out, and a teeny tiny bikini would go a long way to doing that, whether it was for good or bad reasons. I don't need to know which, but if I'm doing it, then I'm doing it right.

I rummage through my suitcase – and it takes me ages to find it, which just goes to show how tiny it is – and put it on. I thought I would feel self-conscious, but I don't (I do a bit), I feel empowered. That's what I need to tell myself. This is empowering. I'm taking charge of my own destiny. I'm going to make Travis wish he was never born (and if I keep saying it, I might believe it).

I stand proud (ish) in the mirror, squaring my shoulders, pulling every spare bit of boob I can from under my armpits, wrangling them up front and centre to maximise my assets.

Let's do this.

Back outside, I walk as confidently (but carefully) as I can. Harry and Owen break out in whistles and woos, which I would have thought might make me feel more self-conscious, but it actually helps.

'Oh, mate, you're in big trouble,' Owen warns Travis.

Travis just laughs.

'Shall we do this?' he asks me.

'Why not?' I reply.

Wading into the cool water provides a brief relief from the sunshine. Travis climbs onto the podium first, his muscles rippling, water cascading down from them as he reaches out to give me a hand up – ever the gentleman. He makes lifting me seem effortless, which you'd think would do wonders for my self-esteem, but he makes it look so easy it just kind of annoys me a bit.

I can feel the girls watching from the edge of the pool, and I know they're banking on me to pull this off.

The podium isn't actually a podium at all, just a small flat surface barely wide enough for two people, and now that we're both straightened up he's right in front of me, our basically naked, soaking wet bodies pressed up against each other. Every time either of us moves so much as a muscle it's like electricity between us. I'm caught somewhere between loving it and it feeling like actual torture.

'Comfortable?' he asks, his voice low and gently teasing.

'So comfortable,' I reply, putting extra emphasis on each word.

Nothing about this is comfortable. His body is radiating heat, and it's impossible to ignore the tension building between us.

I focus on my footing, trying not to look at him too much, but every time I glance his way, he's looking at me.

'This is boring as shit to watch,' Owen calls out from across the water. 'We're going to head inside and play some pool.'

'Yeah,' Nita adds, a suspicious edge to her voice. 'We'll give you two some space.'

I don't miss the knowing look she throws my way before she heads off. Great. I'll bet she thinks I'll be more likely to get my flirt on without an audience – not that I think it will go any better for me, but she clearly believes in me.

With nothing else to do, and with a building urge to bring this round of the competition to an end already, I decide to test Nita's theory, shifting my weight ever so slightly. We both wobble, and Travis not only adjusts, to correct his footing, but he instinctively steadies me too. His hands brush my sides, almost like he's taking my hips in his hands, so I thrust my pelvis lightly in his direction. Honestly, it's like the softer touches are the ones that drive me the most crazy. Here's hoping it's working on him too.

'Careful,' he says, but I can hear the faint trace of nervousness in his tone.

'What's the matter?' I ask innocently, letting my voice dip into something a little softer, a little sweeter too. 'You seem uncomfortable, Travis.'

He laughs, short and low, but there's a flicker of something in his expression – a crack in his usual cool armour.

I lean in just a little closer.

'You know,' I begin casually, not actually knowing what I'm going to say myself, just that I want it to be vaguely flirtatious, 'I'm usually pretty good at these kinds of games. I guess I've just… had a lot of practice… with my body being under this sort of pressure.'

One of his eyebrows raises, only a millimetre, but I notice it. It's working.

'Oh, yeah?' he says, matching my tone. 'And what kind of practice is that?'

I shrug, feigning nonchalance.

'Oh, I think you know what I mean,' I reply – again, I'm not entirely sure what I mean myself, I just wanted it to sound vaguely sex-ish.

Travis chuckles, shaking his head, but I can feel a stiffness in his posture that makes me think it's working.

'You must be pretty good with girls, though,' I say. 'You seem like the type who knows how to keep them interested. And, oh my God, these muscles! They're just so… so big!'

'Ha!' he replies. 'No, not really. It's been a long time since I dated anyone. I went through a bad break-up, so…'

His voice trails off.

His honesty catches me off guard, and for a second, I forget this is a competition. That level of honesty is… unusual? Touching? Or maybe it's a tactic? Maybe he's making this whole story up to throw me off – I wouldn't put it past any of this lot. My brain runs through the possibilities, but the sadness in his eyes really does seem genuine.

'Oh, I'm sorry to hear that,' I tell him.

'It's weird, because it's a long time since we broke up, and it's not that I'm not over it, it's just that we were supposed to be going to the wedding together, so I know there's going to be an empty plus-one seat there, and the fact that I've been single ever since – it's like a milestone, you know? I feel like I should have moved on by now.'

Again, his honesty is as surprising as it is refreshing. I know Dean never used to like to talk about how he felt – unless he was reminding me that he thought marriage was stupid, of course.

'That's rough,' I say simply. 'But you shouldn't be putting pressure on yourself to move on. I, er...'

I pause for a moment. Should I tell him about me? Not that I want to make this about me – I'm always worried that by trying to show people that I relate to what they're going through, I just end up talking about myself – but I want him to know that this is totally normal.

'I went through a break-up too, last year,' I confess. 'Dean, my ex, dumped me because I accidentally thought he was proposing to me – it's a long story, but the misunderstanding was enough to make him end things.'

'Shit, I'm sorry,' Travis replies.

'In my defence, we were eating alone, in a private dining room, and he said he wanted to ask me something at the exact moment he reached into his pocket,' I point out.

'There isn't a jury on this earth that would find you guilty, in that case,' he replies.

'Right?' I say enthusiastically. 'Anyway, it's not so much that but it's had a knock-on effect on my work too. I'm a recruiter, and

I'm trying to find someone to oversee our new product development plans, coming up with new recipes, and someone called Dean reached out, about meeting up, and I thought it was him crawling back so I replied telling him to piss off and... it's a whole thing. Long story short, my boss insisted I take this break, and I really, really need to find someone for the job now, which is why I wanted to work while I was here, but there's no wi-fi and... and... sorry, I've made this about me.'

I finally stop to take a breath.

Travis places a hand gently on the small of my back and gives it a gentle, reassuring rub.

'I'm so sorry to hear that,' he says sincerely. 'And it's not fair, that it's affected your job. What kind of company do you work for?'

'Brookes Biscuits,' I reply – everyone knows Brookes, we're one of the biggest manufacturers in the country.

His face lights up.

'I love Brookes Biscuits,' he says. 'Those ginger shortbreads – game-changing.'

I smile, relaxing a little.

'Yeah, they're amazing. Plus, I get free biscuits at work, which might actually be the worst part about losing my job,' I joke. 'Screw the boyfriend, forget needing an income to live, just don't take my free biscuits.'

He laughs, his shoulders shaking, causing that sexy friction between us again.

'I don't know if I would be more heartbroken about the break-up or the biscuits, if I were you,' he jokes. 'It doesn't sound like he was a great guy.'

'The biscuits, honestly, he was a dick head,' I insist. 'He did me a favour, in the end.'

'Molly, you deserve so—'

Travis doesn't get to finish his sentence. The fountain springs back to life, roaring below us. Then a jet of water blasts upward, and I can't help but scream as it sends me flying into the pool. I bob up for air just in time to see Travis fall off too.

The first thing I notice, after realising I'm not dead, is the boys shouting and cheering.

'Travis wins!' Owen yells, pumping his fists. 'Molly fell first.'

'That's not fair!' Nita storms over, hands on her hips. 'Someone turned the fountain back on!'

Harry shrugs, far too innocent.

'It's probably on a timer,' he tells her.

Travis climbs out of the pool first. His friends grab him, lift him up, shake him like the hero that he is.

I climb out after him, like a soggy piece of seaweed – the loser, washing up last.

'Don't worry,' Lou reassures me. 'We'll win the next one.'

'Yeah,' Nita adds, her expression hardening. 'Even if we have to play dirty like they do.'

I smile and thank them but all I can think about is Travis. What he said, the way he listened. My heart goes out to him, going to a wedding alone when you were supposed to be going with a partner, and seeing that empty chair – ouch.

I know we were up there for the competition but, for a moment, I wasn't thinking about strategy or sabotage. I was just... enjoying myself. Having a deep conversation with a man who is... he seems like he might be really something.

As I wring out my hair – and check that all of my body parts stayed tucked inside my bikini which, thank God, they did – I can't help but think about how great that was, and how I want to do it again.

28

It's amazing how much better sitting out in the sun makes you feel. Sure, I've got a world full of worries, my job is on the line, I'm single, there's no wi-fi – blah, blah, blah. None of it matters right now because this, in theory, is so relaxing that I couldn't care less.

Well, I shouldn't – I'm doing my best.

I'm trying to read my book but I've been stuck on the same sentence for what feels like an eternity. I don't know if it's my eyes or my mind or both, but something refuses to cooperate.

Normally a romcom novel would have me gripped, but it's a dream love story of my own that I've got on my mind. I can't stop thinking about Travis. His warm, sunny smile, his kind eyes. I can still hear the honesty in his voice from our last conversation, and I love the way he laughs at my terrible jokes, and I can't shake the image of his muscles glistening in the sun when he emerged from the water earlier, droplets cascading down his tanned skin like a waterfall, and... oh God, listen to me. I sound like a lovesick teenager.

Honestly though, it's like the image of him in his trunks is burned into my brain, I can see it when I close my eyes, I can see it... right now.

'Hi,' he says simply, flashing me a grin.

'Hi,' I reply.

'What're you reading?' he asks, popping himself down on the sun lounger next to me.

His abs flex as he sits. I need to remind myself to breathe.

'Oh, just a novel,' I reply, setting my book to one side, because the only love interest I'm interested in is right here.

'It must be good, you were biting your lip,' he points out.

My cheeks feel suddenly sunburned. Was I really doing that? So embarrassing.

'Oh, it's, um... just a romantic comedy,' I say. 'More comedy really – which is also how I'd describe my love life.'

He laughs. See what I mean, he laughs at the worst jokes.

'Fair enough,' he replies. 'I won't keep you, I just thought I'd return something you dropped earlier.'

I can't help but look puzzled.

'I wasn't carrying anything,' I reply, gesturing vaguely at my bikini-clad self. 'There are no pockets in this thing, so it was the only thing I had to drop, and thankfully, it stayed on.'

Travis smirks but he doesn't say a word.

'So, I don't think I dropped anything,' I continue.

'It was an earring,' he tells me as he holds out his hand towards me. 'It must have fallen out of your ear.'

I instinctively take what he's offering me and it isn't an earring at all, it's a small, folded piece of paper.

I tilt my head curiously, suspicion creeping in, and I want to ask him what it is but he doesn't give me a chance.

'Anyway, I'll get back to my mates, but I'm sure we'll chat more later,' he tells me. 'Be careful with that earring.'

What in the world...?

My fingers fumble to unfold the paper, and my heart races as I slowly reveal what's written inside. When I see it, I can't help but laugh with delight. It's Nolan's wi-fi password.

I stare at it for a second, a no doubt ridiculous smile fixed on my face.

I guess now he knows how desperately I need it for work, he's gone out of his way to get it for me.

Honestly, he's going to have to stop being so perfect, or I might be in serious trouble.

29

There's something about the relaxing crackle of the firepit. Yep, even with the boys around, I find that if I just focus on the flames, and the sounds, then I can almost block them out. Almost...

After another long day we're all gathered around the firepit again. This time, we're hoping for minimal bloodshed – ideally no blood at all, if we can pull it off. The thing is, with these boys, you just never know.

Tonight, suspiciously, we're all getting on quite well.

The drinks are flowing, no one is making any sly comments, and the battle of the roses (as far as where is better, Yorkshire or Lancashire) isn't even getting a mention now (of course, we all know Yorkshire is the best).

'Let's play a game,' Harry suggests.

'No, come on, we're all playing nice tonight,' I point out. 'Games tend to end in chaos for us.'

'What did you have in mind?' Owen asks him.

Harry pulls a deck of cards from his pocket.

'Lucky Red Black,' he says with a smile.

'I've not heard of that one,' I say.

'That's because it's a game we invented when we all lived together at uni,' Travis tells me. 'It is a real game though, with real rules – we've spent hours playing it.'

'So you'll be better at it than us,' I point out. 'That hardly seems fair.'

'You might think, but this game is pure luck,' Travis tells me. 'There's no skill involved – it's actually quite fun.'

'Tell you what,' Harry says as he shuffles the deck. 'We'll say it's our pick, for the next round of the competition. What do you reckon? Why don't we let fate decide this one?'

Me and the rest of the girls all look at one another. I give Nita a shrug, to say it's up to her.

'Okay, let's do it,' she says. 'But we'll know if you're cheating, or if this is some kind of scam, so don't bother.'

'It's a real game, I promise you,' Travis says. 'Shall I explain the rules?'

'Go on then,' I reply, still unsure whether or not this is a good idea, but putting the competition in fate's hands, even if it's just for one round, does sound like a lot less work than the other rounds have been.

'So, here's how you play,' Travis begins – I need to do my best to listen, because normally when someone tries to explain a new card game to me, my brain goes into standby mode.

'There are fifty-two cards in a deck. We'll play in teams, to keep things moving. So one team goes first, and they draw four cards, but before you draw each one, you have to guess if it's red or black. You get two points for each one you get right. Then the other team does the same. That's round one.'

'Simple enough so far,' Nita says. 'Go on.'

'Right, round two,' Travis continues. 'This time you draw three cards, guessing the suit before each one. For every one you get right, you get four points. Then the other team does the same.'

I'm still following.

'Round three,' he goes on. 'You draw two cards. This time, you have to guess what number or face it is. This time you get thirteen points if you get one right. Then the other team goes.'

'This is actually a great game,' Nita says. 'I thought it was going to be silly.'

'Well, hold your horses,' Travis says with a laugh. 'Because the final round is the one that can change it all, and it's... interesting.'

'Go on,' I say, intrigued.

'So, for the final round, you only draw one card,' he continues. 'And you have to guess exactly what card it is. For that, you get fifty-two points. However, this game has a twist, because if you guess the three of diamonds, and you draw that card from the deck, you get fifty-two million points.'

'What?' Nita blurts.

'It's a game-changer,' Harry says.

'Has it ever happened?' I ask.

'Once,' he says, his eyes lighting up excitedly. 'And believe me when I say, we've played this game thousands of times.'

'So, what do you reckon?' Travis asks us. 'Fancy a game?'

'I'm in,' I say.

'Me too,' Nita replies.

'Yeah, it sounds fun,' Lou adds.

'It sounds daft,' Willow corrects her. 'But I'll play, sure.'

'And you're happy for it to be our round for the competition?' Owen checks.

'Yeah,' Lou tells him. 'It beats playing another sport.'

'It sounded like an actual, adult, sensible, marketable game until you mentioned the fifty-two million points thing,' Nita points out, shaking her head. 'That's just nonsense.'

'It's just fun,' Travis tells her, before swigging his beer. 'It's nonsense until someone draws the three of diamonds. Then it's amazing.'

'And it's happened once?' I check.

'Yeah, in our third year at uni,' Travis replies. 'You should've heard the screams coming from our student house.'

'Okay, let's do it,' I say.

The boys draw first, so that we can learn by watching them play. Travis leads his team with confidence.

'All right, red,' he says, flipping the first card to reveal the six of hearts. 'That's two points.'

'Black,' Harry calls next, but he's wrong – it's the eight of diamonds. No points there.

'Red,' Owen guesses, and he's correct again. By the end of round one, the boys rack up a (what I'd imagine is a) respectable six points.

The girls go next. Nita guesses red, starting us strong with a red queen. I call black and get a black two. Lou's guess of red is wrong, but Willow ends our turn with another correct guess. By the end of round one, the score is tied at six points each.

Okay, so now we have to guess the suit.

The boys go first again. Travis confidently calls 'hearts' and flips the card – he's right. Four points. Harry follows up with 'spades', but it's a diamond. Nolan guesses 'clubs' and scores. They end round two with eight more points, bringing their total to fourteen.

'We've got this,' Nita says, trying to pump us up.

'Diamonds,' I kick things off, and luck is on my side. Four points. Lou follows up with 'clubs' and misses, but Nita scores with her guess of 'spades'. The girls end the round with eight points as well, keeping the score tight at fourteen to fourteen.

It takes round three to break the draw, with the boys finishing up on twenty-seven points, and us trailing behind with twenty-six.

'This is close,' Travis points out. 'So it all comes down to the final card – and you have to guess the exact card so, seeing as though we're winning, and we all love to see it, I'll guess the Lucky Red Black card – the three of diamonds.'

'Ace of spades,' Owen confirms as he flips the card over. 'Tough luck, mate.'

'Nita, you pick,' I suggest.

'Well, obviously I'm going to pick the stupid card,' she says. 'We're losing anyway, and if it's tradition.'

'That's the spirit,' Travis says. 'Let's see.'

I flip the card over on Nita's behalf. The three of diamonds stares back at us like a miracle. For a second, we all sit in stunned silence. For us girls, I think it's mostly because we're waiting for confirmation, but for the boys it's a big moment. As they erupt into cheers and chaos, it's infectious, so we join in. We're screaming, hugging – we're just as excited as the boys are, for some reason.

'I can't believe it,' Harry says, shaking his head. 'That has only ever happened once before.'

'And even then, we thought you cheated,' Owen reminds him.

'I didn't cheat!' Harry protests, though he's grinning. 'This is insane. I don't even mind losing – this is a moment for the history books. Seeing the lucky card drawn is like... spotting a unicorn on the M62.'

'You lot are so weird,' Lou says, but she's smiling.

'This might be the best moment of my life,' Nolan says solemnly, though the twitch at the corner of his mouth betrays him.

'I'm just jazzed that we won,' I say. 'We're neck and neck again.'

'Yeah, well, we'll see about that,' Travis replies through a smile.

'You know, I came up with it,' Owen tells me, muscling his way in front of Travis.

'No, you didn't, we all did,' Nolan reminds him.

'Well, I said it should be the three of diamonds,' Owen says.

'Erm, no you didn't,' Travis says with a snort.

'Ignore them, they're just jealous,' Owen insists. 'Fancy a couple of rounds of Black Jack? Just for fun.'

'Okay, sure,' I reply, amused. 'But it can't be as exciting as that.'

Honestly, when we're all getting on, it's great. I could do a week of this – even two.

In a weird way, it would feel strange here without the boys now – but don't tell anyone I said that, because no one here in this villa could torture that information out of me.

Still, just between us, I am actually starting to enjoy myself. Who knew that was going to happen?

30

'What are you doing on your laptop without wi-fi, playing pinball?' Owen asks.

'When was the last time you used a computer?' I joke.

'They don't have pinball any more?' he replies. 'Anyway, I'm glad you're keeping busy with something. You can keep your secrets.'

I will absolutely be keeping it a secret, that Travis gave me the wi-fi password, lest I risk losing it.

Owen sits down next to me. I'm underneath a pergola, where there's shade, so that I can see my laptop screen.

It's a little quieter over here, a few extra steps from everyone. It's almost like having privacy – but not quite.

'I thought you might like a bottle of water,' he says, handing me one. 'If only because you look absolutely fire in your bikini.'

'You're too kind,' I say with a laugh, taking the bottle from him.

Oh my God. It's cold. Ice cold. I wonder if he's going out of his way to break the rules and do something nice for me, or if he's not even thought about it, he's just grabbed a bottle from the fridge and brought it here.

I try not to reveal my sheer joy at how cold it is, lest he realise his mistake and take it back from me.

Oh boy, that's good. I feel like my eyes are rolling into the back of my head. It's a mad time when a bottle of cold water gets you this lit.

'How's your wedding stuff going?' he asks. 'Everything going to plan?'

'Yeah, I think so,' I reply. 'The only spanner was this booking going tits up, but we've figured it out, right?'

'Right,' he replies with a grin. 'I didn't realise how much pressure it would be, planning a wedding, trying to stop things from going wrong.'

'You're the best man?' I check.

'Yep,' he replies.

'Chief bridesmaid,' I tell him, with a silly little wave. 'I know what you mean about the pressure, of trying to keep the show on the road, keep the bride calm. I just want Lou to have a great day and I'll worry about me later.'

'Are you worried about you?' he asks curiously. 'Tell me to piss off, if you want…'

'Oh, I'm just being silly,' I tell him. 'There's just something… kind of sad, about being the single friend left behind. And no offence, but all of this, it was just so unexpected, which means I've had the extra job of wrangling my lot,' I can't resist telling him.

'So what you're saying is that you and me are the glue holding all of this together,' he jokes.

'Yes, that's exactly what I'm saying,' I say sarcastically.

Owen leans forward, taking my hand in his. His tenderness takes me aback.

'It's not easy, being the lone wolf, standing on the sidelines,' he says. 'But we'll all meet someone, someday. There's a right person out there for all of us. This is Lou's time to shine, to get her happy ending. Yours will come along. Don't forget that, okay?'

'Wow, are you always this good at pep talks?' I can't help but ask.

He glances at me, his expression softening for a moment.

'I've noticed you use humour, to deal with situations,' he points out. 'You don't always have to do that, you know.'

'I mean, I do at least until this wedding has been and gone, and everything is okay,' I say.

'Okay but just know that being single when your friend is getting married isn't the death sentence you think it is,' he says. 'It's an adventure. It's all about perspective. You're not tied down. You're not compromising or settling. You're free to figure out what you actually want. That's a pretty enviable position to be in, if you ask me. Some people really miss being single.'

'Don't let your friend who is tying the knot hear you say that,' I point out – joking, as per. He's right though, I shouldn't always do that. 'But thanks for the perspective. You're right, I'm focusing on all the wrong things.'

'Maybe you are,' he says. 'And maybe, if you stop worrying about being single, stop trying to find the right person, and just let the right person come to you, he might show up when you least expect it – even here.'

'It's hard to imagine my dream guy popping up anywhere,' I reply. 'Love doesn't feel like it should come so easily.'

'Well, then maybe aim lower,' he replies.

I pull a face because is that ever a good idea?

'I don't mean lower your standards,' he insists. 'But if you're always expecting the fireworks, and they don't come, you're going to be disappointed.'

'I bet you say that to all the girls,' I quip.

'And there's one of those jokes again,' he points out with a knowing smile.

'Water and words of wisdom,' I say. 'I really have hit the jackpot today.'

'I'm just that kind of guy,' he jokes. 'But, shh, don't tell anyone we had this chat – it'll ruin my reputation.'

I laugh.

'Oh, I wouldn't dream of it,' I promise.

'If you ever want to chat, about anything, know that I'm here, and I'm a really good listener,' he reassures me.

'I'll keep that in mind,' I tell him. 'And, hey, you too. I'm always happy to chat.'

'I'm going to hold you to that,' he tells me. 'Anyway, I'll leave you to whatever you're doing on there.'

'Thanks,' I reply. 'For everything.'

'Ah, it's nothing,' he replies.

Now that their bravado is fading, and we're all starting to get on a little better, it's starting to seem like these boys aren't so bad after all.

Who knew?

31

Nita leads us into the lounge – aka, the boys' bedroom – ready for our chosen round for the competition.

'This,' she announces as she practically slaps my laptop down on one of the sofas, 'is what we want to do for our round of the competition, and you have to say yes. Boys, allow me to present... the *Sex and the City* quiz.'

I smile to myself. We've got this one in the bag.

'How are you on the wi-fi?' Nolan asks.

'Molly paid for some local hotspot thing, or something – don't change the subject,' Nita insists. 'We're doing this quiz, okay?'

'And you lot don't stand a chance,' Lou continues, smirking. 'We've been training for this since we were teens.'

Harry frowns.

'That's the one with the shagging and the shoes?' Harry checks.

'Oh, you're going down,' Willow replies.

We all sit down on the sofa, after Travis clears his bedsheets from it, and set the laptop down on the coffee table.

'Apparently, it has thousands of questions, but it serves them up at random, so it's all fair,' Nita tells them.

'How is it fair, to quiz us on your favourite show?' Harry asks.

'How was golf fair?' Nita claps back.

'You had Willow Tree,' Nolan points out, still clearly in awe of Willow's driving skills.

'We'll take turns, ten questions each, and whoever gets the most points wins. If anyone doesn't know the answer to a question, the other team can steal it. Sound good?' Nita asks.

She obviously thinks that will be a way for us to get extra points. Honestly, this is going to be like taking candy from a baby.

'Question one,' Nita reads aloud. 'For the girls. In the pilot episode, what does Miranda say her date has a fixation with?'

'Easy,' Lou replies. 'It's models.'

'Correct,' Nita replies as the answer flashes up.

The boys groan, but Owen leans forward, suddenly focused.

'Okay, go on, give us a question,' he insists.

Lou reads it aloud: 'What colour is Carrie's tutu in the opening credits?'

Without hesitation, Nolan answers, 'Pink.'

'I mean, that's just a good guess,' Willow points out. 'What other colour would it be?'

'A point is a point,' Owen reminds her.

The quiz continues, and of course we get our question right, but the boys surprise us again and again, answering questions we thought would stump them. They nail the name of Charlotte's first husband (Trey MacDougal), Miranda's favourite takeout (Chinese), and even the exact designer of Carrie's infamous wedding dress (Vivienne Westwood).

'Come on, how do you know this?' I ask, as they score yet another point.

'Do you really want to know?' Owen asks. We nod. 'We used

to watch it together at uni. We thought it might give us some expert knowledge, to help us with girls.'

We can't help but burst out laughing.

'You watched *Sex and the City* to help you with women?' Willow scoffs, rolling her eyes. 'That's ridiculous.'

'Is it, though?' Owen counters. 'It's helped us win this quiz, hasn't it?'

'An excellent point,' Travis chimes in. 'Also, it's just a great show.'

'You liked it?' I ask, surprised.

'Yeah,' he says with a shrug. 'It's really entertaining. And Samantha is hilarious.'

'That's true,' Nita says, raising her drink in agreement.

Despite our best efforts, the boys stay neck and neck with us until the final question. We need to get this one right.

'Last question for us,' Lou says, her eyes fixed on the screen. 'What continuity error can be spotted during the opening credits of *Sex and the City*?'

We exchange panicked looks. Continuity error?

Willow furrows her brow.

'I didn't even know there was one,' she says.

'Neither did I!' Nita replies, chewing her nail.

Harry leans forward, smirking.

'I think I know this,' he informs us.

'No, you don't,' Willow says with a scoff.

'Give me a chance to steal?' Harry asks.

'Okay, fine, if you're so sure,' Nita says.

Harry grins, and the boys nudge him forward like he's their star player, about to take a penalty.

'The bus that splashes Carrie? In one shot it's got people on it, then in the next, it doesn't,' he says smugly.

Lou checks the answer.

'That is… correct!'

The boys explode into cheers and high-fives, while we sit there, stunned.

'Once you've seen it, you can't unsee it,' Owen says smugly, leaning back in his chair. 'It used to annoy us every time.'

'You're way too smug for someone who learned everything about this show to "understand women",' Nita tells them.

'Oh, come on,' Harry teases. 'You're just gutted we won.'

'Credit where it's due,' I tell them. 'You won fair and square.'

'All right,' Nita says, swirling her wine glass. 'Honest opinions – did you like the movies? I assume you watched them.'

This is just so bizarre.

'I liked the first one,' Willow chimes in. 'But the second one? Absolutely not.'

'Agreed,' Lou says firmly. 'What even was that?'

'I actually liked the second one,' I admit, feeling a little sheepish. 'More than the first. It's just… it's silly and over the top, but it's entertaining.'

'Same here,' Travis says. 'I mean, yeah, it's not deep or anything, but it's fun, and sure, all the Abu Dhabi stuff is… what it is, but I'd be lying if I said I didn't enjoy it.'

'It was awful,' Willow insists. 'It's basically a parody of itself. And I can't believe you two are bonding over *Sex and the City 2*. Think about your life choices.'

Travis and I look at each other and laugh. Clearly feeling a little warm, he pulls off his T-shirt, the muscles in his arms flexing as he pulls it over his head, slowly revealing his abs a bit at a time. Is it me, or is this happening in slow motion? The magnetic pull of his toned stomach – and the fact his eyes are briefly covered by this T-shirt – mean I need something to look at, so his body it is. Of course, my gaze lingers for just a little too long, and he catches me staring. Could the ground swallow me up?

'Are you hungry?' he says – is he reading my mind? 'We were just about to eat – Spanish omelettes. Fancy some?'

It takes us a moment to realise he's talking to us. He says this like it's no big deal, but to us it's huge. Hot food! Imagine!

'Erm, yeah, okay,' I say coolly. 'That would be really nice.'

Nita looks like she can't believe our luck either.

'Perhaps I could make us some cocktails?' she suggests. 'We can all pretend we're the *Sex and the City* girls.'

'Now that I would love,' Harry says. 'Best way to celebrate. Let's do it.'

I can't believe Travis is offering us food. It's such a simple gesture, but it softens something in me. We're really starting to feel less like rivals and more like, well, friends.

We eat, drink, and chat until it's time to go to bed. It's one of those nights that sneaks up on you – fun, warm, and surprisingly lovely. Even as we tidy up to head for bed, I find myself smiling, the boys' laughter echoing in my ears.

Maybe this competition isn't such a bad thing after all.

32

I could honestly get used to doing my job from a sun lounger. Sadly, working for a Yorkshire biscuit company, I'm not sure how often the opportunity will arise. Perhaps when I do find someone to oversee the product redevelopment, I could ask him or her to convince Iwan that we need to do some flavours inspired by other countries, and that the recruiter needs to be the one who travels around doing the market research.

A girl can dream.

I'm lying with my laptop balanced precariously on my thighs, squinting at the screen while the sun glares down at me, almost like it is offended that I'm working under it instead of relaxing.

However, relaxing isn't all that easy when your career feels like it's hanging by a thread.

I've managed to reply to a few emails, clear some admin bits and bobs, and now I'm just checking the work group chats and... oh my God!

> We really need to fill the role ASAP, but the recruiter has gone on holiday.

Oh, lovely, they're talking about me. And being slightly catty with it?

Annoyed, I jab at the keyboard and type out a reply.

> I'm on holiday, but I've found someone.
> Someone amazing. I'll sort it all when I'm back.

I hit send before I think it through. Obviously that's a total lie, and one that I don't know how I'm going to get out of other than by finding someone for the job. You've got to congratulate me though, on finding a way to put myself under even more pressure. Who knew that was possible?

It's fine. Well, it will be fine. I will find someone. I always do. Not finding anyone isn't an option.

I slap my laptop shut with a frustrated sigh and lean back, placing my hands over my closed eyes for a moment, to escape the sunlight that's glowing through my eyelids. There's no hiding from the sun, when it's shining like it is today.

'Are you okay?' Travis asks, his voice snapping me from my thoughts.

He's stretched out on the lounger next to me, but he's turned slightly on his side, propping his head up on one arm. His sunglasses are perched low on his nose, so that I can see his eyes.

He's been next to me for a while now, quietly, and I haven't been sure if it's because he's relaxing or because he thinks I'm working, or maybe he just hasn't wanted to talk to me. I know I would much rather be chatting with him than working though.

My cheeks heat up instantly. Of course he's awake, and paying attention, when I'm having a mini work meltdown.

'All good,' I tell him, trying to sound like it is actually all good, but totally failing.

I resist the urge to stare at his shoulders, broad and golden under the sunlight, or the way his tanned stomach ripples as he moves. Focus, Molly. One thing at a time.

'Well, not all good,' I say, getting back on track. 'I just lied to some colleagues, about having someone for the product development role, and—'

My phone starts ringing. Shit, it's Iwan. I knew I shouldn't have connected my phone to the wi-fi too. I could not answer it, but that will look suspicious, but if I do answer it, what will I say? I guess we'll find out.

'Hello, Iwan,' I say brightly.

'Hi, Molly, how's the holiday?' he asks, in a friendly way, like he isn't the man who sends me stress-inducing emails in the early a.m.

'It's... lovely, thanks,' I reply, trying to sound upbeat. 'So, so relaxing.'

Out of the corner of my eye, I see Travis shift again. He's watching me intently now, smiling slightly, like he's amused by the mess I'm continuing to make for myself.

'Not only are you working while you're there, but I've just heard you've found someone for the job?' Iwan continues. 'I can't believe you've done that, on holiday. That's excellent news. You've really come through for us, Molly.'

'Oh, well, you know me,' I babble. 'Always working.'

'So, who is it?' Iwan asks curiously.

Who is it? Oh, God. That's a very good question, and one that I obviously don't have an answer for.

'Who is it?' I repeat back to him.

'Yeah, who have you got?' he asks again.

I stare straight ahead, my brain scrambling for words, but all I can conjure up are panicked sound effects.

'Well, I'm still... working on him,' I say, my voice an octave higher than usual. 'Just a few Is to dot, Ts to cross...'

'Still working on him? You just said you had someone,' Iwan points out.

'I do have him, I do, it's basically a done deal,' I continue to flounder.

'Are you sure?' Iwan asks slowly. 'Because, if you don't have someone...'

'No, I do, I absolutely do, he's real,' I insist.

I cringe the second I say the words 'he's real' because why wouldn't he be?

'Molly, no one could blame you for not finding someone, while you're on holiday...' Iwan says, offering me an out, but I can't back down now.

'He's real,' I say again. 'He's...'

Before I can make an even bigger fool of myself, Travis's hand suddenly appears in my eyeline. He gestures at me, coolly and calmly, to hand him the phone.

I stare at him. 'What are you doing?' I mouth, but he doesn't say a word, he just extends his hand again, palm up, insistent.

'Molly?' my boss prompts.

I... I don't know what to do. What else can I do? I don't even know why I do it, but I hand Travis the phone, my heart hammering against my ribcage as I watch him sit up, lean forward, and take over.

'Hi, yeah, it's Travis here,' he says smoothly, voice dropping into something confident, casual, and yet totally professional.

He pauses while Iwan speaks.

'Yeah, I'm who Molly's been speaking to about the role,' Travis continues, his gaze flicking towards the horizon, like he's deep in conversation now. 'I've got some experience with product development... I haven't worked with biscuits before, other than being a keen patisserie chef, but I'm looking for a new challenge and I think this might be it. Big fan of Brookes, love all of your products, but I've got ideas, too. Some interesting flavour pairings, seasonal concepts – all sorts, really, my mind raced when Molly told me you were looking to innovate. Maybe the UK market needs a Yorkshire take on lunettes de romans...'

I don't think I'm breathing – am I breathing?

'Yes, Molly is certainly wooing me,' he adds, and then he grins at me – a slow, teasing grin that makes my stomach twist into knots. 'Yeah, I'd say her charms were working.'

What is even happening right now? Is he really doing this? Is it working?

'Yep, okay. I'll pass you back to Molly,' he says, handing the phone to me like he didn't just hijack my mental breakdown and nip it in the bud.

I take the phone, staring at him in stunned disbelief.

'Hi,' I practically croak down the phone.

'Good work, Molly,' Iwan says, clearly impressed. 'He sounds great. Get him for us, no matter what it takes, okay?'

'I can do that,' I reply faintly, because I'm not sure that's true.

We say our goodbyes and hang up.

'You saved me,' I blurt, still in shock.

'Ah, it was nothing,' Travis insists, leaning back. 'I could talk about biscuits all day.'

'How did you blag your way through like that?' I ask.

'Well, I am actually a chef,' he says, stretching out again, his muscles shifting under his skin in that totally distracting way.

Suddenly it seems so obvious.

'Ahh, I should have guessed, when I ate that incredible bagel and it was so good I saw colours,' I joke. 'I thought I was just that hungry.'

'I've bought you some time,' he says with a smile. 'And don't worry, I know lots of people, a few who are actually looking for work. I'm sure I can find you someone perfect for the job – someone even better than me.'

Oh, I seriously doubt that. Someone better than him? Better than my actual hero? I'm not sure anyone gets better than that.

33

It's kind of nice, the four of us hanging out in one room, it's still got that girly sleepover vibe. I thought we might be feeling a bit sick of each other by now – well, not sick of each other, but sick of not really having much personal space, but if anything the physical closeness has only made us, well, closer.

'Are you really not nervous?' Nita asks Lou.

'Erm, not really,' she replies.

'I'd be bricking it,' Nita replies.

'I mean, obviously I'm nervous about the wedding in that I hope it goes well,' Lou continues. 'But as far as getting married goes, nope, not nervous at all – I can't wait.'

'I feel like that should make me feel sick, but I'm so happy for you,' Nita tells her, scrunching up her face anyway.

'Yeah, you and Ellis are perfect for each other,' I add. 'This is just the start of the next phase of your relationship, and it's going to be even better than the last.'

'Yeah, honestly, even if your wedding goes really, terribly wrong, you'll still have such a happy marriage,' Willow chimes in.

We all stare at her.

'What?' she says, furrowing her brow.

A knock on the door snaps us from our conversation. I nominate myself to answer it.

I wonder which boy it will be, only to see all four of them standing there.

The first thing I notice (well, the second, after how good Travis is looking today) is that Harry's shirt clings to him with the unmistakable dampness of someone who's been playing football under the sun for hours. He'd probably stink of sweat, were it not for the fact that they all reek of chlorine. I think they're nose-blind to it now. They've just accepted it and now their nose cancels it out for them. We can still smell it though – big time.

'Uh, quick question,' Harry starts, rubbing the back of his neck as he chooses his words. 'Do you have an iron?'

'Because we're women?' Nita snaps at him.

Travis steps forward.

'No, nothing like that,' he insists. 'It said in the listing that the villa had one, but we can't find it downstairs. We're trying on our suits, for the wedding, and the first thing we noticed is that the shirts are a little creased.'

'I'll have a look for you,' I tell him.

'That would be great, thanks,' he replies.

You can see the gratitude in his smile. It's warm and genuine.

'You guys seriously smell like the pool,' Willow tells them bluntly.

'Cheers,' Owen mutters, shooting her a look.

'Look, you don't want to try on your wedding outfits, if there's a chance they might end up smelling like chlorine,' I start, looking back at the girls briefly, giving them a look. Nita nods in approval. 'Why don't you use our bathrooms first?'

'Really?' Travis replies.

'Yeah, absolutely,' I tell him.

'You have to give us something though,' Nita says. 'Something good – something really good.'

I glance back at her. Do they though?

'What's really good?' Harry asks her.

'A point in the competition,' she says almost instantly.

Oh, so that's where she's going with this.

'Not a chance,' Harry says.

'Not a chance you're using our showers then,' she tells them.

I sigh.

'One sec,' Harry tells her.

The boys huddle in the hallway, whispering together. Finally they join us again.

'Okay, fine, we'll give you a point if you let us use your shower,' Harry says, smirking.

'Deal,' Nita says.

'We would have swapped it for two points,' Harry tells her, trying to wipe the smile from her face.

'I would have let you use the showers for nothing, just to get rid of the stink,' she replies. 'Just do me a favour, yeah? Use someone else's fucking shampoo.'

The boys just laugh – still no admission of guilt, but I think we all know.

'We were actually going to get some air, so feel free to use all four showers,' I tell them. 'You don't have to take turns in one.'

Travis smiles. I can tell he appreciates my more amicable approach.

'Feel free to use our loo, if you need the loo,' Harry says – kindly, but it doesn't quite have the same ring to it.

The boys head off to get their things, so we make a move to head downstairs.

'You don't mind, do you, girls?' I check.

'Of course not,' Nita says.

'Yeah, I mean we basically owe them one for feeding us yesterday too,' Lou adds.

'And they really, really do stink,' Willow says. 'I was going to suggest we turn the hose to them, if there is one, just to try and blast the smell away. I guess this is nicer.'

Er, yeah, just a bit.

I'm the last one to walk downstairs, passing the living room doorway just as Travis is about to head upstairs, his washbag in hand – meaning they do have toiletries with them, at least. I'm guessing using Nita's shampoo was a tactical manoeuvre, to try not to get caught, rather than just to really piss her off. I'll bet that was just a nice bonus for them.

I flash him a smile, but Travis catches my hand in his as I go to pass him.

'Honestly, thank you for this,' he tells me. 'I know we've been quite stubborn but this is really good of you. Sometimes I feel like I'm the only one of my lot that remembers there's a wedding at the end of this, and I did wonder how we were going to clean up. So, yeah, thank you.'

'Ah, it's nothing,' I tell him. 'Consider us even, after the food you made us.'

I lean in close and lower my voice.

'And the other food, and the wi-fi password, and smoothing over things with my boss,' I whisper.

'You're welcome,' he whispers back – his whisper makes him about ten times more charming and at least fifty times sexier. 'If there's anything I can do, for Lou's wedding – if you need anything, or want anything, just shout.'

'I will, thanks,' I say, giving his hand a squeeze.

He releases me and heads upstairs. I hold my hand in, well, my other hand. As soon as he let me go, it was like someone took a little piece of me.

I mean as far as anything I want, or anything I need, I hate to admit it but I think that might be him. Imagine if I hadn't promised not to sleep with the enemy (figuratively and literally). I could follow him upstairs, slink into the shower with him, get all hot and steamy in the bathroom. I mean, that's assuming he would want me to. I could throw my everything into what I imagine is a porn cliché – stepping into the bathroom and asking him if he needs a hand – and he might tell me to get out. Or he might just ask me if I'll scrub his back, just a platonic favour, between one mate and another. You know what though? I'd do it. I'd wash his back. I'd... Oh, Molly, Molly, Molly. You thirsty girl. What is going on with me? If anyone needs a shower, it's definitely me. An ice-cold one.

34

'Okay,' Lou says, holding up her wedding dress, giving it a nervous look, almost like she's suspicious of it. 'Moment of truth. Let's make sure these all still fit.'

There is absolutely no reason to suspect that they don't fit, because why wouldn't they, nothing has changed. But I totally get why we're checking. I'd probably be constantly checking, convinced something was going to go wrong. But I think we'd know from our day-to-day clothes if anything had changed, like a sudden growth spurt, or any of us shirking.

Dutifully, we all slip into our dresses while Lou wrestles herself into her bridal gown.

The bridesmaid dresses are perfect. They're flattering, floor-length, a beautiful sage green, and even though they're floaty, they have structure, which gives us all shape where we need it.

'I really do love this dress,' I say, smoothing my hands down the soft fabric.

'We look hot,' Nita adds, standing next to me to check her reflection. 'Who says bridesmaids can't steal the show?'

'I do,' Lou calls out as she puts on her shoes.

'Well, there's enough spotlight for all of us,' Nita adds, smiling at herself.

'There really isn't,' Lou adds with a laugh. 'Okay, let's see.'

Lou stands up, allowing the skirt of her white gown to fall to her ankles. She looks beautiful, with her lace bodice and subtle sequin detail. Honestly, even without the hair and make-up she has planned, she looks perfect.

'Shit,' she says, sounding disappointed.

'What's wrong?' I ask.

'Since I changed the shoes, to a smaller heel, the dress is too long,' she says. 'I thought it would be fine.'

'I mean, I'd be worried, if you couldn't sew, and hadn't already told us you were bringing a sewing kit with you for situations like this,' Nita points out.

'Yeah, you can fix this,' Willow reassures her.

'I know, it's just not what I needed,' Lou replies with a sigh. 'Molly, can you put it on for me?'

'What?' I blurt.

'We're the same size, same height... it will be easier if someone is wearing it,' she explains. 'I can't exactly wear it and make my own adjustments.'

I mean, she's got a point but obviously I've never worn a wedding dress before, and I didn't think I would until I was actually getting married. Still, my friend needs me, so I need to step up.

'Fair,' I reply, carefully removing my bridesmaid dress. Lou takes off her wedding dress which I carefully put on, trying not to breathe too hard in case I do anything to damage it. It's delicate, lacy, but way heavier than I expected it to be. When it's finally on and fastened I take a look at myself in the mirror.

I suck in my stomach slightly, even though I probably don't

need to, and I know it's probably not going to do much at this point. It's just one of those things we grow up doing, because we think we're supposed to. But I can relax here, with the girls, because I don't have to impress them, they don't care if I'm bloated and, crucially, this isn't my dress, it's Lou's. It's a beautiful dress, sure, but when I think about what kind of dress I'd like to get married in… I don't know, my mind goes blank. I wonder what that means. If I'm not interested in getting married? If Dean has made me feel like I'm unmarriable? Both? I'm hoping, when and if I do decide to get married, that I'll know the perfect dress when I see it. That everything will just click into place for me. Maybe one day I'll find out.

'Oh my God,' Lou says softly. 'Molly, you look incredible.'

'I do not.' I laugh.

'You really do,' Lou insists as she circles me, pins in her mouth as she crouches to check the hem.

'You're stunning,' Nita adds, snapping a picture on her phone. 'You'll make someone a lovely little bride someday.'

'Shut up,' I insist, laughing it off.

There's a knock on the door, followed by Harry's voice.

'Hey, are you lot decent? We need help,' he calls out.

'What kind of help?' Nita calls back.

'Harry's suitcase has torn his trousers for the wedding,' Travis calls back.

Oh, no. Travis.

'Come in!' Lou calls out.

'Wait—' I start, but it's too late. The door swings open, and the boys spill in.

The room falls silent. I can't help but notice that Travis is staring right at me.

His eyes go wide, and his mouth opens just slightly, like he wants to say something but can't quite get there. He looks stunned – absolutely, genuinely stunned – and his gaze travels down the dress and back up to my face.

'I'm just wearing this so Lou can make adjustments,' I insist. 'I'm not some crazy bridesmaid wearing a white gown. Hi, by the way.'

Smooth. So, so smooth.

'Hi,' he replies, still not saying much.

'You okay, mate?' Harry asks him, giving him a nudge.

Travis blinks like he's snapping out of a trance.

'Yeah. Yeah, fine.'

He scratches the back of his neck, eyes darting anywhere but at me now.

'What's happened to your trousers?' Lou asks, cutting to the chase.

Harry holds them up in front of him.

'My suitcase zip ate them. Some of the stitches popped. Can you fix it?'

Lou takes the trousers, inspecting the damage.

'Yeah, I'll sort it. Just let me finish this, then I'll get right on it,' she tells them.

'That's so good of you, thank you,' Harry replies.

'It's sorted?' Owen asks, joining us. Nolan is right behind him.

'Yeah, Lou is going to fix them for me,' Harry tells him.

'Wow, look at you all in your dresses,' Owen points out.

He pauses to stare at me, confused.

'This is Lou's dress,' I say, bringing him up to speed. 'She's making adjustments.'

'It suits you,' he tells me. 'Ten out of ten. Do you want us to give you all a rating?'

'Only if we all get tens,' Nita points out.

'Okay, then let's do this properly,' Harry declares, stepping forward, pretending he has a microphone in hand. He clears his throat dramatically. 'Ladies and gentlemen, welcome to the Villa Fashion Show. Introducing our first contestant... Willow! Representing elegance and grace, she's serving us green silk today, ladies and gentlemen.'

I can't help but laugh. It's the way he's doing it like a boxing ring announcer, rather than someone at an actual fashion show.

Willow laps it up, laughing as she twirls so hard her dress flares.

'Up next, Nita, a solid ten out of ten,' Harry continues. 'Known for wit as sharp as her cheekbones, she's a vision, also in green. Look at that pose. Slay, Nita. Slay.'

'It's all true,' Nita says, flipping her hair and winking. 'It's all true.'

'We'll skip Lou, seeing as though she's wearing a dressing gown, and working,' Harry says in his normal voice, before switching back to ring-announcer mode. 'And finally, our unexpected headliner of the evening...'

He pauses dramatically, gesturing towards me.

'Molly! A vision in white, she's stolen the spotlight – and probably a few hearts. Let's go to one of our experts. Travis, your thoughts?'

I shoot Harry a glare, mortified, but my gaze flicks to Travis.

'No words,' Travis says simply, his voice low but clear as he smiles. 'No notes. Ten out of ten.'

'There you have it,' Harry says, clapping his hands. 'Ladies, take a bow!'

'Don't you bow,' Lou says to me quickly. 'You'll make the hem wonky.'

We all hang out together, while Lou makes her alterations.

The boys can be so much fun, when they want to be. My cheeks hurt from smiling so much – and okay, fine, maybe because Travis's eyes are on me the whole time. I can't say I'm not happy about that.

'I was thinking, to thank you for your hard work,' Travis starts, as the chaos settles into chat, 'I could make dinner for everyone tonight.'

'I don't know if you know this, but he's an amazing chef,' Harry points out. 'He's won awards and everything.'

'It's the least I can do,' Travis says, moving the conversation on from Harry's praise, clearly so modest about it all.

'We'd love that,' Nita says quickly. Maybe too quickly.

'That would be great,' Lou adds. 'Harry, I'll sort your trousers now, it won't take long.'

'Then I'll go get started,' Travis says. 'I'll shout when it's ready.'

'Do you need a hand?' I ask him.

'No, you relax,' he says. 'It's all under control.'

The boys shuffle towards the door, Travis lingering just a second longer than the rest to give me a smile.

Then he's gone, and I'm left standing in the wedding dress, my heart racing for reasons that have nothing to do with the tight bodice.

'Actual dinner made by an actual chef,' Nita says. 'Result. Although presumably, Molly would rather eat the chef, than the dinner...'

'Shut up,' I insist, but I can't stop smiling.

But she's right, the thought of Travis cooking is almost as delicious as the idea of spending more time with him. Almost.

35

I can't quite believe it, but we're out for Lou's hen party, and the boys are out for Nolan's stag party, and we're all hanging out together, in the same place.

Fair enough, there is only one bar in the local town, so without travelling we were all always going to end up here, but we didn't have to come together, and we didn't have to decide to sit together. We're like one big group now, rather than two separate ones – and we definitely no longer feel like warring sides, not tonight at least.

The town bar is adorable – traditional, tiny and completely unpretentious. The drinks are poured generously, the jukebox has nothing we've heard of, and we've got a big table all to ourselves. It's like our own private pad tonight.

The boys claimed the table while we got the first round in – another thank you for another dinner – and now we're all sitting together, hanging out, everyone's laughing like old friends. The tension from the competition feels like a distant memory. In fact, it's hard to imagine why we felt so negatively towards them in the first place (I have had a few drinks though, and I'm sure if I think back to the first days, I could probably recall why).

Nita slides a tray of shots onto the table.

'More drinks,' she announces.

'You're reading my mind,' Harry replies, winking at her as he grabs one. 'Do you know what would go really well with these? A drinking game.'

'Uh-oh,' Lou practically sings – she's had just enough to drink where I reckon she'll go along with it. 'Are you trying to get us into trouble?'

'I'll make sure you don't get into trouble,' Nolan reassures her – I suppose he is the sensible one. Oh, and he's getting married too. There's that.

'They're scared they can't keep up with us,' Harry teases, obviously trying to get a reaction out of one of us.

Nita obliges.

'Erm, excuse me? We are practically professionals. Do you know how much we've drunk over the years?' She nudges me and Lou. 'Remember those nights out before you two got boring?'

'We're not boring,' Lou protests. 'We got boyfriends.'

I notice Travis look at me. I need to say something.

'And I don't even have one any more, so there's nothing to hold me back.'

'You two were legends,' Nita reminds us. 'Why don't we show these boys what they're dealing with?'

Travis leans closer to me, smiling.

'Legends, eh?' he says. 'That's a bold claim.'

'I don't know about being a legend, but I will happily play a game,' I reply.

'I've got the deck of cards with me,' Owen says. 'You girls ever played Decked?'

'Everyone who grew up in the UK has played Decked,' Nita informs him.

There are a few variations of the game, and different people play by different rules, but generally it's just drawing cards, and doing whatever weird or wonderful thing that card means.

'I'll recap the rules,' Owen begins, shuffling the deck. 'First rule: no crying and/or chickening out. That's not in the spirit of the game.'

'And no refusing to drink the dirty pint because you don't like one of the things in it,' Harry adds.

'Let's do it,' Lou says.

I smile to myself. I love how she's embracing the hen party chaos. In hindsight, we should have brought a bunch of penis-y supplies, and L plates, to really see her off in style. Then again, that might be where she would draw her line.

Nita chooses the first card, a king, meaning she starts the dirty pint. She pours a generous splash of her cocktail into the cup in the centre of the table.

'I reckon that's for future you,' she warns, pointing at Harry, flashing him a sinister smile.

Lou pulls a card for 'Never Have I Ever'.

'Okay, okay, okay,' she says, smirking. 'Never have I ever... fancied someone at this table.'

I hesitate. I know, you're supposed to play honestly, but I'm not about to admit that, am I?

As I glance around, I notice pretty much everyone drink, I think everyone apart from Lou. Well, I might as well, seeing as though everyone else is.

'That's very, very interesting,' Nita says.

'What can I say?' Harry jokes. 'It's Travis's cute little bum.'

We all laugh – but he does have a great bum.

Nolan becomes the Question Asker, asking Willow a series of

questions, trying to catch her out by making her say the word 'yes' or 'no' – the only two words you're not allowed to say. Of course, he catches her out right away, by asking her if she knows the rules. She looks furious.

'Drink,' Nolan commands her.

Eventually she smiles and knocks her glass of wine back.

By the end of the game – which really has been a blast, and a bit of an eye-opener – the dirty pint finally claims its victim. Harry. We all scream and cheer as he downs the gross-looking mixture in the glass in the centre of the table. Ew, rather him than me, it smells like sick.

But he does it, like the good sport that he is.

'I'd have that again,' he says, before burping. I'm fairly sure he's joking.

'Have you ever played Paranoia?' Nita asks.

'No?' Harry replies. 'What's that?'

'Basically, one person whispers a question to another, and the answer has to be a person at the table. They answer out loud. Then, the person whose name was said has a choice, they can either play on and ask a question to someone else, or they can ask to know what the question about them was – but, if they do, they have to take a shot,' she explains.

'Love it,' Harry replies. 'Let's do it.'

Here's hoping everyone is gentle, although I have a sneaking suspicion we're about to drink a whole lot more.

As I look up, I notice Travis catch my eye across the table. His laugher dissolves into an easy smile, then a wink. I smile back at him.

Here's hoping no one asks me who I fancy at the table, because I would have to say Travis, and if I do say his name, I get the feeling he would be willing to drink to find out…

36

We pretty much all stumble out of the taxis in a chaotic, laughing heap. We've all had way, way too much to drink tonight. I know we said we'd see who the last group standing was but I don't think any of us are going to be standing for much longer.

'We should keep this party going inside!' Nita declares, her voice bright and full of wild energy as she stumbles slightly into Lou. Thankfully Lou catches her, rather than falling down with her.

'I'll get the music on!' Harry suggests, already halfway to the door, fumbling in his pocket for something.

'I'll get more booze from the kitchen,' Owen adds.

Willow leans against one of the pillars next to the door, looking pale.

'Ugh, I feel so sick. I think I'm going to lie down,' she tells us. She tries to move but she falls back against the wall.

'I'll help you,' Nolan says immediately, ever the gentleman. 'Come on, be careful. I won't let you fall.'

The rest of us filter into the villa, but before I can follow, I feel a hand curl gently around mine, pulling me back.

The warmth of Travis's touch freezes me in place. He's not even holding me that hard, it's like there's a magnet that keeps us together. He holds my hand lightly, his thumb brushing over my knuckles.

'Are you okay?' I ask, keeping my voice soft and quiet.

He exhales deeply, his shoulders rising and falling.

'Yeah, I'm fine. I think I just need a minute to cool down,' he tells me.

I know exactly what he means. The night's been loud and manic and messy. My brain is as tired as my body.

'I could do with a break from the noise, too,' I tell him. I glance towards the villa, where music is already thumping faintly through the walls. 'Fancy a walk?'

'Sounds good,' he says with a smile.

I squeeze his hand before letting it go, feeling oddly reluctant to lose contact.

'Let's go to the secret garden,' I suggest. 'No one will disturb us there.'

The noise from the villa fades behind us as we step into the garden, its winding pathways lit by scattered lanterns that cast a warm, golden glow. The air is rich with the scent of flowers and earth. Breathing it in just makes you feel so much better – like the air is cleaner here, somehow.

The hedges are tall and thick, curving around us like walls, giving us our own private space.

Travis walks beside me, hands shoved into his pockets, his body relaxed but he's just so tall and broad in a way that distracts me.

We're quiet while we walk, and I don't mind it. There's something about being with Travis that makes silence feel easy. Nothing could ruin this moment – except me of course, as I trip on something (or maybe nothing) and stumble forwards.

'I've got you,' Travis says, his arms around me in an instant, steadying me, putting me back on my feet.

His hands land on my arms, warm and steady, as I rest my hands on his body. My face feels like it's on fire as I look up at him, my heart pounding for all the wrong (and, to be honest, the right) reasons.

'Your reflexes are better than mine,' I tell him. 'Thank you.'

'That's okay,' he tells me. 'I've got you.'

We part again but Travis doesn't let go of my hand as we continue walking. His thumb brushes over my skin absent-mindedly, and I wonder if he knows what he's doing to me – how my breath keeps stalling, how my imagination runs away with me every time he looks at me.

We reach the small clearing – I'm sure we can call it our clearing now – where we sat a few days ago, the grass soft beneath our feet. The spotlights don't do much here, under the canopy of the trees, making everything shadowy and kind of sexy.

The quiet wraps around us again, and for a minute, it feels like we're the only two people in the world. And then I start laughing, like the tipsy idiot that I am.

'What's funny?' Travis asks, turning to me with that easy grin of his.

'I was just thinking about the last time we were here,' I say. 'When I was trying to smell your hair, and we ended up sort of wrestling.'

He laughs too, shaking his head.

'That wasn't wrestling. You barely put up a fight,' he teases.

I gasp dramatically, clutching my chest.

'Excuse me? I had you pinned. Actually pinned to the floor,' I point out.

'Erm, no,' he corrects me. 'I had you pinned.'

I narrow my eyes.

'I don't remember that happening.'

Except I do. I remember everything. How it felt being that close to him, how his weight pressed down on me just enough to make me feel all kinds of things.

He tilts his head, his gaze locking onto mine.

'Then let me refresh your memory,' he says, barely warning me.

Before I can argue he leans forward, hooking an arm around me and lowering me to the ground so gently it steals the breath from my lungs.

He's careful. Deliberate. One of his arms holds me up, while his other pins me lightly, his weight balanced just enough to keep me trapped without overwhelming me.

I gaze up at him, suddenly so aware of every little thing. How close he is, how warm his body feels even through his shirt, how his blue eyes look so much darker now, out here.

'See?' he whispers, his voice much lower now. 'Pinned.'

My chest rises and falls in uneven breaths as I stare up at him, my free hand resting lightly on his shoulders, while the other is still held in place above my head. My heart is hammering so hard I swear I can hear it. I think he can hear it too.

My God, I wish I had the guts to kiss him, or that he would just kiss me, put me out of my misery. I part my lips slightly, hoping, and praying, that he takes the hint.

His eyes flick to my mouth, and I see it. The moment he decides.

He leans in ever so slowly, his gaze never leaving mine, giving me every chance to stop him, but there's no chance of that happening. His lips brush against mine softly at first, just enough to send shivers down my spine, but when I wriggle with delight beneath him, he turns up the heat.

His hand moves to cup my face, his thumb stroking gently over my cheek as he kisses me, the slow and steadiness making way for something more passionate, more frantic. It's like when you're running late, so you pick up the pace. This is long, long overdue. We don't want to waste another minute.

I melt beneath him, letting the world fall away. The chaos of the villa, the sound of the wind in the trees, the tipsy feeling – it's all gone. There's only him.

There's only two things you can do in a situation like this. You can de-escalate – which, let's face it, I probably should, because I don't see how this won't end in tears, and I did promise my friends I wouldn't sleep with the enemy – or just give yourself to the moment, jump in, feet first, and give it everything you've got. I just need to give Travis a sign, to show him where I want this to go.

I'm sure I could be more subtle about it, but I'm acting purely based on what I want, and what I want is him, so I reach down and fumble with the button on his trousers. I just about get it undone before Travis takes charge, hitching my dress up around my waist in one swift and impressive movement, before leaning forward again to kiss my neck.

There's no turning back now, I can't put the brakes on – more importantly, I don't want to. Forget what's wrong or right, this just feels right.

I just hope the garden keeps its secrets, but we'll worry about that tomorrow.

37

Oh, boy, my head is pounding. I'm scared to even open my eyes – not just because I think it will hurt, because I have no idea where I am, and I'm scared to find out.

I pry my eyes open, wincing at the light pouring in through the balcony doors. Oh, I'm in my room. Alone. That's... interesting.

I know I had a lot to drink last night, but of all the things I probably don't remember, one thing that I do remember is being in the garden with Travis. It was amazing, perfect, everything I dreamed of. And yet here I am, alone.

My hangover is so rotten that, when I hear the banging on my bedroom door, I actually stop to consider if the noise might be my brain, throbbing against my skull.

'Come in,' I call out, the volume of my own voice making my headache worse.

It's Travis, and I would say I'm pleased to see him, because the fact that he's here means he's not avoiding me, but he doesn't look happy at all. Shit. Is he here to tell me he regrets it? If he does, I'll just have to say that I regret it too.

'I've really fucked up,' he tells me.

Oh, right, bloody charming. I know he might regret what we did, that I might not be everyone's dream conquest, but to file me under 'really fucked up' is a bit harsh.

'Oh...' I say simply. 'I... er...'

'I've lost the rings,' he continues.

He looks genuinely panicked. He's not even thinking about what happened between us right now.

'What?' I reply, wrapping the covers around my underwear-clad body as I struggle to my feet. Yes, now is the time to worry about him seeing me without my clothes, even though he not only saw but touched pretty much every part of me last night. I guess he was drunk then. He's very sober now.

'I've lost them,' he says again. 'I was supposed to be looking after them and... I don't know.'

'You had them?' I reply.

'Owen thought they would be safest with me,' he tells me. 'And, yeah, now we know how that has turned out.'

'Were they in your room?' I ask. 'Has someone taken them?'

'I kept them on me,' he replies. 'So they were with me last night and... fuck.'

'Okay, this is fine, because we went to the bar, and we were... in the garden, so we can just check those places,' I say. 'Go check the garden now, I'll throw some clothes on and catch you up, and if they're not there then we'll just go to the bar and check there. They have to be somewhere.'

'Yeah, okay, you're right,' he says, pausing to puff air from his cheeks. 'Okay, I'll do that. Thanks, Molly, it means so much to me that you're willing to help.'

'It's nothing,' I reply with a reassuring smile.

I mean, I'm reassuring him with my smile, but I'm not sure how confident I feel. He must have lost them somewhere – who knows if they're still there? Could they have fallen into the pond? On the road, as he got out of the taxi? Could he have lost them in the bar – shit, what if someone has found them?

I throw on some clothes, wash my face, scrape my hair up into a big bun on the top of my head, grab my handbag (because I'm pretty sure I'm going to need some painkillers) and head downstairs.

'No sign in the garden,' he tells me as I join him in the back garden. 'And there's more bad news.'

'Go on,' I prompt him, bracing for what he's about to say.

'There are no taxis available to take us to town, they're all booked up for the day,' he says. 'But I did find something…'

Travis walks around the villa, to a shed, where the door is already open.

'Can you ride a bike?' he asks me.

'I could, when I was younger, but I don't know if I still can,' I admit.

'Well, you know what they say, right?' he asks.

'What?' I reply.

'It's like riding a bike,' he jokes. 'Alternatively, one of them has a seat on the back, but you will have to hold on to me.'

Obviously I would love that.

'I think I'll ride on yours,' I say, instantly cringing at my choice of words. 'Just in case, because the last thing Lou needs is me falling off a bike, days before her wedding.'

'Fair enough,' he replies with a smile. 'Let's go.'

Travis hops onto the bike, which has an extra-long seat, making it perfect for two – well, two who want to be up close and personal. As I take my seat behind him, pressing my body up against his, wrapping my arms around him tightly, I swear, we're closer than we were last night. I'm fixed to him.

'Okay, let's go,' he replies.

Travis is safe but obviously terrified about the missing rings, so we don't talk much as we head to town. Time is of the essence, but I'm happy to let him concentrate. From the back of the bike, I can admire the beautiful Spanish countryside in a way that I couldn't from the back of a taxi. In a way I'm sort of disappointed. I know this trip was for Lou's wedding, and not for sightseeing, but I wish I'd got to experience more of Spain. I'll have to come back the next time I go on holiday – whenever that might be. I suppose I'll have plenty of time, if I lose my job…

* * *

Well, they're nowhere to be seen in the bar, and while we're lucky that the barman speaks English, he sadly has nothing to say to us that helps us. He hasn't found anything, no one has handed them in – I don't know what we're going to do. My head is really banging now, I can't think straight.

'I was so adamant I was going to keep them safe,' Travis says to himself. 'What have I done with them?'

I turn to the barman, because I can't go on like this.

'Could I have a glass of water, please? I need to take some painkillers.'

'Yes,' he replies.

As he takes a glass and fills it, I rummage around in my bag for painkillers, but then I feel something strange.

As I remove the small black box from my bag, examining it in front of my eyes, I watch Travis's expression shift as he claps eyes on it.

'The rings,' he says.

A memory hits him like a ton of bricks.

'Oh my God, Molly, I remember now,' he says. 'I knew I needed to keep them safe, and I was worried about having them in my pocket, so I asked you to look after them. I trusted you with them.'

I can't help but laugh.

'Well, I guess you made the right choice,' I reply. 'Because here they are, safe in my bag.'

Travis hugs me and squeezes me tightly.

'Oh, Molly, Molly, Molly, you're my hero,' he says, his voice muffled by my hair. 'There's a shop, next door, that serves food. Let me buy you breakfast, to say thank you – it's the least I can do.'

I'm not sure how much I feel like eating right now, but I can tell that he wants to do something nice for me, so I'm happy to oblige.

'I'd love that, thank you,' I tell him.

I may not be hungry but if it means I get to spend more time with him, one on one, then I'm all for it.

Plus, someone still needs to mention what happened last night…

38

On the plus side, I managed to eat the most amazing seasoned egg wrap for my breakfast. Sadly, though, despite Travis and I having an amazing chat while we ate, neither of us managed to bring up last night. I don't know how he feels about it. He doesn't know how I feel about it. To be honest, I'm not even sure how I feel about it. It was amazing, of course it was, but that was in the moment. I can still feel the echoes of his hands on me, his lips on my neck, his tongue on my body – but what happens now? What about the future? I know, I know, I worry too much about the future, but will I even see him again after this trip? I hate not knowing where I stand.

'And where, pray tell, have you two been?' Nita calls out from her spot by the pool. 'And why is it so bright?'

'It's daytime,' I tell her with a chuckle. 'We just popped to town.'

I take a seat next to her while Travis heads inside – presumably to put the rings somewhere safe.

'I thought the two of you might have been... y'know,' she says suspiciously.

'I promised you I wouldn't,' I tell her, feeling awful about lying.

'I'll believe you,' she says. 'Thousands wouldn't.'

Eventually, Lou comes out to join us. Then Willow. Then the boys show up, and they've got coffees and cakes.

'Travis made these,' Harry tells us.

I take a bite and – wow.

'They're amazing,' I tell Travis as he takes a seat next to me.

'I try,' he replies, flashing me a smile.

I can't help but notice that he's moved his sun lounger, to be closer to me. I wonder if he wants to talk.

'Wow, aren't you a dreamboat,' Nita says to Travis. 'There's something so sexy about men who cook.'

'Well, I think there's something sexy about girls who love to eat what I make, so it's nice to be appreciated,' he jokes.

'Between the dinners and these cakes, we might actually miss you guys,' Nita says. 'We'll never see you again, but we'll always have… whatever this mess was.'

'You'll never see us again?' Harry repeats.

'Not unless you crash another one of our holidays,' she says from behind the privacy of her sunglasses.

'You crashed our holiday,' he reminds her. 'And we kindly let you stay here.'

'We kindly let you stay here,' she claps back. 'But we won't be so kind next week, seeing as though we won the competition.'

Shit, the competition. I'd completely dumped it from my brain. Did we win?

'I thought we won,' Owen adds. 'You don't win just by saying you won. Nolan, you kept score – who won?'

It's like we all forgot about it. I guess we were all having such a good time together that we stopped thinking about it, but this intense… whatever it is, between Nita and Harry, has caused them both to drag it back up, and now we're back to worrying about next week. Who gets to stay? Who has to leave?

'It's a tie,' Nolan says. 'We got three points each and then... just sort of forgot about it.'

'So we need a tiebreaker,' Harry says. 'Let's do it now, let's choose cards.'

'We've already done cards,' Nita says.

'Plus, you can cheat at cards,' Willow adds.

'What about Rock, Paper, Scissors?' Harry suggests. 'You can't cheat at that.'

Nita thinks for a moment. She lowers her sunglasses on her nose, to look Harry in the eye. Honestly, what is going on with these two? We were all getting on so well, now we're competing again, and there's a very real possibility we might not be staying here next week. I feel sick.

'Okay, sure, but only one round,' she tells him. 'One player from each team, one winner, and whatever happens, we have to accept it.'

'Deal,' Harry says. 'What do you reckon – you and me, head to head in the final showdown?'

Nita looks to the rest of us.

'Why not?' I tell her. After all, it will decide on a winner (assuming they don't keep choosing the same things indefinitely), and then it will be over.

'Okay, bring it,' Nita says.

She scoots to the edge of her sun lounger, placing her feet firmly on the floor. Harry sits opposite her, so they really are head to head.

'Ready?' he asks her.

'Let's do it!' she says with a smirk.

You would think, with something like Rock, Paper, Scissors, that the winner would be obvious. And yet...

'Oh my God, I win,' Harry bellows. 'We win. We're staying here, lads.'

'You fucking cheated,' Nita shouts back at him.

'You lost, get over it,' he replies.

'Come on, Harry, we all know you cheated,' I add – because he did.

The mistake we all made was not agreeing on how the game would be played, before we played it, because while Nita went *on* three, Harry was clearly going *after* three. So when Nita made scissors, Harry's hand was coincidentally still in a fist position, and you could tell he was just about to move into paper, before he realised Nita had gone early, but as soon as he saw her scissors he quickly made a fist again, passing it off as rock, and beating her.

'You're just a poor loser,' he tells her. 'And we did all agree that there would be one winner, and we'd all accept it.'

'So you're just going to kick us out?' Willow asks. 'After everything...'

'Yes,' Owen tells her firmly.

'We could try—' Travis starts, but Owen doesn't let him finish.

'Whose side are you on, mate?' Owen asks him, disappointed.

'The lads', obviously, but—'

'But nothing,' Harry says. 'Come on, let's go inside and celebrate, leave these girls to lick their wounds.'

'Can we go to town?' Nita asks us. 'Can we have another night out? Get some food, have some drinks?'

She's so angry she's shaking.

'Yeah, of course,' I tell her. I think the breather will do her good.

'I'm so, so sorry,' she says. 'I had no idea he would cheat. I can't believe they're going to make us leave.'

'They're dicks,' Willow says. 'We've known that this whole time.'

'Let's get ready, head out, and leave them to it,' I say. 'Maybe they are going to make us leave but, if they do, we can do it with our heads held high. We don't need these stupid boys.'

I say this, although I'm not quite sure I believe it.

'Yeah, okay,' Nita replies. 'Let's go. Because if I stay here, I think I'm going to kill someone.'

She really does seem so angry. I actually think I believe her.

39

'See, this is more like how I saw this week ending,' Lou says with a sigh.

'Boys will be boys,' Nita adds. 'Even when you think they're great, or getting better, they remind you that they're not. They're shit.'

'And this is why I'm single,' Willow adds. 'Because they will always let you down.'

'I'm all the more determined to marry Ellis tomorrow without a hitch now,' Lou says with a sigh. 'I'm starting to wonder how I managed to find such a great one.'

'You're so lucky,' I tell her with a smile.

'And you're quiet,' she replies. 'Suspiciously quiet.'

We're all sitting by the pool – our last day not only here, but together too – while the boys are all at Nolan's wedding. It's so quiet without them, and things really took a turn yesterday (and we avoided them for the rest of the day), and now there's nothing but hostility and resentment between us all again.

'I'm fine,' I insist.

'Obviously that's a lie,' Lou points out. 'I can hear it in your voice.'

'Is it about one of the boys?' Nita asks, clearly already knowing the answer. 'One in particular, maybe...?'

'It's not worth talking about,' I insist. 'I thought I liked one of them. Really liked one of them. But they're all as bad as each other, so...'

More than the competition, which is a part of it, Travis hasn't mentioned the two of us hooking up. Then again, neither have I.

'Forget the competition for a minute,' Nita says. 'And tell us how you feel about him.'

'I think he's smart, he's funny, he's kind and considerate. Absolutely, unrealistically gorgeous. Deep, and honest, and I thought we'd been through similar break-ups, that we were both in a bad spot, that maybe we could help each other find our way out the other side. And even if he's a dick head, like the others, stupid me can't help but think about him at Nolan's wedding, watching his friend get married, knowing his ex-plus-one's seat will be empty, reminding him of it all, and my heart still goes out to him.'

I sigh heavily. Am I an idiot? Is he an idiot? Are we both fucking idiots?

'I know we've all been taking this competition a little too seriously,' Nita points out.

'We all have,' Lou adds. 'Even if the boys have just gone way, way further with it.'

'I think we can all tell how much you like Travis, and that it might be beyond holiday romance territory,' Nita continues. 'And, look, we're all furious about the competition, and it's shit that they cheated, and won, and... and really, none of it matters, when you compare it to the rest of your life.'

I chew my lip, deep in thought.

'What we're saying is, don't let a silly game mess up what could be a great relationship,' Lou chimes in. 'It's been a long time since I saw you this happy, and this into someone.'

'Since Dean,' I say with a sigh.

'Let's be real, it was probably not with Dean, he never seemed all that great, generally, or for you,' Nita says, cutting the shit.

'Nita!' Lou squeaks.

'Come on, we all thought it, but Travis is different,' Nita says. 'He's a good lad – the best of that lot – and you can just tell he really likes you too.'

'Shit,' I say softly. 'What do I do?'

'You said he's got a place going for a plus-one at the wedding?' Lou checks. I nod. 'Then go there, turn up for him, support him. And, hey, if it all goes well, there's a place for him at my wedding too.'

'You guys are amazing, you know that?' I tell them, pulling myself to my feet.

'Go, get ready, we'll book your taxi,' Lou tells me. 'If you're fast, you might even make the ceremony.'

Oh my God, am I actually doing this? Making a mad dash to a wedding venue to tell a man that I like him? Who even does that? I certainly don't and yet here I am, throwing on a dress, running a brush through my hair, putting on lipstick…

The girls are right though. I do really like him, a lot, and the competition is just a silly game, but this is real life.

It's time to go for what I want, instead of being sad and scared all the time.

Here goes nothing…

40

Shiiiit, I can't believe I'm doing this.

I'm here, at the entrance to the resort, just trying to take it all in. This place is fancy, and huge – it's like Disneyland for brides. Suddenly I'm not at all surprised that Lou wants to get married here, this place isn't just her, it's everyone. Even my imagination is starting to run away with me, and I've never been the kind of girl to fantasise about her wedding.

Of course, my imagination and my bank balance do not play nice together, so I should nip any thoughts of tying the knot here in the bud, asap. I don't even have a partner, so I'm way, way ahead of myself.

It's virtually impossible not to be impressed by this place, even if I am a woman on a mission. It's just so picture-perfect, like something out of a bridal magazine, and of course the sun is shining brightly in the cloudless sky, ricocheting off all of the shiny surfaces below. I hope tomorrow is this beautiful for Lou – I'm sure it will be.

Hot pink flowers lead the way along the pathway, their petals fluttering in the faint breeze that takes the edge off the heat. Here the air feels just right, warming and cooling at the same time, and I know it isn't true but I can't help but wonder if that's something that is included in the price.

If I weren't so preoccupied, and if I didn't feel like I was going to throw up, I might stop to admire the scenery a little longer, but I need to speak now, or forever hold my peace – that's what they say, right?

I'm walking with purpose, like I know what I'm doing and where I'm going, when in reality I only really know vaguely where I'm headed because Lou has taken me on so many virtual tours of the place, and shown me so many photos, that I feel this odd sense of déjà vu as I walk around. And as for what I'm doing, well, I'm sort of winging it, making it up as I go along, hoping the right words will come to me at the right time.

I'm not usually one for confrontation – even if the only thing I'm confronting is my feelings – and I've never been brave enough to make the first move. Okay, granted this isn't the first-first move, but it's the first one that feels like a big deal. I'm terrified and excited and yep, going to throw up, definitely going to throw up if I don't get this over with soon.

I need to tell him how I feel. He needs to know. I need to know if he feels the same way and, if he doesn't, well, at least I tried. But I can't carry it around with me forever, that I didn't try, so I'm here. I'm trying.

I turn a corner and briefly stop in my tracks when I spot a row of French doors up ahead that is definitely the ceremony room that Lou showed me. Obviously I knew that I was heading here but, shit, I'm actually here now.

I pause outside the doors for a sec, smoothing down the dress that I threw on so quickly with trembling hands. I can't second-guess whether or not it was the right dress now, it's not like I can do anything about it, but I'd be lying if I said I didn't give it a second or two of thought.

I gulp down nothing but air and push the door open, slinking inside, just in case the ceremony has already started.

The light is so soft here, filtered through sheer curtains that dance in the breeze – again, I wonder if you can pay extra for them to make the sun do this, because it's just too perfect.

It's every bit as beautiful as Lou described – even better in real life, perhaps.

I spot Harry and Nolan, standing through a doorway, in some kind of waiting room. Relief floods through me. The ceremony must not have happened yet, so maybe I can talk to Travis first, get this over with, done and dusted without having to sit through a wedding ceremony, photos, maybe even a dinner before we get a moment alone – and that's if he doesn't just tell me to leave.

'Is the groom ready?' a man in a neat navy-blue suit asks Nolan. He's holding an iPad, so I'm guessing he's some sort of wedding coordinator.

'Yeah, just some last-minute nerves,' Harry replies, not that Nolan looks all that worried. 'But he told us he's on his way.'

Wait, what? My chest tightens, my breath catching in my throat. I must have heard wrong. I have to have heard wrong.

'Honestly, what is Travis playing at?' Nolan says to Harry, now that they think it's just the two of them again.

Harry laughs.

'Don't worry, Owen's talking him back into it. He'll be fine,' Harry replies.

Those lying bastards. They've spent all week telling us all that it was Nolan who is getting married, but he isn't, and who is? Travis. Fucking Travis.

The realisation hits me like a punch to the gut, and suddenly

I can't breathe at all. I need to get outside, to get some air. I need to get out of here.

Suddenly so much makes sense in a way that pisses me off so much. He's the one getting married. That's why he cares so much about the wedding. Why he was so worried when he thought he'd lost the rings – they're his bloody rings. This is his goddamn wedding.

Oh my God! It's hard to say which feeling is the strongest: sick, cold, totally fucking stupid. I think that last one might be winning right now.

I head out of the door as quickly as my legs will carry me, but I'm only out of the door for a step or two when I collide with something – technically someone.

'Oi, watch it,' a sharp voice snaps.

Oh, and just when you think things can't get any more awkward I – quite literally, I might add – bump into the bride.

She's perfect, everything you'd expect a bride to be – everything I'm not, if we're being honest. Her dress clings in all the right places, and all the places seem pretty perfect anyway, so that will help. She's model slim, with curves in exactly the right spots. Her glossy brown hair shines like glass in the sunlight, cascading down her back in immaculate waves. Even her annoyed expression just makes her look like a supermodel, on a catwalk, giving attitude.

'I am so sorry,' I tell her, my voice all squeaky and barely audible. 'I was just... I didn't mean... I'm sorry.'

Her frown softens slightly, like she thinks there might be something wrong with me, but she doesn't say anything. She just stares at me until I take the initiative to piss off out of her way.

I'm such an idiot. How could I have been so blind? So stupid? All week, everyone's been talking about the groom, and I'm not going mad, they said it was Nolan. And I, what, just believed them? Have I learned nothing about men during my time on this earth? Clearly not.

Travis could have told me. If not at the start then at the end. Bloody hell, telling me while he was inside me would have been better than finding out like this. Not much, but a bit.

I can feel the tears creeping up on me, my vision is getting kind of blurry, and I'm feeling a bit dizzy.

I should hate him. I want to hate him. He let me believe there was something between us, and maybe there was, but it was never going to work out, was it? He was taken from the day we met – which was only a week ago, so why does it hurt so much?

I really can't face telling the girls yet. I'll just say that I changed my mind, or that I chickened out. I'll let them make fun of me for being a big baby, because that sounds much easier to take than the pitying looks and the angry man-hating, wine-drinking pity party that we had after Dean broke my heart.

Yep, anything is better than the truth, because the truth is that I fell for someone else who was never going to be mine.

God, I've been such a fool. Again. Is it always going to end this way?

41

It doesn't matter how prepared you are for a wedding – you can pretty much guarantee that, on the day, everything is going to go wrong.

I'm not feeling great today, at all. Well, after my big shock yesterday, I've found it impossible to get Travis off my mind. I know the boys weren't great – we all did – but I never thought Travis would lie to me, use me – and then see me kicked out of the villa too. I suppose he needs us gone, really, because we would have soon realised he was the groom, when the others came back, and he went off on his honeymoon.

Now I can't wait to get out of here. It will be so weird, and awkward, when the others come back, and we have to leave. We just need to get the wedding out of the way and then we can go. The sooner the better, except now it seems like the wedding isn't going to plan either…

'What do you mean the road is blocked?' Lou shrieks down the phone.

She's not usually one for shrieking at people for just doing their job, so this must be bad.

She slams the phone down and turns to face us.

'The taxi can't make it,' she tells us. 'There's been some kind of accident, on the road, blocking cars from passing. He said the taxi will be here as soon as it can but I need to get to the venue, my hair takes ages, my make-up – what am I going to do?'

'Look, don't worry,' I reassure her. 'It's a quiet road, I'm sure they'll get it sorted quickly, and the taxi will be here in no time. Let's just get everything ready that we possibly can.'

'We could do your hair, if needed,' Nita says.

'No, thanks,' Lou says a little too quickly.

'Well, you're under pressure, and you're having a bad day, so we're going to pretend you didn't say that like that,' Nita replies, patting her on the head.

'What's going on?' a voice asks, snapping us from our conversation, potentially breaking up a fight.

Shit, it's Travis. So much for avoiding a fight – I want to kill him. Ugh, they all must have come back here last night, after the wedding. I was really, really hoping I would never have to see any of them again – especially Travis though.

'The road's blocked,' Nita tells him. 'And Lou needs to get to the venue, like, now.'

Travis looks as tired as I feel – although he's probably tired from having a fabulous time at his wedding, whereas I sat up all night thinking of ways to find his passport and burn it in the firepit.

'I'll take you,' he tells Lou, quick as a flash.

'The road is blocked,' she reminds him. 'And... how?'

'There's a bike, in the shed,' he tells her. 'Molly and I rode to town on it. We'll be able to ride around the block in the road – I know, I can't take you all, but I can get you there, you can be getting ready...'

Lou runs over and kisses him on the cheek.

'Life saver!' she tells him. 'Get the bike, I'll get my things.'

Nita looks at him like he's lost his mind.

'You are not putting her on the back of a bike on her wedding day,' she tells him.

'He is,' Lou says. 'If it's the only way I can get there, I'm doing it. I can put my dress in my bag, strap it to my body. I'm doing it. You guys can wait for the taxi, you don't need hours having your hair and make-up done.'

I smile, just a little. Whether this is a good idea or simply her only option, it's turned the day around for her, and it's good to see. Well, why panic and wallow when you can be proactive? At least Travis is good for something.

Lou dashes off to grab her things.

'Morning,' Travis says to me with a smile.

'Morning,' I reply flatly. 'I didn't think we'd see you here this morning.'

'Yeah, well, it was a great wedding,' he says, smiling as he rubs his eyes. Then he detects my tone and his smile drops.

'Are you—'

As Travis speaks, he reaches out to touch my shoulder. I violently pull away, freaking him out a little.

Before anyone can say anything else, Lou appears again.

'Lou, seriously—' Nita starts, but Lou cuts her off.

'See you there,' she tells her giddily. 'I'm getting marrieeeed.'

I'm glad that Lou is getting to the venue on time, of course I am, but something about it being fucking Travis who saves the day makes me so, so angry. He's the villain in all of this and yet today he gets to be the hero.

I grit my teeth while he and Lou get on the bike and cycle off, but when they're gone, I can't hold it in any more. I snatch Travis's bag from the hallway.

'He's so fucking smug,' I mutter, storming out back to sit by the pool. 'He thinks he can do whatever he wants, use whoever he wants, get away with everything – and then swoop in for the glory. I hate him.'

'What are you doing?' Willow asks.

'I'm throwing his stuff in the pool,' I say, marching towards the patio.

'Why?' Nita replies, baffled.

'He deserves it,' I tell them, my anger boiling over. 'For being so – so fucking nice and helpful and – and fucking married!'

'What?' Nita asks. 'Travis is married?'

'As of yesterday,' I tell her.

Willow grabs my arm, stopping me just as I reach the pool.

'Hang on, stop, don't do that,' she tells me. 'Molly, you've got it all wrong.'

'Nolan was never the one getting married,' I tell her.

'I know,' she replies. 'We've been, erm, sort of... hooking up.'

'Willow, you scoundrel,' Nita says, impressed. 'So...?'

'So, obviously I'm not going to sleep with a taken man,' she replies. 'He came clean to me, told me who was really getting married – it's Owen.'

For a moment, I just stare at her.

'Owen?' I check. 'But he said he was the best man...'

'Travis is the best man,' Willow corrects me.

'Molly, he really is the best man,' Nita points out. 'In every way. What are you doing?'

'But I...'

'You've got it all wrong,' Willow tells me – I'm surprised at how tactful and supportive she's being.

'Willow, look, I'm impressed in a way, but what about girl code?' Nita reminds her. 'You should have told us the truth, about Nolan.'

'I know that now,' she replies. 'But I, well, like him, and he told me it was a secret, so...'

'Forget it,' Nita says. 'That's not what's important right now. Molly, what are you going to do?'

'I need to fix this,' I tell them. 'I need to go see him, right now.'

'We'll have to wait for the taxi,' Nita says.

'No, we won't,' I reply. 'There's another bike.'

'Can you ride a bike?' she calls after me as I head for the shed.

'I'm going to have to,' I reply. 'I was so awful to him just now. I need to fix this. Plus, how hard can it be? I used to be able to ride one...'

And, you know what they say: it's just like riding a bike.

42

Lou and Ellis's wedding didn't just go without a hitch – which is a miracle, considering how many hitches tried to crop up this morning.

The weather was glorious, the venue was decorated to perfection, the food was unrealistically good (although we have all had a week of not eating as much as we usually would have) and the speeches were spot on, with the right amounts of humour and heart, none of that cringey, comedy roast material I hate to hear.

But to be honest, all those details – the weather, the flowers, the food – don't really matter. Earlier, when everything was hitting the fan, I don't think Lou cared if she had to marry Ellis at the side of the road. At the end of the day, the bottom line, she just wanted to marry him. You could have swapped the Spanish countryside estate for Leeds bus station. Because weddings are wonderful, sure. There's food, music, dancing, everyone looks gorgeous and drinks and dances the night away, but it's a party, a one-off, it's not the till death do us part bit. It's not about the wedding, it's the marriage that matters. Still, I'm so, so glad that Lou has got both.

However, aside from all of the joy and champagne fumes in the air, there's something else too. Thick, scary tension between me and Travis. Yes, Travis, who saved the day, and landed himself an invitation to the wedding in the process. He's sitting at the singles table, because apparently the universe has a sense of humour, and because of course he is.

I need to talk to him, to come clean, and to get it over with ASAP. I can't have it hanging over me for the rest of the evening.

His shirt sleeves are rolled up, his tie is a little crooked, and he's leaning back in his chair mid-conversation with one of Ellis's cousins. She's leaning in too, twirling a strand of her hair and laughing a little too loudly at something he just said. To be honest, you'd think I would be jealous, but I'm not. Frankly, now that I know that he isn't married, or getting married, nothing else seems all that worth getting upset about.

I hover awkwardly on the edge of the table, trying not to look like a groupie. The cousin notices me first.

'Can I help you?' she asks.

'I was after Travis,' I say.

She tosses her hair back with an exaggerated giggle.

'You've found him,' she tells me.

'Hi,' he says, flashing me that devastating smile as he turns around to face me.

'Hi,' I reply. 'Can I have a word?'

'Of course,' he says, jumping to his feet immediately, in a way that makes things feel easier already. There's no playing it cool, no games. I like that.

'Shall we pop outside?' I say as we walk.

'Yeah, sure,' he says. 'I think there's a garden, I don't know if it's a secret one, but I promise we'll behave.'

His joke makes me laugh, and feel even more at ease. I was so worried this was going to feel impossible.

We step out into the garden area, leaving behind the hum of laughter from the wedding. The air out here feels fresher, and cooler, but it's getting dark now. Overhead, strings of fairy lights twinkle like stars, and for a moment, life just feels good.

Travis shoves his hands into his pockets, watching me expectantly.

'I need to say something,' I blurt. 'To confess something, really.'

'Okay…' he replies slowly, like he's bracing for impact.

I take a deep breath. Here goes nothing.

'I made a huge mistake yesterday,' I start. 'I came to find you at what turns out to be Owen's wedding because I… well, I wanted to tell you how I felt. But when I got there, I overheard Harry and Nolan talking, and so I knew you'd all lied, that it wasn't Nolan who was getting married, but what I heard led me to believe that you were the one getting married. So… yeah.'

His eyes widen, horrified and mortified.

'What? No. Molly, no,' he replies. 'Oh my God, I would never do that to you. Or anyone!'

'Yeah, well, I figured that out eventually,' I say, the memory making my face flush all over again. 'But you did all lie, you said it was Nolan getting married, I'm sure you did.'

Travis groans, running a hand through his hair.

'Owen… is an idiot,' he says. 'We asked him why he lied, after he said it, and he told us he did it because he thought Nolan sounded like the "nicer" groom, so you'd be more likely not to kick him out. But, also, for whatever reason, he said he just wanted one last week of feeling single. He loves Suze, he really does, and he'd never cheat on her. I think he just wanted to feel… I don't know. I don't get it myself.'

I kind of do. I think back to what Lou said earlier about

weddings marking the end of that being single, and getting to enjoy one last week of it.

'It's not entirely stupid,' I admit. 'Everyone wants to feel like they're doing what's right for them, and that they're happy about it. At the end of the day, they both chose their partners. We can always make different decisions, good or bad.'

'Speaking of,' he starts. 'You said you came here yesterday, to find me, to talk… what were you going to say?'

'Well, before I thought you were a lying, no-good heartbreaker,' I start, letting him know that I'm joking with a bit of a smile, 'I was going to tell you that none of the stupid competition stuff mattered. That I didn't care about the villa, or the arguments, or anything else. All I cared about was you. Because you…' I swallow hard, trying not to chicken out. 'You're the first person to make me feel really happy since my ex. And I didn't think that was possible. And I like you. A lot.'

The smile that spreads across his face is so genuine.

'Molly, I almost left Owen's wedding yesterday,' he confesses.

'What?' I squeak.

'Yeah. I couldn't stand the way we left things,' he replies. 'I wanted to find you and tell you that… well, you've woken something up in me. Something I thought was gone. I didn't want to waste another minute not being with you. But Owen reminded me, quite fairly, that it was his wedding day, and I was a big part of it, so I stayed. I was going to talk to you, when I got back last night, but you were asleep.'

'I wasn't actually asleep,' I confess. 'I was too heartbroken to sleep and, to be fair, I figured you'd be in a honeymoon suite somewhere.'

'I'm so sorry that you felt heartbroken, even for a day,' he says. 'But everything I wanted to say yesterday, I still mean today. And I'll still mean it tomorrow. Probably forever.'

'Me too,' I whisper.

He takes a step closer to me, taking my hands in his.

'So, what happens now?' he asks softly.

'I guess we just need some time, to figure out what happens next,' I suggest.

'It's funny you should say that,' he says with a grin. 'Nolan and Harry and I had a chat. We really want you girls to stay for the second week. You can keep the bedrooms. We'll share the villa, but we'll do it properly this time, you can use the kitchen. Whatever you want, all that matters to me is that you all stay. What do you think? And no more secrets from here on out.'

'I'd love that,' I reply, mirroring his grin. 'But as far as no more secrets go – did you know Nita's been sleeping with Harry?'

Travis's jaw drops.

'What? Harry? When did that happen? I thought they hated each other...'

'Oh, I'm sure they do, but it works for them,' I say with a laugh. 'And did you know that Nolan and Willow slept together?'

I didn't think he could look more shocked but I stand corrected.

'How am I always the last to know these things?'

'Girls talk,' I tell him.

'Well, that takes care of one problem,' he says.

'What problem?' I ask.

'If we've all paired off then, well, that's the bedrooms shared out,' he jokes.

I laugh, slapping his chest.

'Don't get ahead of yourself, mister,' I tell him.

'Okay, okay,' he replies. 'How about a kiss then?'

I nod my head. That we can do.

Travis smiles and pulls me closer, his hands sliding to my waist. He kisses me and it's slow, sweet, and (as corny as it sounds) charged with possibility – not just for what's to come later, but for the future.

'Okay,' he murmurs when we pull back. 'That's the kiss sorted. Now, how about a dance?'

'Are you a good dancer?' I ask. 'Because I'm really, really not.'

'No, not at all,' he admits with a laugh. 'It's been said that my dancing offends people. But we'll figure it out – we work well together.'

Hand in hand, we head back to the reception and while I may not know where this is going, for the first time in a long time, I can't wait to see what happens next.

43

MAY 2027

Is the altitude different at the altar?

I swear, I feel so wobbly on my feet, like the air is just that little bit harder to take in here.

Realistically, I'm in a church, not at the top of Mount Everest, and the air is fine. It's just me, I'm nervous.

Standing up here, in front of all these people – I mean, there are just so many things that can go wrong, so many potential ways to embarrass myself.

The vicar keeps smiling at me. He's so cool and calm, he must have done hundreds of weddings. I imagine the smile is supposed to reassure me but I wonder if he can spot a nervous customer, if he's worried I'm going to say something, do something – faint, even. Something that throws him off his game.

Or maybe he's just friendly. The most obvious answer is often the right one, right? Not when you're anxious. When you're anxious, the worst-case scenario is happening, so panic, panic, panic.

That said, I thought I was going to fall, when I walked down the aisle, but here I am, in one piece, upright, and I haven't dropped my flowers or popped out a boob or anything. I just focused on putting one foot in front of the other, one at a time, until I got from A to B. I don't know if it felt like it took a lifetime, because I was worried sick, or if I barely even noticed that I did it, because I was so focused on trying to make sure it all went to plan.

Anyway, I'm here now, and so is Travis. Oh, look at him! My God, he looks incredible in his tailored navy-blue suit. He catches my eye and grins, the same easy, heart-melting grin I fell for back at the villa. So dreamy, like a regular Prince Charming, and yet I want to rip his shirt open, pinging the buttons in all directions, pushing him back onto the floor and... God, I shouldn't be thinking this in a church. Or saying God like that – bloody hell. Focus on the wedding, Molly. You can rip his shirt off later.

I love that we've still got that spark, that fiery passion. I thought that was supposed to wear off – it did with you-know-who, if the two of us even had it to begin with – but with Travis it's been almost two years of bliss. Going on amazing nights out together, taking trips – and that's when we can tear ourselves from the bedroom. Oh, and we work together now, so if we were going to get sick of one another, it definitely would have happened already. Travis did what he said, he promised to help me find the perfect person to oversee the revamp at work, and it turned out that the perfect person was him after all. He really is perfect, in every way. I don't know how I got so lucky.

So here we are, together – except this time, the run-up to the wedding hasn't been anywhere near as dramatic or chaotic, which is surprising, given who is getting married.

Finally 'Here Comes the Bride' starts playing. Wow, that was fast. She told us she was going to make him wait at least ten more minutes, just to freak him out.

Nita looks incredible in her bridal gown. Honestly, she's practically floating down the aisle, and I honestly can't ever say I've seen her look quite so happy.

Harry, on the other hand, looks terrified. He's scrubbed up well, and he's even let a professional at his hair, because his usual chaotic, mess-on-purpose look is nowhere to be seen in favour of a sleek, slicked back 'do. Ah, the things we do for love.

As Nita finally reaches him, Harry relaxes, grinning from ear to ear. I guess Lou was right, when you know, you know.

I take my place as chief bridesmaid while Travis settles into his duties as best man.

Here we go...

* * *

'Did you ever think it'd be these two who made it down the aisle first?' Travis says, pulling me close as we dance together.

'Not a chance,' I whisper into his ear, before nuzzling his neck with my cheek. 'Not without one of them being in a coffin anyway. Though I guess it makes sense. They've got too much in common not to work.'

'Well, just wait until they find out who is going to be walking down the aisle next,' he says.

'Shh,' I say quickly. 'We said we'd keep it a secret until after the wedding – I don't want to steal Nita's moment.'

'And that's why I love you,' he tells me. 'And why I want to tell everyone.'

A couple of weeks ago Travis and I went to Spain, to stay in 'our' villa, just the two of us, and while we were there he got down on one knee and popped the question. I said yes – of course I did – but with Nita's wedding imminent I just didn't want to do anything that might overshadow it, so we're keeping it to ourselves, just for now, but I kind of love having a secret.

I really can't wait to marry him, to stand up in front of everyone and say our vows – although I'm sure I'll be terrified, I was nervous enough just being a bridesmaid.

I made a few vows to myself, when I got back from Spain, and I'm proud to say that I've been honouring them. I'm not sweating the small stuff – it's just not worth it. I'm not beating myself up over Dean – we even bumped into him at the cinema, and I was perfectly polite (although it did help that I had Travis on my arm, while Dean was single again). I'm enjoying my work – although I'm not obsessing over it; when I clock off, I'm off, and when I'm at home, I'm not thinking about it. And while I do know for sure that I want to marry Travis, I have absolutely no idea what I want my wedding to look like, and that's fine. We can figure it out together.

Everyone is on the dance floor, joining the happy couple with their first dance – mostly because Harry said he couldn't face doing it on his own, so Nita suggested everyone dance, that way he could just blend in.

As Harry and Nita kiss to cheers and applause, Travis reaches for my hand, threading his fingers through mine. I glance at him, my heart pounding in my chest in that way it always does when he looks at me like that. I hope that never wears off.

'I love you,' he tells me.

'I love you too,' I reply.

It's funny how things work out sometimes. Before we went to Spain, my life was a mess. Of all the things I didn't have, it was my lack of hope that was the most demoralising, and when you don't have hope, it's impossible to imagine finding it again.

I didn't feel like I was on the right track, at all, but it turns out that sometimes the wrong route takes you to the right place. That villa was supposed to be for us girls, the boys weren't even supposed to be there, but in the end it turned out that it took a mistake, for everything to go wrong, to put me in the right place, at the right time, to get everything I wanted, and everything I needed. I'll never sweat my mistakes ever again. Sometimes, they're the key to true happiness.

* * *

MORE FROM PORTIA MACINTOSH

Another book from Portia MacIntosh, *Wish You Weren't Here*, is available to order now here:

https://mybook.to/WishYouWerentBackAd

ACKNOWLEDGEMENTS

Thank you to Megan, and the team at Boldwood Books, for all their work on yet another book.

Huge thanks to everyone who has taken the time to read and review my books – your support means so much to me. I really hope you've enjoyed this one too.

Finally massive thanks to my family for always being there for me. To Kim, Aud, Joey, James, Joe and Darcy. I love you all so much and I don't know where I'd be without you all.

ABOUT THE AUTHOR

Portia MacIntosh is the million copy bestselling author of over 20 romantic comedy novels. Whether it's southern Italy or the French alps, Portia's stories are the holiday you're craving, conveniently packed in between the pages. Formerly a journalist, Portia lives with her husband and her dog in Yorkshire.

Sign up to Portia MacIntosh's mailing list for news, competitions and updates on future books.

Visit Portia's website: www.portiamacintosh.com

Follow Portia MacIntosh on social media here:

- facebook.com/portia.macintosh.3
- x.com/PortiaMacIntosh
- instagram.com/portiamacintoshauthor
- bookbub.com/authors/portia-macintosh

ALSO BY PORTIA MACINTOSH

Off The Record

Love On Tour

Always The Bridesmaid

Drive Me Crazy

Truth or Date

It's Not You, It's Them

The Accidental Honeymoon

Never The Bride

Summer Secrets at the Apple Blossom Deli

Snow Love Lost

Here Comes the Ex

Honeymoon For One

My Great Ex-Scape

Make or Break at the Lighthouse B&B

The Plus One Pact

Stuck On You

Faking It

Life's a Beach

Will They, Won't They?

No Ex Before Marriage

The Meet Cute Method

Single All the Way

Just Date and See

Your Place or Mine?

Better Off Wed

Long Time No Sea

Fake it or Leave it

Trouble in Paradise

Ex in the City

The Suite Life

It's All Sun and Games

You Had Me at Château

Wish You Weren't Here

Too Hot to Handle

Boldwood
EVER AFTER
xoxo

JOIN BOLDWOOD'S ROMANCE COMMUNITY FOR SWEET AND SPICY BOOK RECS WITH ALL YOUR FAVOURITE TROPES!

SIGN UP TO OUR NEWSLETTER

HTTPS://BIT.LY/BOLDWOODEVERAFTER

Boldwood

Boldwood Books is an award-winning fiction publishing company seeking out the best stories from around the world.

Find out more at www.boldwoodbooks.com

Join our reader community for brilliant books, competitions and offers!

Follow us

@BoldwoodBooks

@TheBoldBookClub

Sign up to our weekly deals newsletter

https://bit.ly/BoldwoodBNewsletter

Printed in Great Britain
by Amazon